"Will you let me carry you into the house, Loris?"

As if he awaited her pleasure, he bent low, his forehead touching her shoulder. She heard his sigh, the catch in his breath, and knew a moment of tenderness so great it almost overwhelmed her.

"I can walk up the stairs," she told him softly. "I need you, Connor. I need to know you care about me. I want you in my life." Her pause was long as she enclosed his face in her palms. "Is that clear enough for you?"

"Yes, ma'am. It surely is." He hadn't forgotten how to grin, that sassy twist of his lips that told her he was pleased with her. With a quick movement he snatched her from her feet and carried her into the house.

"I can walk," she protested.

"But I want to carry you! Just kiss me and behave, sweetheart."

* * *

Oklahoma Sweetheart
Harlequin Historical #780—December 2005

Acclaim for Carolyn Davidson's recent novels

The Marriage Agreement
"Davidson uses her considerable skills to fashion a plausible, first-class marriage-of-convenience romance."
—*Romantic Times BOOKclub*

Texas Gold
"Davidson delivers a story fraught with sexual tension."
—*Romantic Times BOOKclub*

A Marriage by Chance
"This deftly written novel about loss and recovery is a skillful handling of the traditional Western, with the added elements of family conflict and a moving love story."
—*Romantic Times BOOKclub*

The Tender Stranger
"Davidson wonderfully captures gentleness in the midst of heart-wrenching challenges, portraying the extraordinary possibilities that exist within ordinary marital love."
—*Publishers Weekly*

DON'T MISS THESE OTHER
TITLES AVAILABLE NOW:

#779 THE LADY'S HAZARD
Miranda Jarrett

#781 THE OUTRAGEOUS DEBUTANTE
Anne O'Brien

#782 CONQUEST BRIDE
Meriel Fuller

CAROLYN DAVIDSON

Oklahoma Sweetheart

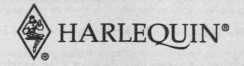

HARLEQUIN®

TORONTO • NEW YORK • LONDON
AMSTERDAM • PARIS • SYDNEY • HAMBURG
STOCKHOLM • ATHENS • TOKYO • MILAN • MADRID
PRAGUE • WARSAW • BUDAPEST • AUCKLAND

If you purchased this book without a cover you should be aware that this book is stolen property. It was reported as "unsold and destroyed" to the publisher, and neither the author nor the publisher has received any payment for this "stripped book."

ISBN 0-373-29380-1

OKLAHOMA SWEETHEART

Copyright © 2005 by Carolyn Davidson

All rights reserved. Except for use in any review, the reproduction or utilization of this work in whole or in part in any form by any electronic, mechanical or other means, now known or hereafter invented, including xerography, photocopying and recording, or in any information storage or retrieval system, is forbidden without the written permission of the publisher, Harlequin Enterprises Limited, 225 Duncan Mill Road, Don Mills, Ontario, Canada M3B 3K9.

All characters in this book have no existence outside the imagination of the author and have no relation whatsoever to anyone bearing the same name or names. They are not even distantly inspired by any individual known or unknown to the author, and all incidents are pure invention.

This edition published by arrangement with Harlequin Books S.A.

® and TM are trademarks of the publisher. Trademarks indicated with ® are registered in the United States Patent and Trademark Office, the Canadian Trade Marks Office and in other countries.

www.eHarlequin.com

Printed in U.S.A.

Available from Harlequin® Historical and
CAROLYN DAVIDSON

*Edgewood, Texas
**Montana Mavericks
‡Colorado Confidential

Look for Carolyn Davidson's
Redemption
**Coming soon from
HQN**

Please address questions and book requests to:
Harlequin Reader Service
U.S.: 3010 Walden Ave., P.O. Box 1325, Buffalo, NY 14269
Canadian: P.O. Box 609, Fort Erie, Ont. L2A 5X3

Chapter One

January, 1893
Kent Corners, Oklahoma

Connor Webster viewed the female standing in front of him. The woman who'd represented his future. He felt the urge to turn his back and walk away, across the porch and into his parents' home. Not that the woman he'd planned on marrying was unfit for the estate of matrimony. Loris simply was far from a suitable bride, so far as he was concerned. Considering that the baby she carried had been planted in her womb by his own brother, her pregnancy made her *totally* unsuitable.

Not that Connor couldn't have accepted another man's child. It was the betrayal by the pair of them that made him angry. And right now angry was too mild a word to describe the surge of hot-blooded rage that poured through him.

"I'm sorry," Loris said, her eyes awash with tears. And no doubt she was. But it was unclear whether her sorrow was due to the pain she'd caused him or because she'd fallen pregnant. Either way, he realized his love for her was a thing of the past. Even the tears that filled her soft brown eyes failed to bring him to his knees.

Loris was not prone to crying. He'd seen her conquer her share of adversity and even admit defeat when fate was against her, but never had he seen her shed a tear.

"You're having a baby. Am I right?" he asked, his voice terse and clipped. "And that baby belongs to my brother. Am I right on that point, too?"

She nodded, twice in fact, and then turned aside, as if she would begin the long walk back to town from his home.

"I know I've hurt you, Connor, and—"

"You don't know the half of it, Loris…." He could barely speak, the betrayal cut Connor so deep. He wondered if he truly could walk away from Loris with no regrets.

"What will I do?" she asked in a soft whisper, turning back to face him again.

For the first time since he'd discovered the truth, he felt a faint glimmer of sympathy for her.

"Maybe James will marry you," Connor said glibly.

"You know better," Loris said quietly. "He was out for a good time, and I fell for his promises. I was fool enough to think…" She shrugged, as if realizing that her excuse was lame, and she'd just condemned herself. "He's your brother, Connor. At first I thought he was only flirting and it was exciting."

"You thought he'd marry you? But you were already betrothed to me, Loris. Why would James fall into that trap? He's smart. Apparently, smarter than I."

"That's not it," she said. "I thought he really loved me. That's where I was dead wrong. I should have known better. Your brother has courted every eligible girl in town—and some that were not so eligible. More than I can count, and I doubt he can keep track either." She laughed, and Connor thought the sound was singularly without mirth.

"So what do you expect of *me?*" he asked, knowing already what her answer would be. She was stuck between a rock and a hard place, and Connor Webster was her only hope of salvation.

"I would like you to honor your promise, and marry me," she said. The words were flat, without expression.

"I'm not a fool, Loris," he told her. "I'd planned a future with you, and that included babies and a farm and years of marriage. You've ruined all of that. I'm afraid you're on your own."

Loris's tears flowed down her cheeks, and onto the front of her dress. Connor felt an unwilling tug of pity as he looked at her. "I'll help you get out of town, if you like," he said. "Do you have any relatives who might take you in?"

"No." She shook her head. "And once my folks find out, I'll be on the front porch with my valise and nowhere to go."

"There's not much I can do for you, Loris," he said bluntly.

"I thought you loved me," she told him, her gaze falling to the snowy ground at her feet. She shivered, as though the sight of the newly fallen snow had reminded her of the chill of the dreary January day.

"I did," he admitted. "We've already gone over that.

But I trusted you with my heart, and you went behind my back—with my brother."

Loris turned away, her foot sliding on the slick ground. He reached to grasp her elbow and held her upright, but she withdrew from his touch.

"What will you do?" he asked.

"I don't know. But for sure I won't bother you again," she told him, walking away, her back straight, her shoulders squared, the road to town before her.

Loris Peterson had thought her life was planned, had been happy in her betrothal to Connor Webster, had thought she was in love with the man. Until Connor's brother, James, had entered her life.

James, was a right good hand with the ladies, a scamp of the first order, her father had said, when he found her speaking with the man in front of the general store one day. She'd been warned, not only by her father, but by her own common sense. And failed to heed the message.

James had been kind and gentle, yet dashing and sophisticated, at least to her eyes. And she had assumed that she was safe with him. After all, he was Connor's brother. As if that had made a difference.

Two brothers could not have been more unalike. Connor was steady, reliable and rock-solid. The sort of man a sensible girl would choose for a husband. And Loris considered herself eminently sensible. At least, she had until James had swung her around the dance floor at Eloise Simpson's wedding. His offer to escort her had been kind, she thought, with Connor gone on business.

James had been gallant, serving her with small cakes and cups of punch, and walking her outside when the grange hall became too warm for comfort, due to the number of exuberant dancers filling the floor.

Outside, he'd been funny, telling her stories that tickled her, probably more so because of the spiked punch he'd coaxed her to drink. He'd halted their progress beneath a tall oak tree, and there in the shadows that surrounded them, he'd kissed her for the first time.

Now, she wished fervently that it had never happened, or that it had been the first and last kiss she'd received from his experienced lips. There was something about a man with experience that appealed to a woman, Loris decided.

James knew how to bend her to his will, knew that his mouth against the nape of her neck would make her shiver with delight. Possessed of blue eyes and dark hair, he was handsome. Gifted with a body that was tall and well-muscled, he was strong, and yet he had a gentle streak that appealed to her as a woman. For surely a man so sweet would never cause her harm.

She laughed aloud as she passed the church, and then stifled the sound, lest some holy presence might strike her dead for her sins. Though that seemed unlikely, for hadn't the Lord himself forgiven the woman caught in sin?

Right now, she was more interested in the forgiveness of her parents, and that was not a likely occurrence. They would be horrified. Her mother would cry and carry on, her father would be stern and judgmental. And she would be forever left with the burden of guilt she carried.

Through it all would be the knowledge that her life was ruined. Ruined by one moment of temptation, one glimpse of pleasure, one man set on having his way with her. And he had. In the depths of her father's barn, where the hay lay soft and deep in a storage stall, he'd talked her out of her clothing, whispered sweet words of appeal, and taken her virginity. That he was very good at what he'd done seemed of little consequence now, for guilt overwhelmed her as she thought of her unfaithful behavior. At the time her thoughts had been of the years ahead, when she and James Webster would spend their lives together.

It was not to be. James had been offered a job as manager of a ranch in Missouri and planned to leave town soon. He'd told her of his opportunity, and she'd looked up at him pleadingly. "What about me?" she'd asked.

"Connor loves you," he'd told her. "He'll marry you."

"I doubt it," she'd said sadly. "I'm going to have your child, James. I've cheated on him. I hate myself. How can I expect him to forgive me?"

"Tell him I forced you into it," James said loftily. "He'll believe you."

"And then he'll tell me to force you to marry me," she said. "And if my father hears of such a thing, he'll get out his shotgun and you'll be wearing a load of buckshot in your fanny."

"That's not gonna happen," James had said. "Connor will marry you, and you're smart enough to never let your father hear my name in connection with this."

Loris turned in at the gate and climbed the steps to the front porch of the big house she'd been born in nineteen years ago. Behind the house was a barn and corral, a henhouse and a garden. The property was not large, but prosperous. She clasped the door handle and turned it. The front door was closed but not locked, for the folks in this town seldom set a bolt on their doors.

People in Kent Corners, Oklahoma, could be trusted

not to infringe on another's property. She'd heard that all of her life, and now she laughed as she stepped into the front hall. Most folks could be trusted, but not James Webster, who had done more than infringe on his brother's property. He'd seduced his brother's fiancée.

Then he had turned his back on his responsibility and walked away. His departure was scheduled for that very day.

Loris climbed the stairs, holding the smooth banister firmly, her legs not seeming solid beneath her. She thought for a moment of her father's shotgun, and wondered how it could be used to put her out of her misery. Then dismissed that thought as not worthy of contemplation. She'd never be able to pull the trigger.

If she had to find a place to live, scrabbling for food, making a way for herself, she would. If Connor was willing to pay for her passage out of town, maybe he'd help her move someplace close by, an abandoned house perhaps. There were several of them west of town, where families had renounced their dreams, and moved on instead to a more prosperous place.

She trudged to her room and sat down dejectedly on the side of her bed, unconcerned for once that she might muss the quilt. Her mother's training went deep and sitting on the bed, or, heaven forbid, lying down on it in the daytime, was strictly against the rules of behavior taught to young ladies who intended to be thought of as women of distinction.

Whether or not Loris held out any hopes of achieving that exalted position now seemed of little concern, for she knew that her position in society would henceforth be that of a fallen woman.

Now came the difficult part, she realized. Talking to her parents was the very last thing she wanted to do, yet was, of necessity, the most important item on her list of things that must be faced.

Suppertime would be the best time, she decided. In the meantime, she'd do well to sort through her clothing and see how much she could carry with her when her father showed her the door.

"You're really walking away from this?" Connor asked. His younger brother stood in the barn doorway, holding the bridle of his gelding, his saddlebags bulging as they hung over the horse's withers.

"What would you like me to do?" James asked. "When the folks find out what's happened, they'll be after me like flies on a manure pile, and I don't fancy being tossed on my ear by Father."

"Why don't you marry Loris?" Connor asked, his heart aching as he thought of the pearl ring she wore. A ring he had put on her finger himself, just six months ago.

"I'm not planning on marriage. Not for a long time," James said, his handsome face twisted in anger.

"A little late to be planning a life as a bachelor, isn't it?" Connor asked, grasping James by his shirt. He'd loved James, been his friend as well as brother. Now pure hatred rose within him as he shook the man who had betrayed him.

"I *am* a bachelor," James answered quickly. "Women are a commodity that men have been buying for centuries, but in this case, I got a girl without much effort at all, and it certainly didn't cost me anything."

Connor released his grip. "Loris is in the family way. Don't you feel responsible?" he asked.

James looked at him and grinned, then his face reddened and he took on a pensive look. "Yeah, I'm responsible, I guess. But I feel worse about letting you down than I do about fooling around with Loris."

"Don't you like her?" Connor asked.

James grinned again. "Of course, I do. She's pretty, she's got a good figure and she's smart. Who wouldn't like her?"

"You don't respect her, though, do you?"

James thought about that for a moment. "Not a whole lot. No, I don't. Trust me on this, Connor. You're better off without her. If you decide to marry the girl, I'll thank you for taking on my child, but I'll understand if you walk away."

"I've already told her I'm done with her," Connor said.

"What will she do?" James asked, and for a moment Connor wondered if his brother was having second thoughts. "Can she leave town, stay with someone?"

"That's what I asked her," Connor said. "I offered to pay her way if she wanted to leave."

"Tell you what I'll do," James said slowly. "I'll give you some cash for her. I've got a bit saved, and I'm heading for a sure job at a good wage. Tell her I said to take care of herself." He pulled a roll of bills from his pocket and placed over half of it in Connor's hand. "It'll keep her for a little while, anyway. Maybe she can find a place to stay. Or a job somewhere."

Connor laughed harshly. "Who'd hire a woman who's having a child without benefit of a husband?"

"Hell, I don't know," James said impatiently.

Connor turned away, holding the blood money his brother had given him, and headed for the house. His mother was crying in the kitchen over James departure. At least she had been half an hour ago, when her favorite son had walked out the door, saddlebags in his hands. He'd see if she was calmer now, ready to talk. And he'd think seriously about filling her in on the situation in which he found himself.

"I'll kill Connor Webster for getting you in this fix," Alger Peterson said loudly, his voice ringing throughout the dining room and probably resounding from the parlor ceiling.

"That won't do a bit of good, Daddy," she said calmly. "Connor isn't the father."

Alger looked stunned, his mouth falling open at her announcement. It was almost as much a surprise as her first declaration, a whispered notice that he would be a grandfather before the year was out.

Not that her father was averse to the title of grandfather, but he'd expected it to be part of her marriage. He'd given his blessing to her betrothal, and welcomed Connor into the Peterson household as an honored guest.

"Connor isn't the father?" Alger's eyes widened as if he'd been observer to an unbelievable sight. "What are you talking about? Of course he's the father. He's responsible for it."

"No, Daddy," she repeated. "He's not."

"Well then, who is?" her mother asked. Silent up until now, Minnie Peterson was nonetheless a woman who always managed to speak her mind. "Whoever it is, he'd better march over to the parsonage and take you along. There won't be a church wedding, young lady, but there *will* be a wedding."

"You're both wrong," Loris said quietly. "I'm no longer engaged to Connor, and it will be official when I give him back his ring. The other person in this situation has already left town, and I won't be marrying him either."

"Left town?" Her father blustered loudly as he marched around the table and gripped her shoulders. Dragging her to her feet, he shook her, then apparently decided that action was not sufficient to express his anger and so delivered two ringing slaps to her face.

Loris stood silently before him, her eyes closed. She could not bear to look on his face, could not abide the disdain he showered on her. Her cheeks stung from his blows, but compared to the painful disgrace she had brought upon her family, the pain was of little importance.

"You can pack your things and move out," her father said bluntly. "You are no longer our daughter."

"Mama?" Loris turned to Minnie and spoke the title as if it were an entreaty for mercy. As indeed it was.

"Your father is the head of this house," Minnie said primly. Even if she'd wanted to side with her daughter, Loris knew that her mother shared Alger's views on such things as family honor.

"All right. I've got my things packed in the tapestry valise, Mama. I knew this would happen. When I'm settled somewhere, I'll send it back to you."

"You can keep it," Minnie said. "I couldn't look at it again."

Loris left the dining room, walked up the stairs slowly and entered her room. She was cold, not due to the weather outdoors, but instead to a chill that seemed to emanate from deep inside her body.

Her warmest clothing was on the bed, a pair of men's long red underwear she'd been given by her father when they shrank in the wash, becoming too small for him. Before this, she'd only worn them when she went to the river to ice skate in the winter time. Tonight, they would keep her from freezing to death. She didn't plan on forcing her parents to buy a coffin for her, so it would behoove her to start out walking with enough clothing on to keep warm.

By the time she'd found her heaviest woolen shirt, donning it over her dress, and then pulling her heavy leather boots on her feet, she was breathless from the exertion of preparing to leave. Or maybe it was just the prelude to a fit of crying that seemed to be imminent.

Valise in her hand, she walked down the stairs and saw her mother awaiting her in the wide hallway. "Here are your mittens and a warm scarf," Minnie said. "I have no use for them. You may as well take them with you."

It was a backhanded gesture of kindness, and though hurt by her mother's words, Loris offered her thanks.

"Let us know where you are," Minnie said.

"Will you really care?" Loris asked, and then bit at her lip. There was no point in estranging her mother from her any more than she already had with her announcement.

"Yes, I'll care, Loris," her mother said righteously, pressing a bundle into her hands. "Here's enough food to keep you going for a day or so." Minnie touched her daughter's shoulder as a gesture of farewell and spoke again. "Just wait until your child is grown and you are hurt by that child beyond measure. You'll find that you still care."

"Maybe." Loris pulled her mittens on, knowing she would be thankful for their warmth, and wrapped the scarf around her neck. The front door opened and she stepped out onto the porch. The sun had set, the moon had risen, and the night was clear and cold. Stars glittered in profusion across the sky, but they blurred as she walked down the steps and made her way toward the street, her falling tears blinding her.

Yet, she cried but little, for she forced herself to blink them away, knowing she didn't have enough energy to waste on feeling sorry for herself. She struck off for the western edge of town, since it was closer to the shelter she sought than walking through the business district. Taking that route raised her chances of meeting someone she knew.

The road was rutted, so she chose instead to walk on the grass at the side, now overlaid with a light covering of new snow. At least her boots would keep her feet from freezing, she thought, shifting the valise to her other hand. It was heavy, but she'd brought everything warm she owned. And then topped off the contents with a quilt that seemed to be an intelligent addition to her collection. It would keep the wind from her, should she decide to wrap it around herself.

For a moment, she wondered just where she would be when she unfolded the quilt and curled in its folds. Maybe in someone's barn. Although the scent of fresh hay in a barn turned her stomach these days. Had, in fact, for three months, ever since the evening James Webster had pressed her deeply into a bed of the fragrant stuff in her father's extra stall. As if it had never happened, James had ignored her for weeks, while her own guilt had nagged at her, as she continued her discreet courtship with Connor.

She'd been a fool. And not for the first time, she cursed the dance she'd shared with James, the kisses he'd offered, the bedding he'd instigated with her full cooperation.

She passed the edge of town and paced steadily beside the road. Trees met overhead, their branches bare of leaves, the faint noise of their rubbing together in the wind contributing an eerie sound to the quiet of the evening. Ahead was a farmhouse, one belonging to Joe Benson, a friend of her father's.

She skirted it, walking on the other side of the road as she passed by the lane leading to the big house. Being seen would be bad enough. Being recognized would be worse. The valise was heavy and she shifted it again, feeling the muscles in her arm cramp.

The next two houses were small, lived in by hired help, men and their families hired by the Bensons to help them on the farm. She walked as quickly as she could without stumbling and falling. She couldn't afford to turn her ankle or twist her knee. It was difficult enough keeping a steady pace while her legs were sound. Making her way in the dark with pain as her companion would be unthinkable.

An hour passed slowly, and Loris walked on, knowing that she had barely begun her trip. Clouds began to appear in the sky, lowering clouds that made her think they might contain snow. The stars disappeared in another hour or so, and the wind came up, its cold fingers cutting through her clothing as if she were barely clad.

To her right, just ahead, she caught sight of a building. It looked to be an abandoned farm, left by a family who'd moved onward and left their house to the elements.

If that were true, she might be able to get inside and build a fire, she thought. Maybe sleep for the night before she walked on in the morning. Turning up the lane that led to the small structure, her heart beat faster, and she peered at the shuttered windows as she rounded the side to where a small back porch offered shelter.

She climbed the steps slowly, fearful of encountering a locked door. But the knob turned readily and she pushed the door open. Darkness met her, but with an innate sense, she knew the house was empty.

In the depths of the room, she spotted the looming bulk of a cookstove and her hopes rose. Taking her mittens off, she approached the black form and felt across the top of the warming oven, hoping for a box of matches. Her search was rewarded by the discovery of just such a find, and she opened the box, finding it over half full.

Lighting a match, she blinked and then lifted one of the stove's burner lids and peered inside. Ashes met her gaze, but on the floor to one side of where she stood was a woodbox, holding a good supply of short pieces, apparently cut to size for burning.

A bit of brown paper was crumpled beneath the first two chunks of wood and she placed it in the stove, then added pieces of wood and a bit of kindling she found scattered on the floor. Lighting another match, she set the paper ablaze, then watched hopefully as it caught the kindling in its path, flaring up around the larger pieces of wood.

With care, she settled the lid in place and hovered over the stove, waiting for some small bit of warmth to reach her fingers. It took but five minutes or so for the fire to penetrate the iron and reach her. She shivered, held her hands over the stove lid and closed her eyes.

Maybe she could sleep right here in the kitchen, she thought. It would be the warmest place in the house, and though sleeping on the floor lacked comfort, she could not be fussy. She looked around the room, her eyes finally adjusting to the darkness. The shape of a lamp hanging over the table on the other side of the room was encouraging, and she carried the box of matches there, lighting one as she lifted the globe from the lamp and sought to light the wick.

It caught, flared, and then softened a bit as she dropped the globe in place. Now the room was clearly visible, and her heart lifted as she saw the kitchen dresser across the room, the doors protecting an assortment of dishes behind the wavy glass.

The bundle of food her mother had pressed on her was in the pocket of her coat, and she brought it forth into the light. Half a loaf of bread, a chunk of cheese and a generous portion of roast beef lay wrapped inside a dish towel. Enough food for at least a day, perhaps longer if she rationed it out.

The floor did not seem overly dirty, she decided, and was certainly warmer than any other room in the house. Tomorrow was soon enough to go exploring. For now she eyed the bare floor and found it welcoming.

Another chunk or two of wood in the stove would warm her for a few hours, and she could replenish the fire during the night if need be. The stove lid clunked dully into place as she fortified the stove, and then herself, for the rest of the night.

Her quilt was warm, and for that she was grateful, pulling it around herself as she curled on the floor, her head cushioned by the valise. From beneath the stove, glittering in the reflection of the lamp, two tiny eyes watched her, and even the thought of a stray mouse could not stir her from the cozy cocoon of her quilt.

"I'll worry about you in the morning, Mr. Mouse," she said softly. "Just stay out of my food," she warned the tiny creature, thankful that she'd tucked the package into her valise.

And then her eyes closed as weariness overcame her. Even the desolation of her shelter was not enough to keep her awake, and she basked in the heat of the stove, her hands tucked between her thighs for warmth.

Chapter Two

The crowing of a rooster woke her, and Loris sat up from her makeshift bed, groaning aloud as she felt the pull of muscles strained by the hard floor. If there was one chicken out there, there might be more, she thought hopefully. And if one was a hen, there might even be an egg or two available.

She rose slowly, aware now of the chill of the kitchen around her. The fire had apparently gone out, and she'd been too tired earlier to replenish it. Lifting the stove lid, she caught sight of glowing ashes and was cheered by their presence.

More wood was placed with care, lest she suffocate the promise of flames, and then as the bits of bark on the sides of the wood caught fire, she smiled and gently put the lid in place.

Shaking out her quilt, she folded it, depositing it over the back of a chair, and then set out to explore her shelter. The house was small, a parlor and two bedrooms occupying the rest of the downstairs. Furniture had been left behind, the owners apparently not considering it worth transporting. But upstairs there were two more bedrooms, complete with beds.

But beggars couldn't be choosers, she reminded herself as she viewed the sparse furnishings throughout the house. At least there were dishes, and perhaps kettles, though what she would find to cook was another thing entirely.

First on her list of the day's tasks was finding an outhouse, she decided. Stepping outside, she saw the small structure standing near what appeared to be the chicken coop. Loris made her way there, walking carefully across the yard, lest she slip on the covering of fresh snow. Only an inch or so whitened the ground, and she was thankful there wasn't any more than that.

Her duties completed, she went to the chicken coop, opening the door to find two hens squatting in the confines of their nests. A barrel of feed had been tipped over, most likely by the owners, who probably felt guilty at leaving the creatures behind. Bits and pieces of feed lay about on the ground, liberally mixed with the chicken's leavings, and Loris felt a surge of nausea at the odor of the pungent manure.

The two hens squawked at Loris's appearance in their domain, and one of them fluttered to perch on a dowel rod apparently placed there for their comfort. In the nest, Loris found four eggs and she gathered them, aware that they might not be fit to eat. It would be easy enough to find out, she knew and given the temperature of the henhouse, they might yet be edible.

Leaving the second hen to cover her clutch of eggs, Loris left the henhouse, spying the rooster as he scurried in through the tiny door leading into the fenced-in yard. He halted before her and cocked his head, perhaps deciding if she were worth his attention.

Before he could lunge in her direction, which the rooster at home tended to do if disturbed, she left, closing the door tightly behind herself, carrying her find to the house. There, she entered the kitchen, appreciating the warmth of the stove, and found a bowl in the cupboard.

Next, she searched for a skillet and came up with one in the depths of the oven. With it were two kettles and she pulled them out, using her mittens as potholders, and put her treasures on the stove burners.

"Things are looking up," she sighed, heading for the sink in the corner, although she doubted that water would be available, given the cold temperature. A small pan sat in the wash basin, its surface icy, and she rapped on it sharply, pleased when a hole appeared and water welled up.

Dumping the scant cup or so of liquid into the pump to prime it, she worked the handle vigorously and was rewarded by a gush of water.

She rinsed and filled the wash basin and carried it to the stove. Opening the reservoir attached to the side of the black appliance, she tipped the clean water inside, knowing it would warm up soon and provide her with a bit of comfort. She filled the basin again, and after filling the reservoir to the top, she set about washing the skillet and kettles, placing them in the basin and allowing the whole collection to heat on top of the stove.

Beneath the sink was a jar of soap, and she carried it back to the stove, not surprised to find the container behind the faded curtain some poor soul had hung to hide the assortment of odds and ends she'd tucked beneath her sink board. It was the same place her own mother kept a supply, and Loris was familiar with the ins and outs of a kitchen.

A glob of the slimy stuff would soon form bubbles in the basin and would give her a semblance of cleanliness when she began washing the utensils and dishes she planned to use. So she settled to wait for the fire to do its work, pulling a chair closer to the warmth and seeking the bundle of food her mother had given her.

The loaf of bread was cold, but she tore off a piece and bit into it. If the meat were warm, it would be more inviting, she decided, and, ignoring the fact that the skillet, by any measure of cleanliness, should be scrubbed first, she pulled it from the basin and rinsed it beneath the pump. With a quick swipe of her mother's dish towel, she placed it on the top of the stove and put her piece of roast beef in it.

Bits and pieces of silverware were stored in one of the dresser drawers, a motley assortment, to be sure, but Loris found that necessity made her overlook much, and she found a knife to cut up the meat, allowing it to cook faster. Adding a bit of water assured it would not burn, and she waited patiently for her makeshift meal to be ready. Apparently the former tenants had headed for greener pastures and left here empty-handed.

A thin layer of gravy formed from the meat and water, and Loris cut her piece of bread in half and placed it to steam atop the slices of roast beef. A fork from the drawer was wiped on her towel, and when the meat had warmed through she placed the skillet on the table, then sat down to eat her breakfast.

The eggs would wait till dinnertime, she decided, and perhaps, if all of them were fit to eat, she'd poach them and eat them with another piece of her bread.

In the meantime, she'd do well to scout up a source of wood for the stove, since she'd already used up almost half of the supply left in the kitchen. Maybe there would be a woodpile outside, or hopefully, an ax in the barn, allowing her to cut her own. Not that she'd ever done such a thing, but it certainly couldn't be all that difficult.

Her stomach reacted well to the food and she took the skillet to the sink, rinsing it with the flowing water from the pump. Filling the container she'd used to prime it earlier, she assured that the pump would be usable, and then set about washing the contents of the basin. Leaving them to dry, she decided to explore the pantry, the doorway of that small room beckoning her from across the kitchen.

It was dark, windowless, and she was delighted to find a candle on one of the shelves, awaiting a match. Within moments, she'd lit it and saw she'd stumbled on a storehouse of sustenance. The owners must have taken only what they could carry and left the rest, for jars of produce lined the top shelf, and partially filled bins of flour and sugar met her gaze. Even a smaller crock of coffee was there, and she smiled with pleasure as she considered the warmth it would elicit.

A dusty coffeepot was there, too, and she carried it to the sink, washed it quickly and then filled it with fresh water. Dumping in a handful of coffee, she settled it on the warmest spot on the stove, and found herself silently urging the fire to do its best to bring the coffee to a boil. An additional log added to the glowing coals insured its performance, and she set off for the back yard, hoping to find enough wood to keep herself in comfort for the remainder of the day and the night to come.

A pile of neatly stacked logs at the side of the house brought a smile to her lips and she carried a load indoors, depositing the wood in the box behind the stove. "This is more like it," she murmured to herself, basking in the heat and congratulating herself on her ability thus far to survive.

"Where is she?" Connor Webster spoke the words in a rush, his appearance on her front porch apparently having struck Minnie Peterson speechless. The woman groped for a reply and finally grasped Connor by the arm and brought him into her front hallway.

"I don't know," Minnie said, her voice breaking.

"She's not here?" Connor asked, and Minnie shook her head.

"She left last evening, right after supper. Not willingly, but her father gave her no choice."

"And what about you?" Connor asked. "Did you just let her go out in the cold without knowing where she could find shelter?" Connor's heart ached as he recalled his own harsh words to Loris.

"I had no choice," Minnie said weakly. "I gave her a bit of food, and she'd packed a valise. What more could I do, under the circumstances?"

"You gave her a *bit of food?*" Connor asked incredulously. "Just what does that mean?"

"Don't get huffy with me, young man. I shouldn't have offered her even a crust of bread, after she brought disgrace down on her family the way she has."

"No? Not even the fact that she is your daughter made a difference?"

"Alger told her she's no longer our daughter," Minnie said.

"And you agreed with him?"

"I had no choice," she said.

"You *had* a choice," Connor told her, as did he. "Now, have you any idea which way she headed?" The urge to find Loris was overwhelming now. And his anger with her was banished by the memory of her vulnerability.

"I watched her," Minnie said. "She walked away from town, toward the open country."

"On the road?"

Minnie nodded. "On the side of the road. There was fresh snow, and she apparently didn't want to walk in the wagon ruts."

Connor was silent, his mind working furiously. If she'd left last evening, after dark, she wouldn't haven't gotten very far, unless she'd just kept walking until she dropped. And in that case she would have frozen to death. The temperatures were below freezing, and last night they'd dropped far lower.

"What are you going to do?" Loris's mother asked as Connor turned away.

"Find her." The words were terse and to the point, and Minnie only nodded as she closed the door.

Connor mounted his horse and rode from the yard, heading out of town at a slow pace, his gaze on the sparse covering of snow beside the road. Several sets of footprints marred the pristine surface, but most of them were heading to town, not in the other direction.

One small set was easy to follow, and he turned his

horse to the grassy area, the better to track them. If it was, indeed, Loris's tracks he followed, she'd slipped several times and he winced as he thought of the harsh wind blowing toward her as she walked. He'd heard it around the house all night, in those long hours when he'd found it impossible to sleep, not knowing what had happened to her. Those dark hours when he'd admitted to himself that his love for her had not died.

The fact that her father had turned her out of the house didn't surprise Connor. Alger Peterson was a harsh man, a man dedicated to all that was right and proper, and the idea of his daughter bearing a child out of wedlock must have struck him a heavy blow.

Connor wondered why the man hadn't tried to understand his daughter's dilemma, at least long enough to provide her with a place to live, and someone to look after her. Instead he'd booted her out.

The footprints Connor followed wove back and forth a bit, as if their owner were uncertain as to the path she took, and well she might have been. Walking away from town would not have offered her much choice as to the shelter she sought.

He passed by the Benson place, saw Joe himself outside, walking toward the barn, and thought for a moment that it would have been a good place for Loris to seek a resting place. But the footprints beside the road told a different story.

She'd bypassed Benson's barn and walked on. Farther than he'd thought she would, for the next two places had been bypassed too, and after that point, hers were the only tracks to be seen in the sparse covering of snow.

Connor blessed that snow, for without it, he'd never

have seen her trail. He needed to find Loris. She'd been betrayed by parents who should have given her love and affection, setting aside the disgrace she might have brought to them. And he, himself, had turned his back on her.

He cursed himself for being so harsh with her, for denying her his aid. He'd offered her money, his help should she want to leave town, but not the helping hand she'd needed. But he'd been so angry at her betrayal, he hadn't been thinking straight.

If he found her by the side of the road, it would be on his head, for he'd been the logical one she could have counted on to give her help. And he'd turned her away. Sleep had evaded him during the night, his memory bringing her desperate plight before him when he would have slept. While he'd been tucked into his bed, she'd been walking through the night, and he felt the pangs of regret strike his soul with harsh lashes of the whip of remorse. Upon awakening, he'd left home to find her.

A wisp of smoke rose from an abandoned house to the south and he touched his horse's barrel with his heels, his heart lifting as he considered the possibility of Loris having found shelter there. The owners, a couple named Stewart, had left town months ago, taking little with them. But the house was still livable, to his knowledge.

His horse trotted up the lane and to his relief, he noted the footprints that went before him. She was here. He'd lay money on it. Somehow, she'd gotten into the house and lit a fire. The prospect of finding her at the side of the road had daunted his spirits, but now he breathed a prayer of thanksgiving as he realized his fears might have been in vain.

The house was small, the windows covered with shutters, but the back porch held a collection of scattered footprints in the snow that covered its surface. Connor drew his horse to a halt and slid from his saddle. The reins were wound around a hitching rail quickly and he stepped onto the porch.

Loris was dozing again, curled into her quilt on the floor, her stomach having found relief from its empty state, the skillet in the sink, soaking in the basin. She'd given in to the sleepy warmth of the stove and found her place on the floor once more, settling down to sleep, knowing that it would do her more good than tramping around in the snow, trying to discover her surroundings.

The sound of the door opening penetrated her slumber and she caught her breath, lying as quietly as possible as she heard the footsteps enter the kitchen. Then the sound of the heavy portal closing told her she was trapped in the room with an intruder.

"Loris?" His voice was low, his tone tentative, and she sat up warily.

It had sounded like Connor, the voice deep and soft, the syllables of her name rolling from his tongue in a sound that reminded her of the breeze rustling though the trees in springtime.

But it wouldn't be Connor, she reminded herself. He'd left her on her own, just yesterday, and he was a stubborn man, not given to changing his mind, especially not overnight, and particularly not about such an important issue.

She'd betrayed Connor. He would hold his hurt pride

like a shield before him, should they meet, and the thought of ever seeing him smile at her again was beyond hope.

"Loris." This time her name was spoken in a commanding tone, and she felt the bidding of the man behind her. She turned in her quilt, her gaze seeking the intruder, and found the face of the man she'd loved for three years of her life.

"Connor?" She whispered the familiar, beloved name of the man she'd planned to marry, and noted the look of relief that washed over his handsome features. Taller than his brother, but not as muscular, Connor had a shock of black hair and the same blue Irish eyes as James. Yet, on this man, they were soft and appealing, and Loris wondered how she'd ever thought James to be the handsomer of the two, how she'd ever been fool enough to hurt Connor so badly.

He stepped closer and squatted beside her. His hands were big, his flesh cold, as he lifted her from the floor, but she did not flinch from him, welcoming his touch instead.

"Are you all right?" he asked quietly. "Are you hungry?"

She shook her head. "Mama gave me some food to take along," she told him. "I've eaten this morning."

"Are you cold?" He seemed intent on her revealing each small bit of information he could drag from her.

"No," she said softly, shivering as the cooler air in the room penetrated her clothing. Curled by the stove, she'd indeed been warm. Now, uncovered and sitting erect, she felt the chill. Her coat was tossed aside, having been used for cover as she slept, and now she reached for it.

"You're shaking with the cold," Connor said firmly, lifting her to her feet, looking down at the coat she held by one sleeve. "Let me help you put that on."

"Just pull the quilt around me," she told him. "And then put some more wood in the stove." She watched him as he released her and did as she asked, adding four large chunks of wood to her fire, and wrapping her securely in her quilt.

He watched her, his gaze hooded, his mouth firm and straight, with no sign of softening on his harsh features. Connor was handsome, she'd long ago decided. He was not a beautiful man, as was James. Connor had features that were knife-sharp, his nose a blade, his cheekbones high and seemingly carved from granite. If not for the blue eyes, she might have feared him, had she not known the man.

But she knew the soft heart beneath the broad chest, the tenderness he could call forth at will, enveloping her in his arms and holding her as he might a treasured creature he claimed as his own.

She'd turned her back on all of that, she realized, the day she'd given in to James's coaxing and offered herself to him. And loved him desperately with a love that had turned to ashes at his betrayal of her.

Now she faced the man who had planned a future for them, who had placed his ring on her finger and offered her his love. *Connor.* The man she had hurt beyond forgiveness. Who had offered her his help, should she want to leave town, who had apparently spent his morning looking for her when she came up missing today.

He watched her closely and she knew he was evaluating her, gauging her condition, allowing her to gather herself before he spoke again.

She bent her head, so that she no longer needed to see his harsh face hovering above hers. "I'm sorry you've gone to so much trouble, Connor," she said. "I didn't think you might be looking for me."

"I never intended for you to be frozen by the side of the road or left on your own, the way you were last night," he said.

"What did you think would happen?" she asked, lifting her gaze to his, venturing bravely to watch his expression.

His brow twitched as he considered her query. And then he breathed deeply, as if his words were hard to come by. "I didn't think your father would throw you out. I thought your mother would defend you. I went to your house this morning to make certain you were all right, and I couldn't believe my ears when your mother said you'd left last evening."

His eyes were icy, the chill of anger gripping him.

"Well, I'm all right, as you can see," she said, fearful of his anger being turned against her. But it seemed there was little chance of that, for he only shook his head in disbelief.

"You're far from all right," he said sharply. "You're alone and about three hours from freezing to death, should that stove not be fed on a regular basis."

"There's some food here in the pantry," she said defensively. "And wood outside. I won't freeze."

"And what happens when that pitiful pile of wood runs out?" he asked. "And when the food in the pantry is eaten?"

"There's enough wood for a couple of days, and I'll look for an ax to cut more."

"*You're* going to chop wood?" he asked. "You'd be more likely to cut your toes off or swing wrong and slice your leg open. And then what would you do?"

"I won't do that," she said stubbornly. "I'll be careful."

"You're a woman," Connor said with a stern look that stripped her of her bravado.

"What's wrong with being a woman?" she asked sharply. "I can take care of myself."

He was silent, his eyes holding hers, his mouth a straight line, giving her no clue as to his thoughts.

"I'll be fine here," she said. "You don't need to worry about me, Connor. I'm strong and able to tend to things."

"You're strong?" he asked, and with one smooth movement, he gathered her against himself and held her tightly, one arm around her waist, the other banding her shoulders.

She was trapped in his embrace, and even though she feared him not, she knew her position was that of a woman who could not move without the consent of the man who held her immobile. "Don't try to frighten me, Connor," she said softly.

"Are you frightened?" he asked harshly, as though his mood had turned to anger.

She hesitated, unwilling to admit the wash of alarm that had indeed sped through her veins. And then she looked up into his face and shook her head. "I'm not afraid of you," she told him. "You're angry with me, but you won't hurt me."

"I want to," he admitted. "I want to shake you and knock you to the floor for betraying me. I loved you,

Loris. I'd planned on a life with you, and you turned your back on all that to seek out my brother. And then you let him make love to you." His nostrils flared as if he could barely contain the pain and rage that coursed through him.

His big hands clutched her shoulders and she braced herself for his harsh touch on her slender form. But he only drew her closer to himself and his mouth claimed hers with a passion she could not refute.

She submitted to his kiss, feeling the bruising of her mouth, the crush of his embrace, the strength of his hands as he held her. His tongue claimed her, sweeping into her mouth, the invasion one he'd never instigated before. Always his kisses had been gentle, tender and welcomed.

That this claiming of her mouth was none of those mattered little. She only stood before him and endured. There was no tenderness in his caresses, for his hands were harsh, clutching at her softness, his fingers biting into her hips, his mouth hard against hers. She tasted blood and knew it came from her lips. She felt the hard ridge of his arousal against her belly, through several layers of clothing, and braced herself for his taking.

It was not to be, for he lifted his head and looked down at her. One long index finger lifted to rub at her lip and she winced at the pain of it.

"Your lip is bleeding, Loris," he said softly.

"I know," she told him. "I can taste it." That the inside of her lips were bruised and cut by the force of her teeth against them was of little matter. Her pain was small in comparison to what he felt, and she would not complain.

But Connor seemed to sense more than she had expected of him, for he touched her mouth with his own again, and this time the kiss was tender, a silent plea for her forgiveness.

"I'm sorry," he said roughly, his voice hoarse as if the words were those of a man who had drunk his share, and more, of whiskey and was speaking past the aching throat muscles of one who had had reason to regret his overindulgence.

She shook her head, offering him forgiveness, for she could do no less. He could have knocked her to the floor. And yet, he'd only spent his anger on her in passion. Even now, she felt his arousal prodding at her, and she backed away from the reminder of his desire.

"I won't hurt you again," Connor said harshly. "Don't be afraid of me, Loris."

"No," she said quietly. "I'm not."

"I'll chop some wood for you," he told her. "And then I'll go into town and get you some supplies."

"You needn't do that," she told him. "Just leave me, Connor. I'm not worth your concern."

"Ah, but you are," he muttered. "James left some money for you, and I'm going to spend it on the things you'll need for the next little while. And then we'll figure out what to do."

"James left me money?" Her mind latched on that bit of information and she felt a surge of anger. "I don't want his money," she said bitterly. "I'd rather starve."

"Well, as long as I'm alive and breathing, you aren't in any danger of starving," Connor told her. He helped her onto a chair at the table and turned away. "I'm going out to chop wood, and I'll be back in a bit. There should be enough in that stove to keep you warm for a couple of hours."

"Thank you," she said softly, unwilling to meet his gaze, lest she begin crying and be unable to halt the deluge. Her tears would not be only for herself, but for the pain she had brought to Connor and his brother. For her own weakness that had forever caused a rift between two men who had been as close as any brothers could be. And for her loss of the man with her now. Connor could never forgive her or love her again, and her heart ached at the knowledge of what she had lost.

Chapter Three

Connor's generosity was surprising—and almost overwhelming. The woodbox had been replenished before he left her alone. He'd gone to town, bought supplies for her and chopped more wood on his return, for over an hour, piling an impressive amount of kindling and good-sized logs on the back porch.

And then he'd left, mounting his horse and riding away without another word, only a casual wave of his hand. Would he return? She doubted it, but then she'd have laid odds that he wouldn't have shown up the first time. But Connor was a kind, gentle man, feeling a sense of responsibility to a woman in need, even if that woman was his former fiancée.

Loris found a fresh loaf of bread in the supplies Connor had carried into the kitchen. He must have stopped at the bread lady's house, a small cottage at the edge of town, where lived an elderly soul, Hilda Kane, who existed on the pitiful amount of money her baking brought to her. She baked daily, and Loris had been sent there almost that often to pick up a loaf or two for her mother.

"I could bake my own," her mother had said more than once, "but she needs the money and I can't make it any better than Hilda's."

Fresh bread was almost enough to make a meal from, Loris decided. She ate the last of the cheese and the few bits of beef left from the morning, and settled before the stove again. The sun had sunk into the western sky and dark clouds hid the moon and stars, promising snow by morning.

But the kitchen was warm, and by tomorrow perhaps she'd feel like venturing into the other rooms, try to settle in a little better. After all, she couldn't sleep on the kitchen floor for the rest of her life. But for tonight, it would do just fine.

The woman was crazy. There was no way she could survive alone in that deserted house. Connor frowned, finishing up the evening chores. He handled twice as many now, with James gone, but they were done automatically, without thought, as if his body was created to perform the familiar duties of a farmer.

For that was what he was. A farmer. Like his father before him, and his grandfather before that, the Webster men lived off the land. He'd been milking these cows and feeding the stock ever since he could remember.

Connor doubted if his life would be any different than those who'd gone before. He'd always thought to find a nice girl, get married and work the homestead, taking care of his parents until they were gone from this world, leaving the property equally divided between the brothers. His children would follow suit, working and living off the land, and there was a solid feel of security there.

The land would never let you down, his grandpa had said. If you tended your soil and fertilized and weeded your crops, you stood to reap a fine harvest. Unless the summer was dry and the rains refused to fall. Like last year, when the dry spell had chased several families from town, unable to cope with the poverty they faced without a harvest.

Now Loris had claimed the right to squat in one of those places left deserted. And a squatter is what she is, Connor thought bleakly, living on property that didn't belong to her, yet was unwanted by anyone else. It could probably be purchased for taxes, Connor thought, but Loris didn't have any money to speak of.

He felt the wad of bills in his pocket, touched the bulk with his palm and recognized that he'd barely made a dent in the cash James left behind for Loris. Maybe Loris would accept the cash more readily if he spent it on back taxes and she could live where she was, legally and aboveboard.

The manure pile was heaped, the fresh bedding spread and the cow milked, all while Connor debated the options left to him. He brought the horses in from the pasture; indeed, they were more than willing to enter the warm barn and find their stalls. The cold was bitter, the wind biting through Connor's coat as he headed back toward his parents' house, a place in which he no longer felt the warmth of home.

"You finished?" his mother asked, dishing up a bowl of stew for him. "Your pa ate already. He's not in a good mood," she said glumly.

And wasn't that the truth. The man had been deserted by his favorite son, had been left with one less pair of hands to keep the place up. He'd no doubt have to hire a man to help out. And that would involve finding a place for that man to sleep. Probably a small room could be made habitable in the barn, or else Pa might just hire someone who lived nearby, close enough to come in by the day.

"All done?" his mother asked again. She'd been crying, her eyes swollen and reddened, her skin shiny as if it had been washed by a multitude of tears.

"Yes, I'm not very hungry," Connor said, rising from the table. Things were different with James gone. He'd always been the joker, the one with a ready wit and a tall tale to tell over the supper table. Now they were reduced to eating separately, for he'd guarantee his mother had eaten standing at the stove. Nothing was the same.

"Did you go see Loris?" his mother asked. "Did she know that James was gone?"

"She knew," Connor said quietly. And then decided he might as well fill her in on the mess James had left behind. "Loris is going to have a baby, Ma. And James is the father."

Peggy Webster's mouth dropped open, but no words came forth. She wiped her hands on the front of her apron, then stuffed them in the voluminous pockets, still silent.

"And before you ask, James knew when he left that Loris was bound to be abandoned by her folks. They kicked her out last night."

"Where is she?"

"In a deserted farmhouse. I followed her tracks and found her this morning. Got her some supplies and chopped a bit of wood for her."

"James wouldn't marry her?" Her voice was dull, her

eyes hopeless, as if she couldn't imagine her son ignoring his responsibilities so casually. "He got her in the family way and just ran off? I can't believe your brother would do that."

"He gave me some money for her, but she doesn't want to accept it," Connor said, deliberately concealing his planned use of the cash.

"And Minnie threw her out? It was bitter cold last night."

"Minnie Peterson doesn't act like she gives a good gol-dern about her daughter, Ma. I saw her this morning, and she was as cold as any woman I've ever seen."

"Maybe she'll change her mind. After all, that's her grandchild Loris is carrying."

"It's your grandchild, too," Connor said softly, and watched as that fact sank into his mother's conscious mind.

"So it is," she said idly, smoothing her apron with a practiced touch. "Would she come here, do you suppose?"

"Loris?" And at his mother's nod, Connor shook his head. "I doubt she wants much to do with any of us right now. She's got pride aplenty, and she's bound and determined to make it on her own."

His mother stood silent a moment, then spoke words that sounded almost spiteful, he thought. "James must have had good reason not to stick up for her. Maybe she's just bad news." She paused and then sighed, rather dramatically, he thought. "But you're going to help her, aren't you, Connor?"

He hesitated, then nodded. "I'll help her, Ma. As much as she'll let me."

He'd go to town tomorrow and check at the tax office, see what was owed on the place where Loris had camped out. Find out if he could pay the taxes and take over the farm.

In the meantime, he'd do well to ride out there and be sure she was all right, staying on her own in a deserted house, with no gun or even a dog to keep her safe. In ten minutes, he'd saddled his horse and donned his heaviest coat. A warm scarf circled his throat and heavy gloves warmed his fingers. From the kitchen, his mother watched as he rode away and he offered her a wave of his hand, causing her to lift her own palm to press against the window. It was a gesture he'd seen many times before, whenever one of her menfolk had left home and she couldn't bear to wave goodbye.

The Webster place was on the opposite end of town from Loris's haven, and Connor made his way past the business establishments. Everyone was gone home for the night, only the saloon still being lit, with voices sounding loudly within.

He passed the home Loris had lived in all of her life, noting the lights glowing in the front parlor and in a bedroom window upstairs. How they could rest, not knowing where their daughter was, was beyond him. Didn't they care? Or did their hurt run so deeply they couldn't allow themselves to yearn for their girl?

He rode on, past the lighted houses where folks were readying for bed. And then he spotted the farmhouse where Loris was keeping warm. He rode to the back yard, tied his horse to an upright post and climbed the three steps to the wide porch. Through the window, he caught sight of a shadowed figure, passing between himself and the lamp glow.

His knuckles rapped twice on the door and he called her name. "Loris? It's Connor. Can I come in?"

She opened the door, just a few inches, as though loath to allow him entrance. "It's late, Connor," she said softly. "I'm about to blow out the lamp and go to sleep."

"Where?" he asked. "On the kitchen floor?"

"It's the warmest place in the house," she told him sharply. "And warmth is what interests me right now. I'll think about using one of the bedrooms tomorrow, maybe. If I can get a fire going in the fireplace, I'll probably use the larger room."

"I'll light a fire for you if you want to sleep there tonight." Something about the woman held him here, and he could not have spoken aloud just what it was. She was brave, willing to depend on herself, and yet he felt the aura of need flow from one to the other of them, a cry for him, lest he turn and leave her alone.

"I'll be all right on the floor. Truly," she said quietly, unwilling, it seemed, to meet his gaze, looking instead down at the floor where her quilt lay. It looked to be a cold, lonesome spot on which to sleep, but it sure beat being outdoors. If it was what Loris wanted, he couldn't force her to do otherwise. Still, he felt the urge to try.

His arms encircled her, his body responded to her as it always had, and his mouth descended to touch hers with a tender touch. "Please, let me help you."

Her eyes were dark and seemed empty of hope. "What can you do? Chop wood? You've already done that."

"I'm going to pay the back taxes on this place, and then I'll make certain that you have enough food to eat and wood to burn for a while. That way you'll have a shelter to live, and I'll rest easier, knowing that you're not going to starve or freeze to death."

"You'll pay the back taxes?" She frowned. "How can you do that? It'll require a lot of money, Connor."

"James is going to provide that for you, Loris. It's bad enough he's deserted you, the least he can do is pay for a place for you to live."

"I don't want his help." Her chin lifted stubbornly and her mouth tightened.

"I didn't ask you," Connor told her. "I'm going to take care of it, and if I have to, I'll stay here with you to make certain you're all right."

"You'll have the whole town talking."

"You think I really care? Not about myself anyway. But, mark my words, if anyone has anything to say about you, Loris, I'll hang him up to dry."

"I didn't know you were so tough," she said, her smile appearing.

"Not usually," he admitted. "But right now, I feel like you've been abandoned by too many people, and I need to stick close and let you know that someone cares."

"You really care, Connor?" Her voice sounded dubious and she looked away from his gaze as if she could not believe his claim.

"You're a human being, hurt and alone. And more than that, you're a woman who's been betrayed by a man. Maybe I just need to make amends for James. I don't know. But I do know that I can't walk away from you."

She felt his arms tighten around her, knew for a moment the joy of being held in a man's embrace. Even if he only felt sorry for her, she couldn't help but rejoice in that fact. She'd been so alone, so close to the end of her rope. And now Connor was here.

"Will you have something to eat?" She motioned toward the cupboard where her store of food for tomorrow rested behind glass doors. "I can fix you some toast in the oven, and there's jam."

"Any coffee?" He looked searchingly at the stove, as though a coffeepot might miraculously appear there.

"I'll heat it in a pan," she offered. "I emptied the pot, so the leftovers wouldn't taste burnt, but it'll only take a minute to bring to a boil."

He nodded. "Sounds good to me. And then we'll talk about me staying here for the night."

She'd meant to send him on his way, but Connor was not easily deterred, for he hauled in his bedroll and the leather pack carrying his personal effects and bedded down for the night at her backside.

Now she lay beside him, aware that he was awake, knowing he had put his reputation on the line by staying with her, and yet was unable to deny the peace his presence delivered to her aching heart.

"You awake?" His whisper was soft, but she smiled as she heard his familiar tones. "Are you warm enough, Loris?"

"I'm fine. Just thinking about my nice feather pillow from my bed at home."

"You don't need a pillow with me here, honey. Turn over and lie on my shoulder. I'll keep you warm."

It was tempting, but she shook her head. "No, I'll be fine here."

As if he allowed her the privacy she'd asked for, he

merely shifted to curl around her, his wide chest against her back, his arm lifting to fit itself around her middle. Through the quilt, she felt the warmth of long legs against her own, and knew the heat of a warm body as it drove the night chill away.

"Thank you." The words seemed but little thanks to express her appreciation, but they were all she knew to offer. And it seemed he didn't expect any more from her, for his arm tightened a bit and then relaxed around the curve of her waist.

"Sleep, Loris." Perhaps another time, she might have considered it a command, maybe even resented it, but tonight, he was here and she was needy of comfort.

The rooster awoke her early, just as dawn was tinging the sky with morning light, and the glow was edging the shuttered windows. The gloom of the room was giving way to dim daylight when she stirred, felt Connor's hand tighten on her waist, and then remembered that she was not alone.

"Turn over here." He left her no room for discussion, only commanded her obedience in a firm voice that seemed rough and raw to her ears.

She straightened her legs and rolled toward him, aware that his body was mere inches from hers, that his arm still enfolded her and his body heat warmed her. Even with the quilt thrown from her shoulder, she was not cold. No great amount of fire still burned behind her in the stove, the last of Connor's forays to add wood having taken place in the middle of the night.

"Now just rest for a bit." His arms enclosed her and she relaxed against him, too thankful for his presence to admit her doubts about the decency of the situation in which she found herself this morning.

She felt his mouth touch her forehead, felt his hands roam her back. Like two hot bricks they left their images wherever they touched, and she could barely contain the shivers that swept over her. His throat was so close, his skin held the aroma of soap and a male scent that tempted her closer, and she brought her lips to rest against whiskered skin. Her lips felt the tiny stubbles of his beard and she shifted to where his skin was softer, nearer his ear, feeling his quick reaction to her caresses.

"Loris?" She thought his voice trembled, and yet could barely place credence in the thought. And then he spoke her name again, more tenderly this time, it seemed, and she lifted her face to gaze deeply into his eyes.

"Don't be giving me this sort of encouragement, sweetheart," he said tenderly. "It wouldn't take much for me to roll over on top of you and make you mine, even without marriage."

"I haven't told you not to, Connor. In fact, I've almost given you the right."

"But I don't have the right. Not now. Not without a wedding. I'm not sure you're ready for that."

"I'm just surprised you even want to be this close to me, after what I did to you," she said quietly.

"That sorta takes a back seat when I'm with you. I've felt a deep hurt, Loris. I won't deny that, but you've been betrayed by my brother, and I can't let that go. And if being with you and helping you make a home here helps to fix the mess you're in right now, then that's what I want to do."

He seemed to be searching for words, and she could

only wish that his actions had nothing to do with James's behavior…that Connor would care for her for his own reasons.

And as if he heard her thoughts and wanted to reassure her, he spoke again. "I'm not out for revenge on James, but I need to make reparation for what happened to you. If helping you is making me happy, then I hope you'll allow me to have my way in this."

"I won't fight you, Connor. I care about you, and I'll never be able to thank you enough for helping me."

He squeezed her tightly, and then released her. "Well, that's settled then. Now let's get up before I get any more…" he paused as if searching for a phrase to describe his condition "…any more randy than I am right now," he finished.

"All right." She would not argue his wisdom in bringing a halt to this scene. She'd gotten in trouble by being impetuous before. There was no sense in making a bad situation worse. And Connor was an honorable man. She respected him.

They ate breakfast together and Connor set off for town, his plans made. He would pay the back taxes, stop at the general store and order a new table from the Sears, Roebuck catalog. A table with long benches for either side, to put in the kitchen.

That done, he bought some warm bedding for the big bed upstairs, then searched out an assortment of warm clothing for Loris to wear. What he hadn't planned on was the curious looks of the storekeeper as Connor's bill was tallied.

"You plannin' on settin' up housekeeping, boy?" Nothing was kept a secret long in this town. That was a given, and Connor's purchases were bound to be the subject of speculation before noon, given the speed of the local ladies' gossip.

"No, just picking up a few things," Connor told him.

"I understand the Petersons tossed their girl out in the snow the other night. You hear about that?"

"I heard," Connor said dryly. "Everyone in town heard by now, I'm sure."

The storekeeper leaned closer. "Did you hear she was in the family way?"

Again Connor nodded and agreed. "Yeah, I heard that, too. Seems like the folks hereabouts are real busy passing the word around."

"I thought you was gonna marry her, back a ways."

"Did you?" Connor dug in his pocket for cash and slowly counted out the amount of his purchases.

"Still gonna take her to the preacher?"

"Are you always this nosy?" he asked, "or is this a special occasion?" His eyes narrowed as he stepped back to observe the man.

"Didn't mean no harm," the storekeeper said quickly. "I was just wonderin'." He pointed down to the scribbling that represented Connor's order for the merchandise from the catalog. "I'll take care of this right away. Should be here in two, three weeks."

"Let me know. I'm in town every once in a while."

"Maybe I can just send word to your folks' place. You're still livin' there, ain't ya?"

Connor's jaw tightened. "I'll stop by when I come to town. Don't be sending any word anywhere. You hear me?"

The man nodded. "Yes sir, I surely do."

Connor felt the bulk of the deed in his pocket as he left the store, although the sheaf of papers could not have weighed more than a few ounces. He touched the front of his coat, heard the reassuring rustle of the paperwork he'd had made out, and grinned. Loris would be pleased to know that she needn't move anytime soon, that the place where she'd taken shelter was her own, to do with as she pleased.

He pulled his horse up next to the Benson's place and dismounted. Within thirty minutes, he owned a cow and a half-grown pup from the litter in Joe's barn. A nondescript mutt, he looked to be part shepherd, and seemed to be gentle, his tongue reaching out to seek Connor's warm skin as they traveled together on the horse.

By the time they reached the farm where Loris had taken up residence, a place she owned now, Connor was feeling pleased with himself. A huge bundle hung on either side of his saddle, a dog lay across his lap and a good milk cow followed behind him on a lead rope. He'd had a profitable trip to town.

Loris came out onto the porch, one hand on her back, her hair askew. "What do you have there?" she asked with a grin. "More work for me to do, I'll bet. What makes you think I can milk a cow?"

"You're a talented woman, ma'am. Milking shouldn't be too big a problem for you to solve. And look here at what I brought you." He dismounted, holding the dog in his arms. Legs dangled helter-skelter, all four of them longer than he'd remembered, and as Loris approached, she was served with a dose of the dog's affection.

"He's just happy to see you," Connor said with a laugh. "Must be he likes ladies."

"Well, I didn't need a kiss so early on in our acquaintance," Loris told him. "I'd just as soon he not be so friendly."

"You'll be glad he's here at night, I suspect. And I don't know just how friendly he'd be should some stranger ride up or give you grief."

"He's really mine?" Her hand lifted to pet the tawny head, and the dog wiggled in ecstasy as Connor put him on the ground and gave him the freedom to roll on his back before his new mistress. She knelt beside him, buried her fingers in the hair on his throat, petted his long legs as if she were measuring their length, and then looked up at Connor.

"Can I call him Rusty?"

Connor looked perplexed. "Where'd you get such a name for a dog?"

"I had a pup once, and my father's horse stepped on him in the barn. Killed him, of course. His name was Rusty, and I always thought—"

"Of course you can. Call this little fella anything you want to. He's your dog, and I have a suspicion that no matter what you name him, he'll come a'runnin' when you yell out his name."

"You think he likes me?" Her words sounded hopeful, childlike almost, but Connor squatted beside her and ran his hand over Rusty's head.

"I'd say it was a sure thing, sweetheart. He seems quite taken with you. He's a male, isn't he?" His look begged a smile from her and she did not deny him his reward for bringing her the pet.

"You don't know how happy you've made me," she said quietly. "He can sleep in the house and look after me."

"I thought that was my job." Connor spoke the words bluntly, expectantly, and waited for her to reply.

"You can share the duties of watchdog, if you like, Connor. I just meant, when I was alone here, he'd be good protection. When you're here, I don't need anyone else to keep an eye on things." She eyed the bundles he'd tied on his horse. "What else did you bring home?"

Connor wondered if she realized how easily that word had slipped out. *Home.* It sounded just fine to him, and he hoped she'd come to feel that this place was truly hers, that it was her home. Now, he undid the straps that held his purchases in place and carried the two wrapped packages to the house.

"Come take a look. I got some warm bedding and a couple of things for you to wear. I wanted you to be warm enough when you go out to milk the cow." His smile lent humor, and he hoped she would not balk at his buying clothing for her.

It seemed she would not do anything to fault his gifts, the shawl, the house shoes, new flannel shirts to be worn over her dresses or with the trousers he'd bought, guessing at the size, aware that they must accommodate a growing figure.

"I got you a belt to hold these up for a while," he told her. "A little later on, they'll stay up by themselves, when you've gotten a little rounder."

"Fatter, you mean." She produced a pout, and he was hard pressed not to bend over and kiss it from her mouth. Leaving Loris alone, not spending his affections on her, was going to be a tough row to hoe, he decided. His first impulse was to haul her up the stairs into the biggest bed on the second floor. But she wasn't ready for that sort of thing, yet. In fact, she might never be. Maybe her heart was still set on James. He didn't know.

"Connor?" She spoke his name softly.

His look was distracted. What had she asked him? And then he recalled her words. *Fatter, you mean.* The thought was so ludicrous, he could not help but smile. "I'll never call you *fat.* Not even plump, Loris. You'll always look good to me. You're pregnant, and that's a whole different thing."

As if he had pleased her enormously, she smiled brilliantly, an expression that brought to mind the girl he'd fallen in love with so long ago. "Tell me that again in five months or so." She grinned at him and reached up to kiss his cheek. "You're a good man, Connor Webster. Too good for me, but if you want to hang around, I'll let you."

He'd already decided to hang around, had already made plans to look after her. But her theory, that he was too good for her, was not to be believed. He was too close to laying claim to her to think himself a saint. And yet, he knew that a man could desire a woman without deep emotional ties connecting them. Only time would tell if his attraction to Loris held even a thread of what it would take to keep a marriage together.

Chapter Four

〜〜〜

"I don't want you living with that girl." His mother's jaw was set, but her eyes held a concern Connor could not deny. "She's trouble, son, and I won't have her dividing my boys anymore than she has already."

"*That girl* has a name, Ma. It's Loris. And she's going to be the mother of your grandchild. You might at least try for peace between you." He walked to the back door, tempted to walk out of his family home and never return, but his love for the man and woman who'd raised him brought him to a halt before he stepped onto the porch.

"The trouble between James and me goes a lot deeper than competition over a woman, Mother. He walked out on his responsibility. And if he won't accept that he has an obligation to Loris and her child, then I suppose I'll have to do something to hold the family's name out of the mud."

"Loris is the one who's dragged her own name in the mud," Connor's mother replied in a caustic tone. "She's got you fooled, son, and I'm not happy about you moving over there and doing for her. She'd better learn to take care of herself right quick. It looks to me like she's got a lot of years ahead of her, chock-full of regret and—"

"That's enough. I won't have you talking about her that way. I don't want to have hard feelings with you, but I have to do what's right, and to my way of thinking, taking care of Loris is the right thing to do."

"Well, don't let her lead you astray. I know her type. She'll take advantage if she can." Her mouth drew down and Connor's mother looked as though she had aged ten years in the past week. Her hair seemed more gray than brown, and her eyes had lost their sparkle. Having James leave had been hard on her. And now her other son was all packed up and ready to move to a farm on the other side of town.

Connor's father had given him an ultimatum, announcing that either he stay away from Loris or else not bother coming back home. Connor had accepted the words with a nod, and now he watched as his father stood in the barn door, waiting for his son to make up his mind.

There was no choice to be made. He'd settled that last night when he slept by Loris's side, curled around her back. He'd made the decision even before that, during those minutes when he'd held her close and felt the desire for her rise within him. Even with all that had happened, he still cared about her. He was too honest to deny it, and too attached to Loris to walk away.

His horse waited patiently, and Connor tossed his saddlebags over the gelding's hindquarters. His clothing was packed tightly in one, his personal belongings in the other. His extra pair of boots took up a lot of space, but they were too good to leave behind. Anything else he needed could be bought from the general store.

"I'll be back to get my horses," he told his father, riding the gelding to where the man stood. "Probably tomorrow."

"You know which ones belong to you." The words sounded harsh, but Connor knew that the man who spoke them was deeply hurt by his son leaving, and he could not blame him for his attitude. Maybe someday things would be set to rights.

And maybe not.

"If Hank Carpenter from Turley County comes by to see me, you can tell him I'm at the old Stewart place, the other side of town, next to Benson's."

"He wantin' one of your horses?"

"Either that or he wants me to train one he has already."

"I'll let him know."

"Thanks, Pa." Above all else, his father was an honest man, and if he said he'd send Connor's new customer to him, he was to be believed. Raising and training horses was Connor's first choice. But farming ran a close second. Fortunately, they could be combined, so long as he had a barn and some land to plant. Even though it wasn't going to be the place where he was born and raised that would receive the benefit of his skills and hard work.

Loris met him at the back door, noted the grim set of his jaw, and merely pointed toward the hallway where the stairs climbed to the second floor. He walked past her, carrying his belongings. She watched him go, thinking how much alike they were in this situation. That her clothing consisted of what Connor had bought her, that she'd come almost empty-handed to this place. And now, he'd left home and family and all else that he called his own to stay with her.

"The second door on the right." She called to him as he reached the hallway.

He turned to look down at her with dark eyes that seemed to see within her, measuring her body and reading her thoughts. "Is it your room? You know I'm planning on staying here a long time, Loris. I'm going to take care of you, and that arrangement starts right now." His gaze was straightforward, giving her notice of his plans.

She drew in a deep breath, and then shook her head. "No, that's not my bedroom."

His eyes narrowed and she thought his knuckles grew white on the bags he held. But his voice was flat and without anger when he spoke again. "Which one is yours?"

"Right across the hall." She held her breath as he met her gaze for a long minute, and then growled words that did not surprise her.

"Then that's my room, too." Turning, he walked through the doorway of the bedroom she'd claimed for herself, and she heard the distinct sound of dresser drawers opening, of his bags hitting the floor, and then the noise of his boots as he walked across the uncarpeted floor.

She was a long way from being upset with him. She'd given him the choice, allowed him the chance to have a room and bed of his own, and he'd turned her down. It was what she'd expected, and though she felt a twinge of unease, her heart sang with the knowledge that he wanted to be with her. Wanted to sleep in her bed…and most of all, he planned on taking his place in this home.

I'm going to take care of you, and that arrangement starts right now.

He'd certainly made that plain enough.

Her lips curved in a secret sort of smile as she returned to the kitchen. She'd put bacon on top of a pan of beans, adding all the ingredients her mother had used for the one-dish meal at home. Onions, tomatoes, brown sugar and a bit of mustard flavored the beans, and the thick slices of bacon made it even more palatable.

"Smells good in here." Connor came back to the kitchen, hat and coat in hand, then hung them on pegs by the back door. He took warm water from the reservoir on the side of the stove and began to wash up, dousing his face and then using the soap to scrub his hands and arms, all the way up past his elbows. His shirtsleeves were rolled up neatly, and Loris had a hard time keeping her eyes from him.

He walked up behind her as she stirred a small skillet of fried potatoes. "Is that bacon I smell?"

She thought for a moment he'd leaned close enough to kiss her neck, but instead felt the brush of his hands smoothing back her hair and then holding her shoulders in a firm grip.

"Beans and bacon. Just like my mama used to make at home. She's a good cook."

"I'd say by the looks of your dog, he thinks you're not bad, either." Rusty had been sitting at her side as she worked in the kitchen, as if he delighted in his responsibility. In return she'd managed to find a few bits and pieces to toss his way, and he peered up at her with a foolish look, his tongue lolling out of his mouth, a soft woof stating his pleasure.

"That dog likes you," Connor said.

"I hope so. At least he seems to think his main job in life is to stick close by."

"That's exactly what I wanted him to do," Connor told her. "Now, how can I help? Maybe set the table?"

"If you want to. I can do it if you're tired and want to sit down with a cup of coffee."

"I'd rather help." He knew his way around a kitchen, she noticed. His hands held the plates and silverware easily, the cup handles riding on his fingers. "Should I wipe off the oilcloth first?"

In answer, she located the dishcloth and rinsed it in clear water, then squeezed it almost dry. A quick toss across the table delivered it to his hand and he grinned his thanks.

Before long Loris had browned the potatoes nicely, the table was cleaned and set, the chairs moved to their proper places, and Connor was back at her side. "When the beans are done, I'll take them out of the oven for you," he offered.

"All right." She was happy to accede to him, preferring to finish off the odds and ends of the meal. "I've already sliced bread and I found a jar of applesauce in the pantry. I suspect we'll have enough to eat."

Connor heaped his plate with the hot food she'd provided and worked his way through the meal without comment, only pausing to butter a slice of bread. He leaned back in his chair finally, his plate clean, his hunger apparently appeased.

"Your mother's cooking must have rubbed off on you, Loris. You made a fine meal. The beans and bacon were good."

"I noticed that Rusty enjoyed them, too," she said archly. "He seems to know a soft touch when he sees one."

"Well, he's a discerning sort of dog. Knows good food when he gets some handed to him."

She felt a flush of success at his words. "Mama tried to teach me how to cook and keep house. I'm afraid I wasn't a very good pupil at some of the tasks she set for me, but I know how to use a scrub board and if there's a pair of sad irons here, I can iron your clothes."

"I saw some in the cellar," he told her. "Though why they were down there is a mystery. Maybe it's just an extra pair. My mother had two pair, one a bit heavier than the other. She said some things needed more weight."

"I'll look in the pantry. There may be a pair there, and it seems like a logical spot to store them. Maybe there's an ironing board there, too, back in the corner."

Connor stood, lifting his plate from the table and turning to the sink. Loris followed him quickly, brushing past him to place her own dishes in the sink. And then, as if they had done these small chores together a hundred times before, she handed him a large saucepan.

"If you'll bring water from the stove, I'll put these to soak while I clear up in here."

He did as she asked, then poured coffee from the pot into his cup and settled at the table once more. Straightening the kitchen was a simple thing to accomplish, but he admired her movements as she worked, watched the swing of her skirts as she moved back and forth from table to cupboard, then to the pantry and back again. She paused to find an old metal pan and filled it with water from the pump for Rusty's benefit.

Her dress moved with a swaying motion and he couldn't be certain if it were something she'd acquired recently. Perhaps he hadn't noticed it before, but now it struck him as enticing, her hips moving a bit beneath the full skirt, her feet skimming the surface of the wide floorboards.

"You walk as if you're dancing," he mused, and was treated to a quick glance in his direction, as her cheeks grew rosy and her eyes sparkled.

"You're imagining things," she said tartly, but her pleasure at his words was visible. Her mouth tightened in an inviting fashion, one he'd noticed before, luring him into her presence. It was a simple thing to stand and approach her as she came from the pantry. Her hands were empty, the bread stored on a shelf, the butter placed into a covered dish for the night.

He gave her little choice, his arms enclosing her lightly, as if he were about to dance with her, and for a moment, he thought he almost heard the music that would accompany them.

Loris looked up at him with a smile that encouraged him in his pursuit of her. Her lips curved and her blue eyes darkened, even as he watched. "You make me feel…safe, as though I'm at home here with you," she said softly.

"Feeling *safe* is not what I want you to think about when I hold you this way. I'd like to know that I tempt you a bit." He grinned down at her uplifted face and planted a damp kiss on her forehead. "Surely you know you're a temptation to me, Loris."

"I can't—"

"I don't expect you to," he said, interrupting her as if he knew what her next words would be. "I won't take your body until we're married. And in the meantime, I'll be content with warming you at night and spending my days doing what needs to be done here."

Wasn't that a tall tale, he thought. He'd not be content until he had the right to love her as a husband would, even though the thought of James being there first was hard for him to swallow. Knowing that the babe she carried belonged to his brother might present a problem when the time came, but for now, he tried his level best to scourge it from his mind.

"I didn't know that marriage was a part of this picture." Loris watched him closely, her eyes widening as if she had made some new discovery. He hadn't mentioned marriage, only that he would take care of her. Perhaps now was the time to set her straight on a few things.

"Of course it is. Did you think I'd ruin you totally by living with you without being your husband?"

"You told me before that you wouldn't—"

"Never mind what I told you. Whatever happened in the past doesn't apply to us now. This is a fresh start for both of us, Loris. And marriage is definitely in my plan."

He thought she looked stunned and then she proved him right. "I can't think about that now, Connor. Your family will surely be opposed to such a thing, and I won't come between you and your folks. I'll lay odds that they hate me for dragging you into my mess."

"What they think doesn't mean nothing to me," he said doggedly. "What I choose to do is my business, and I choose to marry you. We'll raise this baby and someday have more. We'll need a few boys around here to take over the farm one day."

"What about James?" She hit his sore spot squarely, and he felt his teeth grit in anger.

"James has nothing to do with this any longer. He could have married you and had the joy of raising his own child, but he preferred to stay a bachelor and walk away. He's not going to be welcome here. Ever."

"Will your parents ever come to accept us together?" She was close to tears. He could sense that much more of this would set loose the waterworks. He preferred to see Loris happy, or at least contented.

"They'll have to, if they want to see their grandchildren." Including the one she carried now, he thought, one that would bear the family name, but would be labeled as James's child.

"Do you think *my* folks know where I am?" she asked quietly.

"I wouldn't be surprised. When I paid the back taxes on this place, I didn't try to hide my plans. I'll bet they've heard already where you are, and that I'm here with you."

"They always liked you, Connor. I think that's mostly why they were so angry with me. They thought I'd done irreparable harm to you, and I deserved everything that came my way because of it."

"I'll decide what's best for you now," he said.

"And what's best for all three of us."

"I heard at the barbershop today that our daughter is living with the Webster boy."

Alger's lips compressed in anger as he told Minnie his news. "She's done nothing but disgrace us in this town, and I won't have it."

Minnie looked at him sadly. "We shouldn't have put her out the front door. It would have been better if we'd kept her here or sent her to your sister Edna in Dallas. As it is, she's bound to have to accept help from any direction it's offered. And if that means the Webster boy is accepting his responsibility, so much the better."

"She's with Connor. James hit the trail, according to what the men at the barbershop had to say. Connor paid the back taxes on the old Stewart farm for her, so she'd have a place to live, and now he's moved in with her."

"Maybe he'll marry her and give the baby a name." Minnie sounded hopeful, but Alger's scornful look seemed bound to deny her that bit of light at the end of Loris's long tunnel of darkness.

"It's not his. Why should he take on the responsibility?" He hung his coat and hat on the hall tree and voiced his main concern. "I hope we're not having meat loaf for supper. I ate it at the hotel today for my dinner."

"No. I put a piece of pork in the oven and made creamed potatoes." If Minnie sounded sour and unhappy, it wasn't because of her menu, but the attitude of her husband, who cared more about the state of his stomach than the welfare of his only daughter.

"It's bedtime, don't you think?" Connor stood in the wide doorway, looking in at Loris as she sat in the parlor. The sofa was well-used, but sturdy, as were the other remnants of furniture left behind by the owners. A book on her lap had remained open to the same page for more than ten minutes, and she seemed faraway. As if her thoughts were focused on the uncertain future she faced.

He was proved to be right when she turned her head and he caught sight of eyes that almost overflowed with tears. "I'll bet my folks will never want to see me again." She looked too sad to be believed, her face drawn and pale, her hands clenched into fists as she brought them from her pockets to scrub at her eyes.

"You're going to hurt your eyes that way," he said, walking in the room to settle beside her on the sofa. Reaching out, he gripped her fists in one of his big, wide palms, and then held them to his lips. His mouth made a feast of her skin, his teeth barely touching her knuckles, his tongue tasting a bit of the soapy residue left from the dishes she'd washed.

She looked at him, mournful now. "Connor, I've made a real mess of things, haven't I?" And then her mouth curved a bit. "The funny part is that I'm already attached to my baby. I can't blame him for any of this. His mama made a big mistake, but I can't regret that I'm to have a child. Do you think God makes us able to accept the retribution for our sins? In this case, I'll have a baby without a father, but I'll certainly do my best to raise him up right, even without grandparents."

"I think God loves us, Loris. Especially those of us who make mistakes and then regret them as you do. But I also think that He loves every child born into this world, whether it is legitimate or not. The baby *will* have a name. I'll see to that."

"After everything I've done to you, how can you want to marry me?" Her words trembled out of her mouth. Her tongue emerged just a bit, touching her top lip, dampening the surface. "I won't hold you to that," she said. "If you just stay here and take care of things till the baby comes, I'll figure out what to do afterwards."

"I asked you to be my wife last summer. And I meant it. I'll never walk away, not once you're my wife. And that means more than just a wedding ceremony. I hope you understand that. I won't be satisfied with just a good-night kiss. I'd prefer to wish you good-night about an hour after we go to bed. Okay?"

She swallowed convulsively, and he watched as her face flushed, a dark blush that ran down her throat. It was all he could do not to pull open her dress to see where that blush ended.

"Okay, Loris?" He repeated the word, knowing that once she made a commitment to him, she would stand by it. And a lifetime obligation was his goal. If she swore on the Bible he knew she kept by the bed, muttered a word of acquiescence in his direction, or even nodded, he would accept it as holding as much value as the wedding vows themselves.

"Yes. Okay." And then she frowned. "Why an hour after we go to bed?"

"When I'm done loving you."

"Loving me?" She seemed to be in a trance, and Connor knew exactly what to do to make her understand his plans. With a smooth turn of his arm, he circled her shoulders and scooted her closer to him on the sofa. Then with another unexpected movement of his body, he carried her to the sofa seat beside her, her head resting on the arm. He leaned over her, his kiss hot and needy, his lips opening over hers.

Unless he was mistaken, she'd not been kissed this way before, for she seemed innocent in her response. And then her own tongue joined with his, stroking his with long slow motions, finally seizing it and suckling with a gentle pressure.

He thought he might explode, and he broke the kiss to view the woman beneath him. She was breathless, and she opened her mouth to breathe. She looked just the way he'd imagined. Her hair was coming undone from the pinned-up mass she'd concocted on the back of her head, and her eyes were wide with wonder.

Well, maybe not wonder, he decided, but at least it was surprise he saw in her face. He'd take surprise for now, and hope for ecstasy some other day. He watched the rise and fall of her breasts, full beneath the bodice of her ordinary dress, and once more he sought the fullness of her lips.

Her dress was dark blue and, when he lifted from the kiss, he thought it matched her eyes almost exactly. How a dress could look so appealing to a man was a question he didn't stand a chance of solving. For it wasn't the dress that held him in thrall, but the shapely form of the woman who had donned it this morning and would remove it tonight.

In his bedroom.

"Connor?" She sounded just a bit apprehensive, perhaps even frightened, and he set about putting her at ease.

"I won't hurt you, Loris. I promise to wait until we're married to make you my bride. I only want to kiss you a bit and maybe touch you a little. I miss how we used to please each other when we were courting."

Loris blushed as she remembered, then hesitated. "Y-You won't hurt me? Will it be different after we're married? James said—"

She halted abruptly, as if speaking his brother's name aloud might set off a fuse in Connor. But he knew without her going any further what she wanted to ask. And so he gave her the answer she sought.

"It usually only hurts the first time a woman makes

love, Loris. After that, her maidenhead is gone and the pain with it. I'll not hurt you. I'll wait until you're ready for me, and I'll be careful. Especially with you carrying a baby."

She blushed again, and he allowed himself the right to view the sight he'd denied himself just a while ago. Her buttons came undone easily, though one hand came up to encircle his wrist as he took his time with the enjoyable task.

"What are you doing?" Her whisper was truly frightened now.

"Looking, sweetheart. Just looking at you. I want to see just how far your blush goes. I'm willing to bet it reaches almost to your belly button." And then he laughed aloud as the last button gave way and he pulled her vest up to reveal her midriff.

It was pink. Not as rosy as her cheeks, but definitely more so than was her usual color. He pushed it higher and her hand dropped from his wrist and she lay quietly beneath his exploration. The very peaks of her breasts were firm and puckered, whether due to the unveiling he'd instigated or because she was aroused by his kisses, didn't matter much. It only mattered that he had, one way or another, had an effect on her.

He touched her breast, circled the crest gently with one long finger, and then bent his head to take the darkened bit of flesh into his mouth. She jerked beneath him and whimpered. "What is it?" he asked, fearful he'd hurt her.

"Don't…"

"Don't what, sweetheart?" He bent closer again and kissed her lips with tenderness as his goal. Whatever his brother had done to her, apparently she hadn't enjoyed having her breasts touched, and a surge of anger swelled within him. "I'm sorry, Loris. I didn't mean to hurt you. I only wanted to kiss you, snuggle a little."

"You didn't hurt me, Connor. I just thought..." And again she halted, her words fading into silence.

He cupped her breasts in his palms and held them close together, then bent to draw a line with his tongue down the crevice he'd brought into being. She shivered and he felt an easing of her tension. Her hand moved to his neck, then slid through the darkness of his hair, holding him in place.

"You like that?" he asked softly, blowing on the dampness his tongue had left behind.

"Yes." A single word, but it carried a meaning he relished. She would come to him eagerly, when the time came. Until then, he'd leave her untouched. For Connor Webster was an honorable man, and if he'd done this to her in the big bed upstairs, he wouldn't have been able to stop until her tender body belonged to him.

Chapter Five

In the big bed, Connor was warm, tucked firmly against her backside, and Loris awoke feeling a deep sense of security. Knowing he was with her was a comfort. More than that, it lent a bit of credence to his claim upon her, his promise to marry her. Not that she would demand such a thing, but knowing that Connor desired her to that extent was balm to her woman's heart.

"Sweetheart?" He stirred, his leg stretching, then finding a nest between her knees. "You awake?" he asked, and she heard the awareness in his tone, knew that he was mindful of her state of confusion.

"It's time to get up." She wasn't leaving anything to chance. Dallying around in bed would get a girl in deep trouble. Heaven knew that dallying in a stall in her father's barn had done more than that, on that afternoon over three months ago. "I'll fix breakfast while you do the chores."

As if it were an offer he welcomed, he pushed the covers back and slid from the mattress. "Well, hello there, Rusty," he said with a grin. "Fancy seeing you here."

"He slept beside the bed all night," Loris told him.

"I noticed he slept on your side," Connor told her.

"That's where the rug is," she said, sitting up and sliding her feet to the floor.

Connor yawned and stretched. "I'll just get dressed and be on my way. Any chance of sausage and gravy?"

"I think we have everything we need," she told him, doing a quick mental inventory of the pantry as she spoke.

"How about if I stick some wood in the stove on my way out? It'll give you a head start."

She nodded her thanks, wondering at his thoughtfulness. Her own father had never done such a thing, only hastened to do his morning work and then hustled back to the house, demanding his breakfast, unhappy if it wasn't ready when he thought it should be. But then, Connor wasn't her father, had shown no signs of impatience with her, had not lost his temper or treated her in any way unfairly.

"I'll have it ready when you come back in," she told him. "I'll hurry."

"If it isn't on the table, I'll have a cup of coffee and watch you, Loris. In case you don't know it, that's become one of my favorite pastimes lately."

"I can't see why." Truly puzzled, she leaned over to make the bed, and then turned her back abruptly as his naked form came in view. "Connor! I didn't know you were still parading around without your clothes on!" she exclaimed.

"You'll see me this way from now on, sweetheart. You might as well get used to it. I don't plan on sleeping in my drawers after we're married." He sat on the edge of the bed and pulled on his stockings.

"Speaking of which, how about taking a trip to town

and finding the preacher today? I'd like to make this baby mine as soon as we can."

"It'll never really be yours," she told him, feeling her throat close on the words.

"You're wrong," he said, his voice almost harsh, so solemn was his mood. "This is my child from now on. James has nothing more to do with us, or with the baby you'll bear. The only thing he'll have in common with our child is his last name. They'll both be called Webster."

"Are you sure you really want to do this?" She felt a twinge of shame as she thought of Connor taking on the child, one not of his doing.

He walked around the bed and reached her quickly, drawing her into his arms. He kissed her, slowly and thoroughly, his mouth soft and tender against hers. "I've never wanted anything so badly in my life. Since the moment I met you, I've wanted to live with you and take care of you and make a home with you, Loris. I don't know how to say it any other way."

"If you're sure…" And if he was, it would be a happy day. She'd loved Connor for years, had even loved him deeply during that time that James had turned her head and taken her virtue. The difference between the two brothers was enormous. Connor, the eldest, was kind and steady. James was used to having his own way, even when it involved the woman his brother had pledged to marry.

And she, like a fool, had given in to his persuading, had allowed him to take from her the gift that should have been, by rights, Connor's. She regretted it bitterly, rued the day she'd let James kiss her. Her father was right. The man was a scamp and a rascal and she'd done nothing to discourage his pursuit. She'd only been intrigued by his attentions. And in the long run she had hurt herself, along with Connor, a fact she would always regret.

"I'm sure." His answer had been a long time coming, but she knew it was sincere, that once it was spoken aloud, he would hold himself to the vow.

"All right. We can get married today, if you want to. I'd like to stop by my folks' house and pick up a few things first if that's all right. I only brought some old clothes with me when I left, and my dresses are mostly in my closet."

"I'll buy you what you need," Connor said harshly. "You don't need anything from your father's house. He gave up the right to take care of you, to provide for you, the night he put you out in the cold. I doubt I'll ever forgive him for that."

"He's a harsh man," Loris agreed. "He knew what he was doing that night, Connor. All he could think of was that I disgraced the family."

"I promise you, Loris. I'll be a good father to our children." Connor's voice was strong, and his eyes held anger as he spoke, and then he kissed her.

The wedding was quiet, with only the pastor of the small church officiating and his wife serving as witness. Far from the fancy doings her mother had talked of, it nevertheless held a world of meaning for Loris. For the man beside her spoke his vows with sincerity, the look he bestowed upon her spoke silently of affection, and the devotion with which he promised to cherish her was honest and forthright.

She vowed words of love, which came easily to her

lips. Of honor, a word she associated closely with Connor, for he was indeed an honorable man, and then came the difficult part. Obey. It was a word that had bothered her upon hearing it in other ceremonies. Its meaning would influence her future. Once she promised Connor her obedience, she was pledged to him forever. Connor Webster was not a man to break his vows, nor would he allow her to turn her back on him, ever.

She was well and truly wed. Loris Webster, a name she'd once craved to own. And now she wondered if she deserved to bear it. Connor's mother surely would not think so. Nor his father. She put the thought from her mind, and concentrated instead on the man who stood beside her.

"You may kiss your bride." The words sounded as if from far away, and for a moment, Loris thought she might fall in a heap at Connor's feet. His arm was strong around her waist though and he drew her close, offering her a chaste kiss, holding her close as if he would cherish her and keep her safe her whole life.

"Congratulations, Connor." The pastor's wife was smiling, her eyes suspiciously shiny as she offered her hand. "You have a beautiful bride. I know you'll be happy, son. You've done the right thing."

And Connor nodded, his smile satisfied, his stance tall, as if he'd assumed larger proportions during the ceremony, as though the cloak of marriage sat well on his shoulders. "Thank you, Mrs. Wilson. I plan on being a good husband."

"You're a lucky girl, Loris." Her attention turned now to the bride and she leaned forward to kiss Loris's cheek. "I surely wish your parents had come to see you married. They'll be sorry one day that they missed this."

"I don't know about that," Loris said sadly. "But I'm sure glad I didn't miss it."

Connor hugged her close to his side. "We're going on a shopping trip now, and then heading home."

"Every bride needs something new," Mrs. Wilson said. "Though Loris looks pretty in anything she wears."

Wasn't that a kind thing for her to say, Loris thought. For already her dress was snug around the waist, and her bosom was pressed into the bodice tightly. She needed something larger, something that would wrap around her and conceal the growing child she carried. Although it would not be concealed for long, no matter what she wore. And in less than six months she would hold this baby in her arms and pray that Connor could truly accept him.

As if he sensed her thoughts, Connor took her arm and hustled her to the front door, then down the steps and to the buggy they'd ridden in. She'd been surprised to find that he owned, in addition to his farm wagon, a buggy and eleven horses. Four of them were up for sale, he'd told her, and he'd already bred the four mares to his stud. Come the first of next year, they'd have a whole batch of young foals in the barn.

His own riding horse was sacrosanct and would never be sold, he'd told her, and he intended to choose just the right horse for her use, too. The beginnings of a business, he'd called his horses. And she felt his pride when he spoke of them.

Now they rode in the buggy, pulled by a sleek mare, down the middle of the town's main street, pulling up to the general store with a flourish. Connor lifted her down and held the door open for her to enter the Emporium. Inside, several ladies looked their fill, and he noted the blush that stained Loris's cheeks.

As though claiming ownership, he circled her waist with his long arm and spoke to the storekeeper. "My wife needs a few things. And we could use some supplies for the pantry while we're at it."

He chose two dresses, brightly flowered and cheerful. One was called a wrapper, and he understood the reasoning behind the name when he saw it held before him, the abundant skirt capable of being folded around Loris's body in a wraparound fashion. The other dress hung from a high waistline, gathered abundantly and capable of holding several more pounds and inches than she currently bore.

She protested at his extravagance and he privately chose two other dresses for a future visit, during which she would be gifted with more clothing, whether she was with him or not. Their pantry supplies were easily chosen, Loris content to cook whatever Connor liked. He carried them out in two large boxes, stowing them at the rear of the buggy, then carried the bundle with her dresses under one arm as he loaded her up onto the high seat.

She held the bundle in her lap and looked straight ahead as Connor drove his mare through town. A glimpse of her mother on the sidewalk was ignored, Loris turning her head away.

"Your mother waved," Connor said quietly. "Just a small movement of her hand, but I think she wanted you to look at her."

"I don't intend to ever see her again." Surprise at her

own surly tones made Loris frown. "She wouldn't have cared if I lived or died, Connor. How can I feel anything for her ever again?"

"Never is a long time, Loris. You may change your mind."

"I don't think so. She turned me out, Connor. Do you have any idea what that does to a person, to know that her own mother doesn't want her in her home. Not to mention the way my father treated me."

"They thought they had good reason," Connor said. "Even though they were harsh, I think they really love you, Loris. Someday they'll come asking forgiveness. Be ready for that."

"I won't welcome them." It was a final statement so far as she was concerned. The hurt delivered by their actions had leveled her to the ground, and she felt no leanings toward the family who had deserted her when she needed them most.

Only Connor had been there. Only his strong arms had held her, only his warmth had kept her safe. And now, she owned his name, his loyalty and one day, maybe even his love.

"Home?" he asked.

"Home." The word tasted like honey in her mouth. The old farmhouse had indeed become a refuge, a place of sanctuary, a place in which she could give and receive the love that would one day come her way.

The evening chores were done, and Loris had even churned a batch of butter while Connor did the feeding and milking and gathering eggs. She looked into the depths of the wooden churn at the results of her efforts and felt a glow of pride. Turning out the heavy lump into a wooden bowl, she worked at it, forming it and squeezing the water from the bulky mass.

In less than fifteen minutes, she'd cut it into two large pieces, formed them neatly and placed one on the kitchen table, beneath the lid of the butter plate. It was a gift from Connor. He'd caught her looking at it among the assortment of china at the general store and picked up the two pieces, holding them to the light and examining them closely.

"Would you like this?" As if her expectant look was enough of an answer, he placed the pieces of china on the counter beside his assortment of food items and asked the storekeeper to add it to their purchases.

Now she examined the finely wrought blue flowers that decorated the two pieces of china. It added a note of luxury to her table, she thought, lifting the lid for a moment, examining the round of butter beneath it, and then replacing it with a small clink of the china top meeting its mate.

"All done?" Connor came in the back door, Rusty close on his heels. His eyes were focused on her, his smile telling her of his pleasure in the gift he'd purchased for her. He strode to the sink and washed his hands and arms, then splashed his face and reached for a towel. "You're a good wife, Loris. I didn't realize you knew how to do so much in the kitchen. If you like, we'll get the rest of the dishes to go along with that thing." Pointing at the butter dish, he awaited her reply.

"You're too extravagant, Mr. Webster." She grinned at him, her pleasure easy to read. "I've never had anything so pretty. If we can afford it, I'd love to have the set of dishes to match. I won't need all the pieces, just plates and a platter and a bowl for vegetables."

"If we get it," he said firmly, "we'll get the whole kit and caboodle. You can have most anything you want, Loris. Anything I can afford. And let me tell you now that your husband is not a poor man. I have a growing business. What with my horses and now with this place to farm, we'll do well." He halted and looked at her questioningly. "I hope you don't mind my assuming that we'll run this farm together."

"You paid the taxes, Connor. You can do anything you like here. Just let me have the house and babies to put in those bedrooms upstairs and I'll be happy."

His heart sang at the words she spoke, as if her only thought was to please him, to make him happy. He'd done the right thing, marrying Loris, moving in here. No matter what his parents thought, no matter how angry they were at this move, he knew it was right and proper that he look after her. More important that he be her husband and a father to her child. His mother could just chew on that for a while, he decided.

"I'll give you all the babies you want," he said softly, approaching her with care. "Maybe not for a year or so, but one day we'll have half a dozen children running around here, making a racket and giving us gray hair."

He held his arms out, the invitation obvious, and she responded, walking into his embrace and circling his neck with her arms, clinging to him as if he represented a lifesaver in the storm of life. He bent to her, kissing her with affection, and then it was not enough that he brush her lips with such care.

His mouth opened over hers and he fit their lips together, then tasted the edges of her mouth with his tongue. She opened to him, and he felt a depth of pleasure sweep through him that filled him almost to overflowing. So readily she gave to him, so easily she offered herself. For that was surely what her kisses meant, that he could take her to his bed now, that she would not hesitate, but would willingly, gladly, become his wife.

But he wanted confirmation, his male instincts needing the assurance that she was amenable to his loving. And he was not disappointed, for she leaned closer, her breasts soft against his chest, her hips nestling within the notch of his legs, where his hardness made itself known. "Loris?"

"Yes, Connor." Whether it was a simple affirmation, or a response that offered him what he craved, he didn't care. Right now, if Loris was willing, he'd be foolish not to accept her offer.

With a quick movement, he picked her up and walked toward the long staircase.

"Connor, what about supper?" She whispered the words, sounding bewildered, as if his action had taken her by surprise. That was just what he'd intended, catching her unaware.

"We'll eat later." He knew his voice was gruff, his actions abrupt, his mouth avid against hers, but he seemed unable to halt the progress of this moment. Seduction was not in his plan, but he doubted right now that Loris would offer any protest to his loving.

"All right." She sounded satisfied. "The biscuits will wait in the warming oven. I'll bake them later, and the stew is simmering on the back of the stove."

"I plan on being hungry afterwards," he told her, his feet setting a steady pace on the stairs, his arms holding her firmly, lest she feel unsafe in his hold. He closed the door behind them, shutting Rusty out in the hallway, and then laughed as the pup howled his displeasure.

"That's enough, Rusty," he called sternly. "Any more and you go outdoors."

Miracle of miracles, the dog ceased his racket, and Loris laughed with delight.

"You can tame most anything, can't you?"

"Not you, Loris. I don't want you tamed. I like you as you are. Spunky and independent and capable."

"All of that?" she asked as he slid her to her feet beside the bed.

He hesitated to answer, only bending to kiss her thoroughly as he placed her on the wide mattress. He followed her down to the quilt, happy that he'd taken off his boots by the back door. Now he only had the task of undressing her and shedding his own clothing.

Removing Loris's clothing would be another lesson in patience, one he sorely needed right now. For he vowed he would not rush her, would not hurt her in any way, would only give her the benefit of what wisdom he'd gathered in his very few encounters with women. Loris was different, for he'd never loved another woman, never offered his pledge to anyone else before now.

Love. It was a word almost unfamiliar to him. And yet, he knew it was the exact word for what he felt now. He loved Loris, with a deep and abiding tenderness. No matter what had happened before, this was the beginning of their lives together, and he promised never to make her think of herself as anything less than perfect in his sight.

He unbuttoned her dress, then the vest beneath it, spreading the edges wide, the better to see her lush bosom. His mouth touched her gently, with care, and she responded as he'd hoped, trembling in his arms, yet eager to accept his caresses. Her hands reached for his head, clasped together at his nape and held him close. Even his mouth opening against her skin seemed not to upset her or cause her to be fearful, for she sighed and wiggled beneath him.

"Loris? If I do anything you don't like, or if I hurt you in any way—"

"You won't hurt me, Connor." Her words were firm. "I trust you."

He was shaken by her faith in him, knowing that at one time or another, he would surely bring her anxiety or even pain, whether through word or deed. "I love you."

She stilled beneath him, and he wondered if she had heard his confession. And then she smoothed his fears away, as if she'd taken the wrinkles from one of his shirts with a hot iron. "And I love you, Connor. I've never stopped loving you. Not for a single minute. Not even…"

"It's all right, Loris. I know what you mean. I just wanted you to know that what we do is a part of our marriage, that this act is sanctified by the vows we spoke. I'll never hurt you, sweetheart."

She lay quiet beneath him, having pulled his long, lean body atop her own, and he fit himself into the cradle of her femininity, then reached between them to unbutton his drawers and push them from his body, kicking them off onto the floor. "Let me take off your clothes," he said, and somehow, without losing contact with her body, he managed to strip her dress, then her underthings from her warm body.

A shiver passed through her and he bent to cover her with his heat. His mouth formed against her throat, his lips traveling to her cheek, then beneath her ear. She spoke softly, words he barely heard, but her tone was that of a woman who is content, knowing she is safe and loved.

"Say that again," he murmured, hoping against hope that he'd heard her aright.

"I never felt this with James," she said quietly, holding him fast against herself. "I never knew such contentment with him, so great a connection as I do with you. You give me so much, Connor. Not just things, but you give me yourself. You make me know that you care about me, not for what you can take from me here in this bed, but for what you can give to me. And if it includes what we do here, tonight, I'll feel rich beyond measure."

"It does." He felt enriched by her words, that she would liken his need for her to a treasure he would bestow on her. And so he would, and in so doing would accept her body as his just due, as her husband and the man who had promised only today to honor and cherish her all the days of his life. The loving would be simple, for he'd never stopped feeling that enduring love for her, even during those days, when she'd hurt him almost beyond bearing. The rest of his vows would be equally easy to fulfill, and for a moment, he pitied James that he had walked away from the beauty and grace of this woman. That he'd scorned all she had to offer and had left her alone and bereft.

Yet, he owed James a debt of thanks, for without his abandonment, Loris would not have been where she was right now, and the fact that he held her beneath him, that he felt the soft curves of her body against his, made Connor a most happy man.

He was able to feel the almost imperceptible bulge of her stomach against his, the proof that she carried a child, a reminder that he must travel this path with care. And so he rolled from her, bringing a cry from her lips as though she felt abandoned.

"Hush, sweet," he murmured. "I only want to make this good for you. Please just trust me."

And she did, obviously and willingly, for her arms circled him, her lips sought his and she was all that was warm and loving in his embrace. He explored her body with hands that trembled in thankfulness that she would allow his touch so readily. His mouth blessed each spot he touched with palms and fingers, and she lay beneath him, lost in the pleasure he brought to her.

She was damp, more than ready for him and he touched her belly again, his palm lying across from one hipbone to the other, as if he measured the breadth and height of the child within her. It would be all right, he decided. She was not so large as to be uncomfortable beneath him, and he would take her with care for her comfort.

He lowered himself to her and she widened her legs, making a place for him, unhesitating as she reached for him and clung with the strength of a woman who is seeking the possession of the man she loves. He did not disappoint her, for he lifted her legs, holding her close, yet providing her with room to move, should she find her position uncomfortable.

With a long, smooth move, he penetrated her, then halted just inside the entrance to her body. It was all he could do not to thrust deeply, to take her with passion, but the thought of the harm he might cause kept him controlled.

"Connor? Is it all right?" She sounded confused, he thought, and he would not have it.

"More than all right, sweetheart. Feeling you around me, knowing your heat and the tight feel of your body—it's wonderful." He shifted just a bit and she responded to him, matching his movements, meeting his thrust, gentle as it was. "Be careful, love. Don't push too hard."

"I'm fine," she assured him, her voice sure and certain now. "I want you, Connor. Fill me, make me yours. Love me."

He did, carefully, with control, yet with a passion that was unmistakable. His desire was overwhelming, his body aching for release, yet he paced himself, waiting till she joined him in the culmination of this dance. His hands touched her with care, lifting from her so that he could reach her most tender places, bringing her to the brink of delight, and then heard her soft cries as she tumbled into the place where love carried them, her joy in him complete.

It was only then that he gained his own pleasure, still cautious as he claimed her body, even as he gave her his own.

* * *

It was time for plowing. The fields were ready for planting, and Connor spent a whole day getting his tools in shape for the task ahead. Loris came to the barn and watched, amazed at his knowledge of the job he performed.

"How did you learn all that?" She leaned forward as he cleaned the rust from a plow he'd found in the hay-mow, and he glanced up with a grin.

"Doesn't take much know-how to figure this part out, sweetheart. Getting the horse to pull the thing will be the problem. I don't own a plow horse, and I'll have to use one of my team for the job. He should catch on pretty quick, though, and if I need to I can use a pair of them."

"Do all men just *know* how to farm? Or did your father teach you?"

He looked aside and then shot her a look filled with pain. "He taught me. James, too, for that matter. I spent a lot of hours doing what you're doing right now, keeping my eyes open and filing away everything in my mind, so I wouldn't forget what he'd done."

The plowshare seemed to suit him now, for he angled it and viewed it with eyes that judged it ready to use. Setting it aside, he lifted the harness from the barn wall and held it in his big hands. It slid with ease through his fingers, and he halted its progress several times to check the wear on a certain piece, and finally picked up one long length of harness, the rein that connected to the bit, and examined it closely.

"What's wrong with that?" Loris bent closer as he held it, sliding it through his fingers.

"I'm not sure. I think it just needs to be mended here

where the ring holds these two pieces together. It looks like the stitching has come loose."

"Can you fix it?" And if he could, it would be one more thing to add to the list she'd formulated in her mind of Connor's many skills.

"Not much to it," he said. "My pa used to have me fix harnesses all the time. I was in charge of the tack room at home."

"Can I help with the plowing?" She feared he would turn her down flat, but she had to ask, the need to lend a hand burning within her.

"If you'll bring me out dinner every day, that would be wonderful," he told her. "I'm gonna get the Simpson boy to help me for a couple of weeks. He can handle the heavy stuff, things that a woman doesn't have the strength for." He shot her a warning look. "And don't be looking at me that way. You're strong and tough, but you're not a man. And for that I'm very thankful. I rather admire your feminine qualities, ma'am. Like fixing sandwiches or soup for me to eat at noontime every day."

"Can I ride out in the wagon?" And even as she asked, she wondered how she would harness the horse, or whether there would be a draft horse to harness, if Connor used him for plowing.

"You'll have to use a mare. I know you can ride, but are you afraid to get up on a horse now?" He leaned back and looked at her. "I don't want you or the baby hurt."

"I love to ride, Connor. I've been doing it all my life. My father had two riding horses and I used to take one out on Sunday afternoon every week for long rides. Sometimes in the evening, too." She decided on confession then. "I don't know much about saddling a horse though. I may have a problem with that. But I can ride bareback."

Connor frowned. "I don't know if that's a good idea. I'll have to think about it."

"You might think about having the mare saddled before you go out to the field. Or else send your young man in at dinnertime to do it for me. In fact, he could come in and get your dinner if you want."

His look was dark. "I want to see you, sweetheart. That's the whole idea of you bringing it to me. Either we figure out a way to do it easily, or I'll come back to the house and eat. It's that simple."

"Whatever you say." She was secretly pleased that it was so important to him that he see her during the day, and giving in on this matter was simple. But it seemed he felt it was an issue he'd won.

"Well, I'm glad we didn't have an argument over that one," he said, his voice smacking of satisfaction. "Maybe this love, honor and obey stuff is going to work out just fine after all."

She swallowed the words that begged to be spoken and instead smiled, gritting her teeth and trying her best to look affable.

"I'm teasing," he whispered, his grin luring her.

It was simple to respond, and she approached him gladly. Her arms circled his neck, and she bent down to kiss him. "I think you're enjoying yourself, mister. You'd better know right now, though, that if I didn't want to agree with you, I wouldn't. And that's a fact."

He tilted his head back and his lips brushed hers, and then with a quick move, he pulled her onto his lap. "Do you know that this barn has a haymow?" he asked.

"All barns have one," she said haughtily.

"This one is very nice."

"What's so nice about it?" And even as he stood her on her feet and then rose beside her, she played his game. "A haymow is just part of a barn. Only good for mice and owls to live in."

"You'll soon find out another use for ours," he said, ushering her into the long hallway and across to where the ladder stood. "Now, climb up there, and I'll guarantee you'll like what you see."

She knew exactly what was in the hayloft, knew what he wanted her to see, and to her credit, did as he asked. And if anyone had asked, she'd have had to admit that the man was right. The use he found for the mounds of hay was much to her liking.

Chapter Six

The corn was coming up, tiny spears of green visible above the dirt, hilled in neat rows, thanks to the work of the three who spent hours at the task. Buck Simpson turned out to be a knowledgeable young man, well suited for the hard work required, and much to her surprise, Loris found enjoyment in the sight of her own field of corn thriving, partly due to her own efforts.

She spent most of the mornings in the house, cleaning and cooking, getting supper started, usually a one-kettle dish that could simmer on the back of the stove during the afternoon. Then at noontime, Buck showed up at the door and loaded her and a heavy basket or two into the wagon.

Rusty seemed torn between running behind the wagon to the fields each morning, or staying with Loris in the house. Connor put a stop to that with ease, pointing to Loris and telling the dog to watch her. Rusty was remarkably intelligent, and he only went to the fields when Loris rode on the wagon.

Today's dinner was welcomed by the men, with

enough shade trees along the hedge rows to protect them from the hot sun as they sat and ate their fill. Cotton gloves helped to protect Loris's hands, and even though Connor grumbled at the sight, she took her place in the cornfield, and for two weeks worked the hills into existence. Her arms turned brown, her face assumed a rosy pink across her cheekbones, with a few freckles tossed in. The biggest drawback was her utter fatigue by the time the sun went down.

Connor carried her up the stairs to bed more nights than not, and tenderly settled her on the wide mattress. He loved her well and often, expecting nothing and luxuriating in her caresses as she responded to his. She was happy, living with the man she loved, doing a job she knew would bear fruit for the winter months to come.

And she wore her happiness like a glowing cloak of rainbow hues, even at her most weary, smiling at him, and providing for his daily needs. She cooked and kept the house clean. Hoed by the hour in the fields, plus planting and caring for the garden outside the back door, until Connor finally protested firmly.

"You're going to hurt yourself, Loris. You do too much. We're gonna have to draw the line here somewhere. I don't want anything to happen to that baby because of me. And that's what's gonna happen if you don't stop wearing yourself out this way."

"I feel good," she responded brightly, even as her back ached from the strain of bending over the kitchen garden, hoe in hand. Her vegetables were coming up nicely and she felt a sense of pride at the neat plot she'd managed to put in.

"I know exactly how you feel," he told her. "I've

seen you in the evenings when you can barely put one foot in front of the other."

She tossed him an impudent smile. "I can still chase you around the house, mister."

"Is that what you call it?" He grinned at her. "You're almost too tired for that these days. And mind you, I'm not complaining. You're loving and warm and good to me, sweetheart. Don't ever think I'm unhappy with you. I'm just glad the corn is well on its way and we can sit and watch it grow for now. Buck and I can use the cultivator on the weeds once a week or so for the next little bit, and then watch the ears form."

"What's next?" she asked, eager to know what his plans involved. Hoping they would include her.

"We need to cut hay. There's about ten acres ready to mow right now, and it'll take a couple more men to do it the right way. I've got Buck's brothers coming for a week, starting Monday, and we'll have it cut by the end of the week. Then it dries and we go out and put it on the wagon and into the barn."

"What if it rains?"

"We're not gonna think about that right now," he told her. "It takes a good few days to dry, and it has to be turned over to expose the bottom layers to the sun. We'll be busy out there."

"Should I plan on bringing out your dinner every day?"

"If it's not too much for you. But just know that you're not working in the field. I won't have the folks in town talking about me working you to death."

"Pooh! The folks in town aren't the least bit interested in what I'm doing out here. They've got other things to gossip over."

"Don't count on it." He sounded gloomy and she frowned.

"What have you heard?"

"Just that you're working your fingers to the bone, and I'm taking advantage of you. Buck went to a dance on Saturday and we were part of the discussion going on."

"I'm going to town and let folks see me, Connor. They need to know that I'm fine, that I'm happy and that you're the best husband I could have ever asked for."

He stood from the table and looked down at her. "Did I ever tell you that I love you, Mrs. Webster?" He crossed to where she sat and lifted her from her chair. His arms were long and his touch was gentle, yet she felt the desire that bubbled near the surface whenever he held her close.

"You've told me. Probably more than I deserve, but I sure like to hear it, mister." She melted into his long body, her arms circling his waist, her head nestled in the hollow beneath his shoulder. His heartbeat was strong and regular against her ear and she felt a moment of pride that this man was hers, that he'd committed himself to her for a lifetime.

The kitchen was flooded with the light from the setting sun, a brilliant wash of color against the dishes that were stacked in the sink. Connor tipped his head toward the hallway and carried a bucket of hot water up the stairs for her use. Even though she had washed and changed clothes before supper, getting ready for bed required a warm cloth to rinse away the residue of perspiration she'd gathered throughout the day.

He watched as she washed piecemeal in the bowl, his eyes intent on her every move, and when she began to peel the clothing from her body, he rose from the bed.

"Let me help you finish," he offered, and she only smiled at him, knowing the joy he gained by the exercise.

His hands were tender, the cloth was warm, constantly dipped into the heated water, and then applied to her throat, then her back and finally down her legs. "I hadn't planned on being naked," she told him, reaching for her nightdress.

"I had," he told her firmly. "This is the way I like you best. I want to see your nice round little tummy and the way your breasts have grown, and the long, sleek lines of your legs."

"All that?" she asked, widening her eyes and teasing him as he snatched the gown from her hands.

"You won't need that." His movements were deliberate as he placed the gown on a chair and then used the towel to wipe the final drops of water from her back. The soft fabric caressed her belly, and his hand eased beneath the burden she carried to hold it in his palm, murmuring quiet words of praise in her ear.

"I don't know why a woman who looks like this should appeal to you, Connor," she said, blushing a little as he made a production out of wiping down her legs.

He looked up at her from his position on the floor, kneeling at her feet. "Don't you? You're as feminine now as you'll ever be, Loris. You're going to have a child, and a woman is made for that. All of your body is involved in the process, and I find you the most beautiful creature on this earth."

She fought the tears that gathered, and cleared her throat, knowing that Connor hated to see her cry. "You're too good to me. I owe you so much, and you just give and give to me. I feel like I'll never catch up with you."

"I'll give you a chance," he said, grinning mischievously as he folded the towel and then lifted her in his arms. Sitting on the edge of the bed, he held her close, rocking her to and fro, almost as if she were a child needing comfort, and she was at once sheltered, yet seduced, by his actions.

His hands roamed over her body, and she reveled in it. His palms cupped her breasts, his fingers sought out the warmth of her womanly parts and he plied her with kisses that pleased her. She was loved, and the knowledge was almost too much for her to understand.

"This is what I always wanted in life, Connor," she told him. "This feeling of being at home, of having someone of my own to love and cherish."

"Then you oughta be downright happy, ma'am," he teased. "I'm all yours."

"Lie down with me then, and I'll show you how happy I am." Her eyes lured him closer, her hands pulled him down beside her on the sheet and she clung to him with the strength she'd gained during the long weeks of hard work.

He did as she asked, as if willing to accede to her wishes in this, and when she set about using her limited knowledge of enticement to his advantage, he laughed beneath his breath and did as she asked of him.

It was as it had not been at any time during the months of their marriage, a time of giving and receiving, a time of loving and demanding the return of that love. Most of all, it was a learning experience for them both. For Loris found that pleasing Connor was more important in this moment than allowing him to give her the pleasure he was wont to devote to her body.

Connor seemed to recognize that his wife needed these moments of loving to establish a claim on him, to draw him into her web in such a way he would never seek to be released. Her claim on him was total, and he responded as would a man who had found his destiny. A man who would not be deterred from the maintaining of those bonds that connected them as husband and wife.

They luxuriated in each other, kissing, caressing, and spending a languid hour of loving as the sun set. It was twilight, that magical time of day when the birds sang in the trees, the animals sought their slumber in barn and coop, and when man and woman clung together in the midst of their loving and found perfection in those moments of peace and harmony.

The hay was turned and then turned again, the hot sun drying it to perfection, and Connor was pleased with the results of his labors. The Simpson boys were sturdy young men, eager to earn their wages and ready right after breakfast to work in the fields. Loris cooked enough food for all of them, and Connor knew she enjoyed the sight of the four men sitting around her kitchen table, putting away the food she readied for them.

Dinnertime found her with baskets packed, quilts folded and ready for them to sit on, and Mason jars filled with water to quench their thirst. One of the young men hiked back to the house or rode a saddlehorse to the barn to collect her, and after hitching the team to the wagon, helped Loris atop the wagon seat for the ride back to the hayfield.

They sat in the shade, eating fried chicken or roast beef sandwiches or left over meat loaf and potato salad.

Loris blossomed with the praise heaped on her cooking skills, and she managed to empty her baskets most days.

She was deeply involved with the child she carried, aware of every movement as the tiny being shifted and turned in the confines of her body. It took her breath sometimes, the thrill of knowing that her baby was alive inside, that she was providing a safe haven for it and causing it to grow and develop in her womb.

It was something she'd not thought to experience yet, and if she'd ever considered the idea, it was Connor's child she'd thought to carry beneath her heart. That he would accept James's baby seemed more than she could expect of him, but he'd said it was to be, and Connor did not lie. Perhaps this child would resemble him, and maybe Connor's parents would come to accept their grandchild.

And maybe pigs would fly.

She laughed bitterly to herself as she lifted the iron to test its heat. She dampened her index finger against her tongue and then touched it to the sole plate. It sizzled satisfactorily and she plied it on the shirt she held. Having been rolled up in her laundry basket, next to the rest of Connor's clothing and her two new dresses, it now awaited her touch, lying across the ironing board.

Ironing was not her favorite job, but Loris took pleasure in caring for Connor's clothing. Scrubbing over a washboard was hard work, but sending her laundry out to have it done, as had her mother, was not an option. Fortunately, she'd learned to use the sad irons and a scrub board was not totally unfamiliar territory to her.

Dinner would be ready by the time she finished the ironing, and she cast a glance at the stove, where a kettle of soup simmered. The haying was almost done, the rows having been raked into order, the wagon piled high with the dry grass and the hay mow almost half full already. Connor was pleased with the results of their work, hiring the Simpson boys on to help for the rest of the summer.

Her own garden was fast heading toward harvest, the green beans already fit for the kettle, and radishes and early sweet peas gracing the table. She'd cooked a big kettle of beans with a ham bone last night for supper, and Connor had grinned his delight with her skills.

"You're a wonder, Loris. I don't know how I got so lucky as to have married you. You're a good wife, sweetheart, and a wonderful cook." He'd come up behind her and hugged her as she stood at the sink, washing dishes, and then had snatched up a dish towel and dried the plates and silverware as she rinsed it.

"What comes next after the hay?" she asked. "Will you need me to help in the fields?"

"No, the boys and I can take care of the corn. We've got about five acres planted, and the corn crib will be full, not to mention a lot of good eating as we go along. I'll use the stalks for silage and the ears of corn for feed."

"I'll just work at the kitchen garden then, and dig out some jars for canning."

"You sound like a farmer's wife," Connor said with a wide grin. "I wasn't aware that you knew how to put up preserves."

"I watched my mother for years. She had a garden out back, and I helped slip tomato skins and cut up vegetables for the canning jars. We usually put up over a hundred quart jars and as many pints every year. What my mother didn't grow herself, she bought from one of the farm wives outside of town."

"Are there jars here?" he asked.

"In the fruit cellar, under the house. I found them the other day when I went down there to explore. If you'll help me carry them up to the kitchen, I'd appreciate it."

"I don't want you carrying anything," he said, his voice carrying a harsh edge. "You're not to lift anything heavy, Loris. And no going into the cellar without me."

"All right." If it made Connor happy to treat her like spun glass, she'd let him. She was perfectly capable of doing a woman's work, but he seemed to have a blind spot where she was concerned. And she wouldn't argue the point with him. It felt good to be pampered a bit.

"Are you ready to begin tomorrow?" he asked. "I'll go down tonight and bring up an assortment. How many do you need to begin with?"

"A couple of dozen quarts and the same number of pint jars. I'll do the beans and begin the tomatoes. They're coming in pretty good now. I probably have a half bushel about ready to pick."

"I'll help with that, or else leave one of the boys up here at the house to help you."

She thought of the work awaiting him in the fields and shook her head. "I'll let you know when I need help."

He looked dubious, but remained silent. His eyes scanned her thoroughly, and she felt the heat of his gaze as if it penetrated her clothing. "You're getting bigger, Loris."

"That's what happens when a woman has a child," she told him crisply. "I'll be bigger than this before I'm done. I've another month to go."

He went to the back door and opened it wide. "I'll go down and get the jars now. There's a bushel basket down there that should hold enough to begin with."

"I'll heat water to wash them," she said, pumping a cool stream into a large kettle. "If I get a head start, I'll be able to do more in the morning."

She heard the door of the cellar thud as it was thrown back against the ground, then silence as Connor apparently descended into the dank area under the house. Holding a pile of withered potatoes and another of carrots, it was a necessity for a farmer's wife. She'd gone down there several times to replenish her kitchen with vegetables to cook with, and finally brought a bag of onions to hang in the pantry, along with the last of the potatoes from last year's garden.

She was thankful for the woman who had so carefully stored the bounty of her work beneath the house. Now it was almost time to replenish the storehouse for the coming winter.

"Here you go, sweetheart." Connor came in the door, sidling through the entryway with the basket held before him. "As many as I could carry," he told her, bringing the basket closer to the sink.

She unloaded it, filling the sink and the cupboard next to it with jars that were dusty and even inhabited by spiders in some cases.

"Want me to rinse out the bugs?" Connor leaned over her shoulder to inspect the insects that had taken shelter in the Mason jars.

Loris tossed him a scornful look. "Spiders are a fact of life, Connor. I've been rinsing them from Mason jars for years. The trick is not to get bitten. You just slosh the water around inside the jar and pour it down the drain."

Connor laughed aloud. "I knew you'd make a good farmer's wife. I thought all women were afraid of bugs and mice."

"Not me. Not of bugs, anyway. I've picked off tomato worms by the dozen and chased potato bugs from the plants for years. I don't like them, but they don't frighten me."

"How about mice?" His words were soft, his eyes twinkling as he questioned her again.

"Mice are dirty little creatures and they don't belong in a kitchen, or a house, for that matter. I've been thinking we need to get a cat around here."

"The bread lady has a litter of kittens about ready to give away," Connor told her. "I'll get one for you if you like."

"A female, please. A tabby cat is a better mouser than a male."

"Women and all sorts of female critters have their place in this world," Connor said judiciously. "If a tabby cat is what you want, I'll do my best to get one for you."

"And where is my place, Mr. Webster?" she asked, unwilling to allow his remark to go unnoticed.

"Right next to me, Mrs. Webster," he answered quickly. "Right where I can find you without having to go searching. Right where I can reach out and hug you and warm myself with your curvy little body curled up next to me."

And then, as if he would turn his words to action, he approached her again and held her close. "Just like this," he murmured against her ear.

She felt her body form against the solid lines of his, her breasts finding a home against the muscular chest, her hips settling nicely into the warmth of his loins. It was like being held securely in an embrace that was the answer to all of life's questions.

"I won't argue with you," she said softly, lifting her face to his. "I love you, Connor. I've loved you for longer than I can remember. You're the best thing that ever happened to me."

"You're not mad at me for telling you that you have a place in this world?"

"No. You were right. My place is here, with you. I won't argue that."

Deep within her, the child she carried rolled and twisted, kicking out in protest at the confinement of being held between two bodies. Connor inhaled sharply and looked down at her.

"The baby?" His eyes were lit by an expectant look she'd never seen before, as if he'd just discovered something new and wonderful.

She nodded. "He moves quite a bit now."

His mouth tightened then and he bent to her. "I'm so glad I'm sharing it with you, Loris."

"The baby seems more real to me now," she said softly. "I'm anxious to see him. Or her. Whatever it may be."

"I hope it's a girl, Loris." Connor's words were firm, his expression sober. "And I hope she looks like you."

"I hope so, too. It's bound to have some of the Webster characteristics. If it's a boy, we'll call him Connor, for you. Is that all right?"

"He'll be my son." And as if that settled the whole question, Connor nodded abruptly.

* * *

Peggy Webster stood in front of the general store, watching as her son approached. He'd spied her there as soon as the wagon rolled close to his destination, but Connor waited for a signal that his mother was going to acknowledge his presence. She focused her gaze on him as he climbed down from the wagon, then watched silently as he climbed the two steps to the wooden sidewalk.

"Mother." His head nodded quickly and he swept off his hat before he opened the door of the store. He was not generally so formal with her, but somehow had lost the warmth of feeling he'd once known with her.

"Connor, I didn't expect to see you in town today."

"If you'd known I was going to be here, you'd have stayed at home. Is that what you mean?" There was anger in his voice but he did not regret the emotion. No matter that the woman before him had given him life, her words of scorn regarding Loris had bitten him deeply and he could not forgive her the pain she'd caused. And all because of the actions of his brother. James was a man who had proved to be faithless, a scalawag to the core.

"No. I didn't mean that," she returned, clutching her purse tightly against her waist. "I came into town to get supplies and I'm waiting for young Thomas to carry them out to my wagon."

She turned her head to watch him as he entered the store. "Connor."

He halted and looked over his shoulder at her. "Yes?"

"Are you all right? Do you need anything?"

"Nothing. My wife and I are doing well. Our horses are thriving and the hay has been cut. Loris is putting up the kitchen garden right now. In fact, I'm here to buy some more Mason jars for her."

Peggy Webster swallowed, a convulsive movement that spoke volumes to Connor's eye. "And is Loris doing well?"

"Are you asking about Loris or your grandchild?"

She tipped her head a bit and smiled, a stiff movement of her lips. "Both."

"They're fine."

"I got a letter from James," his mother said after a moment.

"And what was his news?"

"He's talking about coming back to town for a visit. He asked about you, and about Loris."

"Have you answered his letter?"

She shook her head. "Not yet. I hate to tell him you've married that girl."

"That girl's name is easy to speak aloud, Mother. And whether you like it or not, I'm her husband."

"I don't like it. Not one bit. You've tied yourself down with a tramp, and I wanted better than that for my son."

"Nothing will change my mind on this matter," Connor told her. "If it comes to a choice between my wife and my parents, she'll be the winner, hands down."

His mother darted a look of malice in his direction. "We'll see."

If that was a threat, Connor would not be surprised. Although what his mother could accomplish was beyond his imagination. But the fact remained that if she could cause trouble for Loris, she would.

He approached the counter and gave his list to the storekeeper, then walked slowly around the premises, picking and choosing small items from the household goods on display. Two plates and mugs in the blue-flowered pattern Loris liked so well were added to his pile of purchases, and he nodded at the inclusion of the two dresses he'd chosen for her weeks before. They were both generous in cut and he decided she would look lovely in them, even though she fretted over the size of her rapidly expanding waistline.

"I'll just carry these out," he told the storekeeper, lifting two large boxes and heading for the door.

"I'll give you a hand." Without hesitation, the owner of the general store followed him, carrying a double armload of merchandise. They settled it all in the back of the wagon, and Connor followed the gentleman back into the store. He pulled out his wallet and paid the amount due, then chose a handful of candy for Loris. She'd developed a sweet tooth lately, and he thought to indulge her a bit.

He'd never known anyone so easy to please as his wife. Anything he did for her was greeted with exclamations of pleasure, and she made it enjoyable to think up new ways to give her delight. Thinking of the response he would get when he showed her the candy, he opened the big doors and stepped onto the sidewalk.

His mother stood outside the door, as if waiting there for him. He nodded brusquely at her and went on down the steps toward his wagon.

"Connor? Will you be visiting soon? Are you coming home to see your father?"

He turned, amazed at her words. "No. I won't be coming back to the farm. I have my horses, my clothing and my gun. There's nothing else there that interests me."

As if someone had put a pin into her and allowed her to deflate, she slumped against the wall of the building. "We won't be seeing you again? Has that woman turned you against us so thoroughly?"

"Loris has nothing to do with the way I feel about you and my father," Connor said bluntly. "Other than the fact that you've chosen to ignore her as my wife, and I'm going to spend my life with her. You've made the choice, not I."

He climbed atop his wagon seat and lifted the reins. His mother's words followed him then, and he stored them in his mind for future inspection.

"She'll be sorry one day."

Muttered in a low tone, harshly, it sounded strangely like a threat to him. As if his mother planned some sort of revenge on the girl who had married her son. And had come between two brothers—a rift that might never be repaired.

Chapter Seven

The time was right for the baby to be born, according to Loris's calculations. The July heat was miserable, the days moving slowly as she felt the heaviness of pregnancy take their toll on her body. The garden was too much for her to handle any more, and Connor had taken over the task of keeping it up. He worked hard, and she felt guilty as she watched him grow weary under the load he'd assumed.

She'd thought the end of July would be a happy time in her life, but when the signs of impending labor appeared, she felt a deep depression set in, and her heart was burdened with a heavy hopelessness she seemed unable to conquer, no matter how she tried to berate herself for feeling so down.

"What is it?" Connor looked at her with concern and she only shook her head. "I can see you're upset, Loris. Is it the baby? Aren't you feeling well? Shall I get the doctor?"

"I think that might be a good idea," she said finally. "I don't feel right, Connor. The baby hasn't moved in two days and I'm feeling sickly, nauseated and dizzy."

"Will you be all right here by yourself while I go to town?" He approached her as she sat in the rocking chair by the window, kneeling down before her, clasping her hands in his.

"I'll be fine." The grin she managed was weak, but she couldn't come up with a full-fledged smile, no matter how much she tried. The pain in her back was becoming more intense by the minute, leaving her for minutes at a time and then returning with a vengeance.

"I'll hurry," Connor said, rising to his feet. He snatched up his hat and opened the door, and then returned to her, bending low to kiss her mouth with a passion born of fear. She felt his apprehension as surely as she felt her own, and managed to work up a watery smile for his benefit.

"I'm going to get washed up and put on my nightgown," she told him. "I'll probably be upstairs when you come back."

When he returned an hour later, the doctor in tow, she was indeed in bed, her hair clinging to her temples and cheeks, damp with sweat. Her fingers clutched at the sheet, her hands rigid as if she feared letting go. She was hot, yet chilled at the same time, and the sight of the old doctor from town was welcome.

"What's going on, young lady?" he said kindly, bending over her to brush the hair from her forehead. "You're having quite a time, aren't you?"

"I hurt pretty badly," she said. "Mostly in my back."

"Any movement?" His eyes sharpened as he ran his hands over her swollen belly.

"Not for a couple of days." Her words broke as she uttered them, wondering if that were a sign of danger, that her child had been resting.

"Let's see what's going on." The doctor washed his hands thoroughly in the basin of warm water Connor provided and then began his examination.

It was embarrassing to Loris, but he was kindly and quick, dealing with her as if it were an everyday occurrence to him, and indeed, it probably was. He sat on the edge of the mattress and took her hands in his.

"I don't like the lack of movement, Loris. I'm not sure what's going on, but you're definitely in labor."

And with that another pain rolled through her, from her back to the front, clutching her in hot talons of agony, and she groaned aloud. "How long does it take to have a baby?"

"Hours, sometimes. In your case, I think it'll go pretty quickly. You're already in the final stage."

"It's been hurting pretty bad for hours already. I don't mean to complain, but—"

She broke off suddenly as another pain clenched her womb in an iron fist. She rolled to her side, calling for Connor, certain he would not hear her, so weak was her voice.

She was wrong. He came through the bedroom door, a towel draped over his hands. "I'm washed, Doc," he said. "Soaped up real good and scrubbed up with the brush for a couple of minutes."

"Good. I'm going to need you, son."

Loris thought the doctor's glance in Connor's direction was forbidding, but Connor only nodded, walking toward his wife's side. "I want you to let her grip your hands. She'll need to pull against your strength, Connor. I want her to bear down on the next pain, and it won't be but a few seconds coming along."

He was right, and the harsh contracting of her womb tossed Loris into another world, a painful place where she only thought of pushing the child from her body, a place where agony such as she'd never known existed, now dwelt.

It seemed hours before she pushed for the final time and the doctor murmured softly, encouraging her as he delivered the child. Beside her, Connor drew in a sharp breath, and she fought against the darkness that overwhelmed her, struggling to see the baby.

"Is it a boy?" Her words were slurred, her voice trembling, and through the mist of pain, Connor's face looked down at her, his eyes filled with tears.

She must be mistaken. Connor never showed his emotions in such a way. He looked up at the doctor and his jaw clenched as the doctor spoke only two words.

"I'm sorry."

Those words vibrated in her head, swirling in a gray cloud that threatened to overwhelm her. *I'm sorry. I'm sorry.* Over and over they resounded, and before consciousness slipped from her, she knew the meaning they conveyed.

"Loris? Are you awake?" Connor was close, his mouth touching her cheek, her ear, and finally her mouth. She whispered his name, groping for some knowledge of her whereabouts.

"Where am I?"

"At home. In bed," he answered. "You're going to be all right, sweetheart."

"The baby?" And before he answered, she knew. Knew with a deep despair the fate of her child. For whatever reason, she had been robbed of the joys of motherhood. Perhaps in retribution for her sin, perhaps because she'd failed Connor so miserably. Whatever the reason, she knew her child was not alive, and she buried her face against Connor's shoulder and wept.

"Our baby died." It was a pronouncement of the very worst kind, a death knell that seemed to render her soul. "He wouldn't have been a healthy child, the doctor said. But he thought you'd be able to carry more children later on."

"God is punishing me," she cried aloud. "I was bad, and He's making me pay for the trouble I caused."

Connor held her closely, shaking his head. "No such thing, honey. These things happen sometime. The doctor said it was just one of those things that can't be explained."

"I tried to make up for it, Connor. You do believe I love you, don't you?"

He nodded quickly, but his eyes were dark, and she felt a distance between them. "Of course I do," he said. "And you're not being punished for anything, Loris."

"You don't believe me, do you?"

He gathered her into his arms. "Of course I do. I don't want you to worry about it now. Just sleep for a while. I've got some things to tend to."

"Where's my baby?" It was important to see him, to lay eyes on the tiny form, just once.

"He's downstairs. I'm building a coffin for him. I'll let you see him when I've finished."

"No. Now." She said the words emphatically, determined that no one should keep her from the child. With a sense of futility, she struggled to sit up in the bed, stretched her legs over the side of the mattress and fought to get to her feet.

"No, Loris. You can't get up. The doctor said you

must be careful and lie quietly. He doesn't want you to bleed any more, and if you start trying to get up and walk, you'll run the risk of hemorrhage. I can't let you do that."

"Then bring me my baby."

Connor sighed and arose from the side of the bed. "All right. Lie down and wait a minute. I'll be right back." He went from the room, picking up a small blanket as he passed by the dresser. It was one Loris had hemmed by hand herself, blue flannel with feather-stitching around the edges. She swallowed the lump in her throat as she thought of the hours she'd spent on the small gowns and blankets she'd made during the past few months.

And then as Connor appeared once more in the bedroom doorway, a tiny bundle in his hands, she sobbed anew. The soft blue blanket was wrapped securely around the baby he held, only wisps of dark hair showing as he placed it in her arms. She moved the corner of the flannel aside and looked at the tiny face, the small nose and the rosebud mouth. His ears were flat against his head, his hair curling against his scalp.

"He's beautiful," she murmured. Her lips touched his forehead and found it cool to the touch. One small hand rested atop a fold of flannel and she traced the length of fingers that would never reach for her, hands that would never touch her face.

"I wanted him," she said, holding back the tears.

"I know you did," Connor whispered. "I never doubted that for a minute. He would have been well loved by both of us."

"I don't think God is angry with me," she said after

a moment, looking up into Connor's blue gaze. "Maybe this baby was just not meant to be, perhaps life would have been too difficult for him. No matter how much we loved him, it might not have been enough. Life is cruel as it is, and when a child has the stigma of—"

"Hush." Connor spoke the single syllable, cutting her off before she could say more. "Don't even think that, Loris. There would have been no stigma attached to our son." He bent low to press his lips where Loris's had so recently felt the cool touch of death. "Let me take him," Connor said. "I'll fix him up in his coffin and then carry you out to the orchard. We'll bury him there."

She only nodded, allowing Connor to take the babe from her arms, watching him walk from the room. "This should make your mother happy, Connor," she whispered. "And my folks will be downright pleased that they don't have to explain away the existence of a grandson they never wanted."

It was a solemn occasion, Loris sitting on a quilt beside the short, narrow grave, Connor holding the tiny, hand-hewn coffin in his hands. He stood beside her, his voice deep, a bit gruff, as if he held back tears, and then he placed the box on the ground in front of his wife.

"Do you want to say anything?"

She looked up at him, recognizing the signs of grief on his handsome face, the lines drawn in his cheeks, the narrowed eyes, his mouth twisted into a grim crease across the lower part of his face. Almost as if it were truly his own son in the coffin he'd put together. As if he mourned the child, as would any father who felt the bereavement of his son's death. A death that had not allowed the child to live, never to know the love of parents and the joys inherent in being part of a family.

"Only to tell him goodbye," she whispered, placing her hand on the top of the box, feeling the smooth finish of the wood he'd sanded and stained in such a short time.

"I can't give him your name," she said. "We'll save Connor for our first son, when he comes along."

"This is our first son," he said, correcting her gently. "But we'll name him something else if you like."

"We'll give him his father's name. He'll be James." And with that she lifted tear-filled eyes to him, begging his compliance.

He gave it, quickly and generously, a simple nod of his head answering her unspoken plea.

In a few moments, he'd lowered the coffin into the grave, holding it on two ropes until it rested on the earth at the bottom of the gaping hole. He pulled the ropes free and looked down.

"I wish he were going to be mourned by his grandparents, too," he said carefully. "They might have come to love him, had he lived long enough to steal into their hearts."

Loris stood up, holding a small basket of flowers she'd picked in front of the porch. "I want to put these on top of him," she said, bending over to scatter the blossoms atop the small box. And then she watched as Connor picked up the shovel and began moving the pile of dirt back into the hole. He made quick work of it, as if he knew that every scoop of soil thudding against the coffin created a pain felt deeply by them both.

"Can you make a cross for him, with his name on it?" Loris asked. "Just his name and the date."

"I can do that." It was the least he could do for the

precious child. For a moment he thought of James, of the man who would never see his son. There was anger in his heart towards his only brother, for so many things. The chasm between them had grown so wide, Connor doubted it could ever be mended.

"You have no more responsibility toward me," Loris said firmly. She sat at the table, watching as Connor ate his meal. She'd mended well after the birth, begun her usual tasks a week ago, and now felt capable of caring for herself. "I won't hold you to our agreement," she said, noting the color that washed over his face. He was angry. Without warning, she was telling him he was welcome to leave and return to his family if he wanted to. As if he could leave after being there just six weeks ago at the birth of their son.

"You don't want me here anymore?" he asked harshly. "You're done with me?"

"I want you to be free of encumbrance," she told him. "You needn't feel tied down by me any longer. I'm giving you the freedom to leave and make a fresh start for yourself, and mend your family ties. I know you've missed your folks, and I don't want to be the cause of your problems with them."

"You want me to leave. Is that what you're saying?" He stood, outrage apparent in every bone of his body. He was tall, towering over her, and for a moment, just a quick second of time, she felt a jolt of fear touch her heart. And then it was gone. Connor would never hurt her, never cause her pain deliberately. She knew that, knew it without a doubt.

"I want you to make amends with your parents," she said firmly. "I've done enough damage."

"And what about you? What will you do? Go home to your folks, too?"

She shook her head. "No, of course not. They put me out, disowned me in the middle of winter and have never made any attempt to see me again. I wouldn't waste my time on them. I can take care of myself, Connor."

"You never really loved me at all, did you?" he asked angrily. "You lied to me from the beginning when you said you loved me. And I was fool enough to believe you. I wondered sometimes, but you're very convincing, Loris. I'll give you that much."

"I did love you," she whispered. *I still do. I love you, Connor.* The words resounded in her mind as she watched his face, saw the doubt in his eyes, knowing that he would leave, and bit her tongue to keep from retracting the words she'd spoken.

"I'll leave, since that's what you want," he told her. "I'll be gone tomorrow. And I'll sleep tonight on the sofa."

She swallowed the apology that begged to be spoken, then saw the harsh light in his eyes that told her it was too late, that he'd taken this chance to go back to his old life, without the responsibility of a wife to tie him down.

It was a long, lonely week. Loris spent it cleaning up the garden plot, digging the potatoes and carrying them into the cellar for the winter. She pulled the remaining carrots and shook the dirt from them, then carried them to join the potatoes. The onions were huge, the crop was good, and she congratulated herself on the garden she'd planted and brought to harvest.

The last of the tomatoes lay on the ground, the vines withering above them and she gathered them in a basket, took them in the house and cooked them until they were ready for the canning jars. She should have used pints instead of quarts, she realized suddenly. Without Connor here to cook for she'd be wasting a lot of food, opening quarts of vegetables and throwing half of them away.

Perhaps she'd just drink milk from the cow, eat eggs from the chickens and forget about regular meals. It was a good thing Connor had made her learn how to milk the cow or she'd be in a fix right now.

She eyed the jars of tomatoes on the cupboard and could not repress the feeling of pride at the accomplishments that had been so much a part of her life during the long summer. Mostly because of Connor. He'd encouraged her and praised her for each small thing she managed to do, to the point where she felt truly confident of her abilities. She could do this, she could take care of herself and run this house alone if need be. If only she didn't miss him so much.

If Connor came back, that would be a bonus, and if he didn't…well, she'd think about that another time. It was for certain she wouldn't coax him to return should he come to her or make him feel guilty for her being alone. It had been her own choice, and if Connor was mending fences with his family, it was all to the good.

She woke early the next morning, a feeling of apprehension filling her as she dressed and cooked her breakfast. She'd baked bread the day before, only the third time she'd tried, but the result was better than she'd expected. The bread was crusty, but soft in the middle. Almost as good as the bread lady could make, she thought, slicing it and putting two slices into the oven to toast.

Her coffee was poured and her eggs taken up on her

plate, when she heard a horse whinny outside. "Connor." His name fell from her lips without hesitation and she sat almost frozen at the table, willing him to walk in the kitchen door. It was not to be, although the tall form of a man crossed the porch and then she heard a knock on the door.

She rose and opened it warily, not knowing who to expect. James stood before her, his hat at his side, his eyes searching the room beyond her. "Is Connor here?" he asked. "I need to see you both, Loris."

She shook her head and stepped back from the open door. "Come in, James."

"I've had a long time to think," he said. "I came home for a few days," he said bluntly. "I need to tell you how sorry I am. I went into town and the bank manager told me you were living here, that Connor had paid the back taxes on this place for you." He paused and looked down at the floor, as if he could no longer meet her gaze.

"Are you all right, Loris?" he asked.

"You're a little late asking me that question," she told him. "I've been better, to tell the truth, but I'm all right now."

"What does that mean? I heard in town that you and Connor were married. Is that true? If so, where is he?"

"He's gone back to live at home, I think," she said. "He married me to give your child a name, and now that we no longer need to keep up the pretense, he's gone."

"What are you talking about? What pretense? Where is the baby? I know it's past time for it to be born."

"Do you really care about the child?" she asked bitterly. "Does it make any difference to you what happened to him?"

"It's a boy?" He almost smiled, and then seemed to think better of it.

"Yes, I gave birth to a son, James. He's buried in the orchard. Connor made him a coffin and we buried him the day he was born. He never caught his first breath. The doctor said he'd been dead for a couple of days."

"What happened?" He looked truly dumbfounded, she thought, stunned by the news that his child had not lived.

"The doctor said it was something that happens sometimes, no reason for it, just a failure to develop properly."

James leaned against the wall as if he could no longer hold himself upright. "May I see the grave?" he asked quietly.

Loris didn't hesitate. It would be too cruel to deny him such a thing, and she nodded. "Yes, I'll show you where he is."

Together, they walked out to the orchard and approached the small cross. When Connor had brought it back and put it at the head of the gravesite, she didn't know, but one morning this week she'd awakened, looked out the window and seen it there. He must have come during the night, unwilling to see her.

James looked down at the words carved carefully on the horizontal piece. *James Webster, born July 19, 1893. Laid to rest, July 19, 1893.*

"You gave him my name," he said unbelievingly, turning to look down into Loris's eyes. "Why would you do such a thing? Especially after I'd abandoned you the way I did."

Loris shrugged and smiled tightly. "He was your son, James. For all that you didn't want him, even though you walked away from me, from us, he still was your child. I couldn't ignore that fact."

"Did Connor agree? To name him after me?"

She smiled then. "What does it matter? No one will ever know except for the three of us. Neither your folks or mine give a good gol-dern about him. I was left stranded last January, the day you left, when my father kicked me out of the house and I walked to this place."

"I can't tell you how ashamed I am of what I did, Loris. I was wrong, and I've been miserable, thinking about you and the mess I left you in. I'm glad Connor was able to help."

"Yes," she said briskly. "He bought this place for me, chopped wood and worked the fields, and took care of me till the baby came."

"It's only been six weeks or so since then," James said. "Are you able to be up and around?"

"I seem to be," she told him, turning to walk back to the house.

He caught up with her and grasped her arm. "Wait, Loris. I need to talk to you about something. Connor is gone and I want you in my life again, honey. I'm so sorry I made a mess of things. I hope you'll be able to forgive me and let me make amends. I've done a lot of growing up and I want to take care of you."

"I can't believe you're saying these things," she said, rounding on him and glaring at the penitent expression he wore. "Forget it, James. I have no interest in another man. I've had one husband. That was enough. Just go away. You've accomplished what you came here for. Now leave."

He reached for her again, holding her hand in his as

he spoke quickly. "You can divorce Connor. I'll have the lawyer in town put together a bill of divorcement, and since Connor has deserted you, there shouldn't be any problem having it legalized in the court. Then we can get married, Loris. Make a fresh start."

"I don't think you've listened to me, James. I don't want you for a husband. I'm still married to Connor." Her breath caught in a sob and her words quavered with the force of her grief. "Until Connor asks for a divorce, I'll remain his wife," she said firmly. "Just leave me alone, and don't come back."

"You don't mean it." He stood before her, his stance stubborn, his jaw jutting forward, and his face crimson with anger.

"I mean every word I say. I want you off my land. Get on your horse and get going, or I'll get my shotgun and fill you full of buckshot." She jerked from his grasp and took two steps backward, out of his reach. "Is that plain enough for you?"

"I'll go, Loris. For now, anyway. I know you're upset, and I don't want you to be angry, but I'll be back. I'm going home to visit my folks and talk to them about this, and I'll be back to work things out with you."

She turned on her heel and marched to the house, her back aching, her legs weak, the stress of the confrontation making her almost physically ill. The man was hopeless. He couldn't take no for an answer, and she was determined not to speak to him again.

The shotgun stood in the pantry and she snatched it up, then walked back to the porch. "Now do you believe me?" she asked. "I know how to shoot this thing, and I'm giving you about three seconds to be on your way, James."

He swung into his saddle with haste, held his reins firmly and touched his heels to the horse's barrel. The animal set off at a fast trot, and Loris watched him go without a speck of regret. To think she'd ever thought herself in love with the man was almost more than she could conceive. He was shallow. Shallow and devoid of any pretense of honor. He'd said his apology very nicely, and she knew he hadn't meant a word of it.

If he went to the Webster ranch, he might be in for a big surprise.

The afternoon held a passel of work, as usual, and right after dinner, Connor went to the barn to exercise his horses. He missed the fields at home, where he could look up at the farmhouse and sometimes spy the slight form of a woman watching him. Even at her most cumbersome, Loris had a natural grace about her, a way of moving that revealed her femininity.

But here, at his parents' house, there was no wife to entice him, no reason to hurry with his chores, lest he miss a chance to spend time with Loris. He took the lead rope and led his pinto mare from the barn, looking at her with pride. She was a sweetheart, a mare who would one day breed him some fine-looking colts. For now, though, she was only two years old and he wouldn't breed her for another year. In the meantime, she would get to know the feel of a saddle and the weight of a man on her back. Tall and well-formed, she was a beauty. In fact, he'd thought to train her for Loris.

He walked from the barn, leading the mare behind him. Near the house, a horse stood, reins attached to the hitching rail. There was something about the animal that took his eye. The color, the conformation, the way he tossed his head and whinnied, long and loud.

And then, from the kitchen doorway, he caught sight of a man, a man he'd thought never to see again. His fury arose within him and he felt a surge of madness that enveloped him in a cloud of heat. How James could return, walk in the house and expect a welcome was more than Connor could fathom. The man was insane. He'd have done better to stay in Missouri.

Slowly, he tied the mare he led to the barn door, then stalked toward the house. James looked up at his approach, propped his hands on his hips and waited. His face was drawn into a somber frown, as if he had not expected to see his brother.

"What are you doing here?" Connor growled. He neared the house, watching as James stood on the porch, almost as if he waited for his brother to make a move.

Connor stalked up the steps, grasped James by the front of his shirt and hauled him from the porch. Fists battered him about the head and shoulders as he manhandled his brother, but Connor felt none of the bruises that began to form, even as he made his way toward the barn, James in tow.

Fury lent strength to his muscular arms and he burned with rage. "You walked away, James. You should have stayed in Missouri."

"I went to see Loris," James said with a sneer. "We talked about her divorcing you and marrying me."

"Fat chance." Connor was beyond anger now. That his brother dared to mention Loris by name was an insult to the woman. "Loris is my wife. She'll always be my wife. We're going to spend our lives together." Suddenly the truth struck Connor. No matter what happened, he was in love with Loris. She might think she could divorce him and tag after James, but he wasn't about to let her go.

First, there was the matter of trouncing James that required his attention. He held his brother upright just inside the barn door and drew back his arm. The first blow hit just below the bridge of his nose, the second closed James's left eye. From then on it was a losing battle, the anger and pent up frustration providing Connor with a strength he'd not known before. Within ten minutes, he'd reduced his brother to a broken heap, sprawled on the barn floor.

From the house, Peggy Webster called, "Connor. You leave him alone. I want to talk to you. You come here right now."

"Sure." With a triumphant grin, Connor left the barn, not looking back when he heard his father's voice trying to raise a response from James. He strode to the house and faced his mother. She was furious, giving Connor the sharp side of her tongue in no uncertain terms.

"You had no right to assault your brother that way. And all over that little snip of a girl. You should be ashamed of yourself. Blood runs thicker than water, and James is your brother. He said he spoke to Loris and made things right with her. You have no reason to beat him so badly. I want you to gather up your things and leave. You're no longer welcome here."

"I'd planned on leaving anyway," Connor told her. "Give me ten minutes and I'll be out of your way. In the meantime, you'd better carry your fair-haired child up here to the house and give him a good dose of your pampering. He's probably missed it for the last few months."

"You'd do well to get that girl out of the area," his mother said harshly. "She's going to pay for this. You mark my words."

"You touch Loris, and you'll deal with me," Connor told her.

"You don't scare me, sonny," Peggy said with a scornful laugh. "She's just a tramp and you're no better than she is. Once you get tied up with trash, you wear the stain for the rest of your life."

Connor felt a horrible urge to strike the woman who'd given him life. But restrained his awful impulse. She was his mother. She'd borne him, loved him, but once James had been born, Connor had been relegated to second place in his mother's eyes. Perhaps his father's too. For some reason, James had been the favored child, ever after.

Connor's hands curled into fists and he plunged them into his trouser pockets, lest he let loose his temper on her. With a muttered curse, he went past her, through the house to his bedroom, where he quickly snatched up the most important of his belongings. The horses could wait until later. For now, he would leave on his saddle horse. Tomorrow was soon enough to get the rest.

Seeing Loris was of the utmost importance. He needed to hear from her mouth the words that could put his love to death. And unless she denied all that James had said, he would forever rue the day he'd married the woman.

Chapter Eight

"What do you want done, Mrs. Webster? And how much are you payin'?"

Howie Murdoch was nondescript, his clothing soiled, his beard scruffy. Even his horse looked a bit the worse for wear, but Peggy Webster was not interested in his qualifications as a gentleman. In fact, she was more set on finding out just how far he would go for a hundred dollars. Though she hadn't seen him in over twenty years, he was still mean—through and through.

It was a lot of money, but she'd already decided that no amount was too great to guarantee Loris's absence from the county. "I'm willing to pay you a hundred dollars. But I'd appreciate it if you forgot my name. I was never fond of you, even when I knew you in school, and that hasn't changed," she said sharply. "You're only the means to an end, as far as I'm concerned."

He was desperate and greedy. As if the mention of money had struck sparks, his eyes lit at her price and she frowned. He probably would have settled for less. Too late now. "I need to have the woman frightened enough to leave this area. If you can scare her off, make her think her life is in danger, I'll pay the full amount. I don't want you killing her." She shrugged, rethinking her goal. "Well, only as a last resort, if you've tried all other ways to do this."

The man was crafty. "Who is she?"

"Her name is Loris. From what my son told me, she's living in a farmhouse outside town. You can probably find out from one of the gossips in front of the general store which one."

"And where's your son? He still living at home?"

"He's not here right now, but he'll probably show up again, once he gets over being mad. He and his brother got into a fight and Connor left."

"I'll see what I can do. When do I get the hundred dollars?"

"As soon as you show good faith. As soon as something's accomplished to get that girl out of the way."

"What's her last name?"

"Peterson. Loris Peterson."

"I'll find her."

"What kind of promise did you make to James?"

Loris had never seen Connor so angry, as when he stormed into their house, and she was sure she'd been treated to an exhibition of his bad temper more than once over the past weeks. Though never had it been aimed at her in this fashion.

Nevertheless, she felt no fear as she faced him. "What right do you have to ask me such a thing? You left me to go home with all your belongings, and now you're back here questioning me about James? Why do you care?"

"You told me to go," he roared, then fought for control. "Just give me an answer, Loris. I want to know what you talked about, what sort of promise you made him."

She laughed aloud, and tilted her chin at an angle. "I promised him I'd fill him full of buckshot if he didn't get on his horse and leave me be. The man came here and offered me marriage. Wanted me to divorce you and go off with him."

"And you turned him down?"

She glared at him. "Of course I did. Do you think I'm a fool?"

"That's exactly what I wanted to hear you say," Connor told her.

"But you didn't *expect* me to say it, did you?" Rusty, sitting by her side, growled low in his throat, as though he sensed some sort of threat to his mistress.

Connor flexed his big hands and slid them into his back pockets. "I'd hoped."

"You've never really trusted me, Connor. I don't know what James told you, but I'm telling you the truth. Believe it or not, as you like."

"I do believe it. He's a liar from away back, and he was trying his best to get under my skin. Told me you were willing to run off with him, as soon as you could divorce me." He looked down at the dog. "Tell Rusty I'm not going to hurt you, Loris."

"First I want to know why you believed him."

"I didn't say I did."

"You didn't have to. You came here all puffed up and ready for a fight with me. I thought I wanted you back, but I suspect I've changed my mind, Connor. Go back home where you belong. Your mama will be downright happy to have you out of my house."

"My mama wouldn't be happy with me right now, no matter where I hang my hat. I had a rousing fight with James, and she's probably nursing his bruises even as we speak."

She stepped closer and inspected his face, Rusty forcing his way between them. "I don't see any bruises on you." And then she looked down. "Go lie down, Rusty. Everything's all right." With a low growl, the dog did as she said, but he looked unhappy.

Connor watched the dog for a moment and laughed. "He took me at my word. I think you have quite a watchdog there, ma'am. As to my bruises, I have a few, but not where they'll show. He clipped me a good one on my shoulder, and banged my arm pretty good."

Loris reached out to him and he pulled his hands from his pockets and placed them in hers. She bent her head, then touched the scraped surface of his fists with her index finger. "You're going to have a couple of bruises here, too," she told him curtly. "But I can't find it in me to feel your pain. I have enough of my own to deal with."

She stepped away from him and turned to walk up the porch steps. "You didn't even give me a chance to say anything, Connor. You got off your horse and asked me about James. *'What kind of a promise did you make to James?'* I believe those were your exact words."

"Yeah, they were." He reached for her and she evaded his touch. "Please, Loris. Just listen to me for a minute. I don't want our marriage to end this way. I want to stay here with you and make a success of things."

"Really? And how will you go about doing that?"

"I'll move back in and take over the outside work again. We've got the last hay cutting to tend to, and you can't do it without help. I'll bring my horses back and I'll see to it that the folks in town know that we have a real marriage going on here."

"A real marriage? A union that falls apart as soon as your brother spouts his lies in your ears? I don't think so, Connor. I want a marriage in which two people trust each other and believe each other and stick together. You've all but accused me of—"

"That's enough." His cool demeanor was no more. Now he hauled her off the porch step and clutched her to himself. "I didn't accuse you of anything. I asked you a question, and you gave me the answer I'd hoped for. I trust you, Loris. I do. And I want to be your husband."

"But will you trust me the next time? Will you know my heart and recognize my love for you, without me begging for your understanding?"

His mouth tightened and she watched as a crimson hue painted his cheeks. "I'd never make you beg. You know better than that."

"Do I?" She stood in his embrace, stiff and unyielding.

"*I'm* the one begging now, Loris." His eyes were deep-set and as dark as the midnight sky. His jaw was set in a harsh line and he still wore the ruddy stain on his high cheekbones. A desperate man, willing to lay his pride on the line for her.

And then his arms loosened a bit. "If you want to escape me, you only have to step away," he told her. "I won't hold you against your will. I won't do anything to you that you don't want me to."

He swallowed, and she watched as his throat moved

with the effort. "I'll have to admit that I want to carry you inside right now, Loris, up those stairs to our bed. I want to hold you and feel your soft curves against me, and I want to remind you in the best possible way that we're married and it's gonna stay that way."

"I'm too heavy."

He blinked, and his forehead furrowed. "Too heavy for me to carry?"

She nodded. "I've only lost a few pounds since…" Her words trailed off and she bent her head, focusing on his shirtfront.

"Since the baby was born? Say it, Loris. That baby was real. We labored together to give him birth, even though I only held your hands and tried to give you comfort. We'll never forget the little mite. He'll always be in our memories, a part of our marriage. Even when we have more children, he'll be the first."

"Connor." She spoke his name, knowing he would understand the message she strove to deliver.

"Will you let me carry you into the house, Loris?" As if he awaited her pleasure, he bent low, his forehead touching her shoulder. She heard his sigh, the catch in his breath and knew a moment of tenderness so great it almost overwhelmed her.

"I can walk up the stairs," she told him softly. "I need you, Connor. I need to know you care about me. I want you in my life." Her pause was long as she lifted her head and reached for him, enclosing his face in her palms. "Is that clear enough for you?"

"Yes, ma'am. It surely is." He hadn't forgotten how to grin, that sassy twist of his lips that told her he was pleased with her. With a quick movement, he snatched her off her feet and carried her into the house, the dog at his heels.

"I can walk," she protested.

"I'm aware of that. But I want to carry you," he muttered with more than a shade of arrogance coating his words. "Just kiss me, wife."

She turned her face into his throat and felt his life blood throbbing against her lips. Her kisses were hot and openmouthed against his flesh, and the words she murmured told him of her love.

"I'm not sure I'll make it to the bed," he muttered. "This stairway didn't seem so long the last time I climbed it, Loris."

"I offered to walk, but you wouldn't have it." Her voice sounded smug, she thought, and not for a moment was she repentant. It was satisfying to see Connor eager for her kisses, and she felt joy bubble up within her as he held her possessively, as if unwilling to loose his hold on her.

"I thought I only wanted to hold you in my arms." He slowed his pace a bit and sidled through the doorway to their room, then bent to place her in the middle of the big bed. "Now I'll show you what I really want to do."

His hands were instruments of pleasure as he stripped her clothing from her. His fingertips were knowing and clever as he touched the tender curves and hollows of her body. And when his manhood found its place within her, it was most welcome.

Loris reveled in the happiness he brought her, knew a moment of joy as he whispered words of love in her ears and found herself once more the focus of his loving.

"As reunions go, I'd say this one was a rousing success," Connor said, almost an hour later. He lay beside her, his arms holding her against him, his expression eminently content. Lifting from his embrace, she studied his face, noting the smile he aimed in her direction. Satisfaction gleamed in his eyes, and a primitive look of possession marked his features.

"You're mine, Loris. You always will be. We'll never let anyone come between us again."

"I never told James—"

"I know that," he said sharply. "I knew it before I came here. I was just hurting so badly, thinking he'd spoken to you and perhaps…well, never mind. It didn't happen."

"I showed him the baby's grave," she said quietly. "He wanted to see it and I thought he had the right. Maybe I was wrong, but I felt almost sorry for him. To have lost his first child without ever holding him or seeing his face."

"He wasn't James's child. He was ours."

With those words, Connor put an end to the discussion. And Loris was pleased to do as he said.

It was as it had been. They worked together, Connor repairing the fences in order to keep his horses in the pasture without worrying about them running off. Loris brought his dinner to him on the days he worked till noon and beyond. Other days, he appeared in the kitchen before she could pack up the food for their picnic.

The house sparkled again, not only with the sheen of wax, but with the air of love and devotion of two people totally committed to each other and their marriage. Only when she looked from the kitchen window toward the orchard did Loris feel the sense of grief that had been her constant companion during earlier weeks, when the raw earth had drawn her eyes like a magnet.

Now the grass had grown over the small mound, and she'd planted flowers there, Rusty at her side, as if he offered comfort for her grief. She felt somehow that her child would be better honored by the presence of flowers she planted. Not that the baby would know. But his mother did, having marked his grave with her tears of sorrow that had fallen as she set down the fragile roots into the soil.

Connor built new stalls for the foals that would be born after the first of the year. One oversize stall was designed for the mares in foal, a large area where they would be kept as their time drew near. His excitement knew no bounds, and Loris shared it with him, knowing that he saw success just over the horizon. Three men had brought him three-year-olds to train, and he spent hours at the task.

Finally, the last cutting of hay was in and Connor said they were ready for winter, with grain and hay aplenty for the livestock. Pride filled him, and Loris was well aware of how hard he'd worked. The new stalls and the tack room he'd put together were impressive, and she inspected them thoroughly late one afternoon.

"I'm proud of you, Connor."

"Everything I do is for us and our future, Loris." He blew out the lantern, leaving the barn in a dim light. The sun had set, and twilight was upon them as they walked together to the house. Supper was a meal of leftovers, and they ate contentedly together, washing the dishes and cleaning the kitchen afterward in their usual manner.

Bedtime was early, for dawn was the accepted time

to awake. The daylight hours were growing shorter every week, and Connor wanted to get all that he could completed before bad weather arrived. They lay in the middle of the big bed and whispered quietly together. Loris heard a soft snore beside her and her lips curved in a tender smile, knowing that Connor slept the sleep of weariness.

She closed her eyes and rolled to face the window, aware of the stars in the sky, the faint cast of moonlight through the screen. She was almost asleep, hovering on the edge of dreams when she awoke with a start. No longer did the stars glitter through the window. Instead a brilliant flame lit the midnight sky, and she pushed herself upright in bed, then slid to the floor and darted toward the window.

"Loris? What's going on?" Connor rounded the foot of the bed and halted behind her. His words were hoarse. "The barn! It's on fire!" Without another word, he found his trousers and pulled them on, snatched up his shirt, then ran for the door.

Loris wrapped her robe around her, tied the belt and followed him down the stairs. She picked up his boots from beside the back door and carried them out with her, running across the yard to where crimson flames engulfed the barn. From inside, she heard the scream of horses, and then Connor came through the doorway, two mares behind him, two more animals coming through the barn door ahead of him. He chased them outside, and then turned to Loris.

"Here, tie them up somewhere," he told her, handing her the lead ropes, even as he disappeared once more into the flaming structure. Loris tried to calm the frightened animals, and tied them firmly to the hitching rail near the house. By the time she'd run back to the barn, Connor was again leading horses toward her, and she took them from him, and tied them to the tree near the watering trough.

The fire looked to be increasingly dangerous, with flames shooting from the hayloft, where their winter supply was going up in smoke. This time when Connor burst from the barn, with the last of his horses, he was breathing heavily, his face sooty, his clothing smoking from his proximity to the flames.

"Don't go back in there, Connor," Loris cried.

"I didn't get the cow," he told her.

"You're more important than that cow any day of the week," she said sharply. "I don't want you to die because of a stupid cow."

He stood beside her, the lead lines of three horses in his grasp and shook his head. "I don't know how this thing started, Loris. I swear I turned off the lantern before we came in the house."

"I know you did. I watched you do it." She reached for one of his mares and the animal jumped to one side, shuddering and twitching from stem to stern. "Will they be all right?" Loris asked. "They won't lose their foals, will they?"

"They might." Connor blew out a mighty breath. "We're just lucky you woke up when you did. We'd have lost them all in another ten minutes."

"Damn the horses. All I care about is you." Her heart pounded heavily as she considered what might have happened. One of the boards from the hayloft might have crashed down on his head while he was rescuing the horses. Or the fire might have blocked his way out of the barn. "Connor, we'll build another barn. It's all right. We can buy another cow."

"Your draft horses are most likely gone, too," he said quietly. "I opened the door into the corral, but I don't know if they went out or not. Horses are terrified of fire, and they may have just stayed in their stalls."

"Let's take care of these, for now," she said, turning to where she'd tied the first of the lot. "Can we put them out to pasture?"

"I'm thinking they might not be safe there," Connor told her, "and I'm in no shape to stand guard."

"What's wrong?" He'd sounded strange, but she'd expected him to be distraught, knowing his animals were in danger. Now she looked up at him, noted the smoldering of his shirt. "Turn around, Connor." She allowed him no choice, but grasped his shoulder with care and tried not to hear the gasp of pain he uttered.

"I'm only scorched a bit," he told her, and then with a sigh, he fell at her feet, his strength gone, his body giving way to pain. She knelt beside him, noting the absence of a shirt covering his back, only the charred edges to prove he'd worn one tonight. In the glow of the flames from the barn, she saw ugly blisters rise on his smooth flesh, and she tore the remnants of the burnt fabric of his shirt from his back.

Men suddenly appeared around her, her neighbor, Joe Benson, who had sold them the cow, accompanied by three of his hired hands. The noise of the fire had apparently blocked the sound of their arrival, and she turned her head to look at the men with appreciation.

"I saw the flames and came as soon as I could," Joe

said, breathing heavily. "It looks like we're too late to do much, don't it?"

"You can take Connor's horses home with you and tend to them for a few days, till we decide what to do," Loris told him. "I know it's an imposition, but Connor's burned and I'll be busy taking care of him."

"Let's take a look," Joe said, squatting beside her to view the damage. "Tell you what. Why don't we carry him indoors, and then I'll send one of my hands to get the doctor? And I think we need to get hold of the sheriff while we're at it."

"I'd really appreciate that," Loris told him, loath to move Connor, lest his pain increase. She watched while three of the men picked up Connor's heavy form and then ran ahead of them to open the door, allowing them to enter. "Upstairs, if you can," she called out. "Either that or bring down a mattress."

"That's a better idea," Joe said. "I'll put it on the parlor floor, and you'll be able to tend him there."

"I think we can rescue some of that hay, boss," one of the men said quietly after Connor had been deposited on his stomach on the mattress.. "The floor's come down and piles of hay with it. It's not afire yet, and we can pull it free."

"Don't take a chance on getting burned," Joe told him. "If you can pull some away, go ahead." He watched as the three men ran back toward the barn, then turned to Loris. "The hay was pretty tight in the loft. They may be able to save a bit for you."

"I don't want them hurt," she said. "It's not worth it."

"They'll be careful." Joe stood and looked down at Connor. "You'd better put some wet towels on him. It'll help take the fire out of his back. I'm going to get the doctor, ma'am, while my men work out back. I'll be a while. I'll have to find the sheriff and he may be home in bed, if he hasn't got anybody in jail that he needs to be looking after."

Loris nodded, doing as Joe had ordered, wetting towels at the kitchen sink and then applying them carefully to the burns. Connor lay on his stomach, his head turned to one side, his eyes closed. Yet, she sensed he was conscious, and was proved to be right when he spoke her name.

"Loris? You didn't get burned, did you?"

"No, I'm fine," she said quickly, her tears blurring her vision. How like Connor to be concerned for her well-being instead of his own.

"How bad is it?" he whispered, and she touched his face, then bent to kiss his cheek.

"You're blistered across your back. It looks like your shirt caught fire and stuck to your skin."

"I can smell it." His nose wrinkled as he spoke and she suddenly became aware of the acrid scent of burned flesh. "Doctor?"

"Joe went to get him. They won't be long."

"Hope not. Burns like hell." He was pale beneath the scorching of his skin, his eyes looking like those of a raccoon, she thought. But he had rallied and seemed to only be burned, not near death as she'd thought at first. *Only burned.* What a thought. And yet, it was better than if he'd been crushed by the floor of the hayloft coming down on him.

Before long Joe came in the back door, directly to the parlor, and behind him stood two men, one of them wearing a silver star prominently on his shirt. "Mrs. Webster?"

"I'm over here," she answered, recognizing the second man as the doctor who'd attended her during labor. "I've been changing the wet towels every five minutes. Connor's awake."

"I'd rather have him unconscious," the doctor said bluntly. "As it is, he's gonna be in a lot of pain for a while. We'll give him something to make him sleep."

Connor stirred and opened his eyes, seeking out Joe. The neighbor knelt beside him and touched his arm. "Someone set the fire," Connor said. It was a simple, yet shocking statement, but Joe did not dispute it.

"I kinda figured that myself, knowing how careful you are, Connor. Now we just have to find out who it was. We don't need anyone else's livelihood going up in flames."

He looked up at Loris. "I'm takin' those horses back home with me, ma'am. It looks like a pair of draft horses are out in the pasture. Connor must have untied them and shooed them out the back door."

"He said he opened the door, but he was afraid they wouldn't go out because of the fire. I know we lost the cow, but it couldn't be helped. I fear Connor would have died if he'd gone back in there again."

"I got a dandy little heifer you can have, once you get a place to put her," Joe said.

Connor closed his eyes again, and shifted on the mattress. A low groan sounded from his lips, and the doctor pulled a container of ointment from his open bag. Kneeling by the injured man's side, he lifted the wet towel and looked closely at the burns.

"Not too bad," he told Connor. "You'll live, that's for sure. Just gonna burn like the dickens for a while. This salve will help. It'll take the fire from your skin."

"Sure hope so." His words were barely a whisper as Connor's mouth twisted with pain.

"I'm gonna have your wife get some water for you and I want you to swallow some medicine. Can you turn over?"

"No." His reply left no room for doubt, and the doctor only grinned at Loris.

"A man who knows his own mind," he said quietly. "We'll have to get the medicine in his mouth and let him swallow it where he is."

"I'll get some reeds from the pond for him to suck the water with," Joe offered.

"I think you'll do better to tend him down here, rather than try to carry him up the stairs, ma'am. Besides, you're too soon out of childbed to be goin' up and down the steps much anyway." He looked at her sharply. "Are you doin' all right?"

Loris nodded. "I'm fine." *And wasn't that a lie to end all.* She'd never felt so puny and washed-out in her life. Maybe caring for Connor would pull her out of the depths of darkness she'd been inhabiting since the baby's death.

"I'll look after him," she said. "Just tell me what to do."

"Let that wait for a few minutes," the sheriff said. "I need to talk to Mrs. Webster first." Tall, middle-aged and fit, Loris had known Sheriff Paul Logan for almost all of her life. She turned to him now and he led her from the parlor and into the kitchen.

"What happened, ma'am?"

"I woke up," she began, "and saw the flames. By the

time Connor and I got out there, the barn was hopeless. Connor went in and got all the horses out he could."

"Any ideas how the fire started?"

"I only know that Connor put out the lantern when we left the barn earlier. He's always careful about fire, especially with the hayloft filled and all of his livelihood tied up in those stalls. He's certain it was set by someone, but I have no idea who it could have been, or why anyone would want to hurt Connor this way."

"Maybe it wasn't Connor they were after, ma'am," the sheriff said slowly. "Anybody got it in for you? Anyone who'd like to have you out of the way? To make you so discouraged you'd leave here?"

Loris looked at him, dumbfounded by the idea, and then words came into her head. "The only person I know who hates me enough to chase me out of town is Connor's mother. She's been angry ever since James left town. Then when he came back and Connor had a fight with him, she blamed me. I think she considers me at the root of all her problems with her sons."

"Mrs. Webster's always had a mean streak, as long as I've known her," Sheriff Logan said. "And you're right about James. She was madder than a wet hen when she had to call the doctor to tend him after he fought with Connor. Doc said she kept spouting off about wreaking vengeance. He made it a point to tell me about it, should anything happen to Connor. But I don't think she'd have set a fire herself. Maybe she's hired someone to do it for her."

"Well, if she was behind this, I think she was aiming at me. I don't think she'd have purposely hurt her son. I'm the one she's angry with."

Paul Logan got to his feet and patted Loris on the shoulder. "I'll look into it, Loris, and we'll see what we can come up with. Go take care of your husband now. He needs you."

Peggy Webster was furious. "You were supposed to chase the girl out of town, not put my son's life in danger!" She might be angry at Connor, but in no way did she wish him dead.

The man she'd hired stood before her, hat in hand, his eyes filled with rage. "I did what you told me to do. My thought was to burn the barn and take away her livelihood, let her know someone was out to get her."

"Well, that's not what you accomplished. You've injured my son."

"I understood you weren't any too fond of him, anyway," Murdoch said cunningly. "I don't know what you're so all-fired mad about. Maybe he'll take the woman and vamoose now."

"Not while he's laid up, he won't," Peggy answered. "You need to come up with something else to scare Loris off. And next time, don't involve my son in it."

"Where's my hundred dollars?" he whined.

"You'll get it when she's gone, and not before."

He turned and walked toward his horse, muttering beneath his breath. And Peggy Webster considered whether or not she should pay her son a visit.

"Your mother is here." Loris stood in the parlor doorway, and her words were sharp, not a welcome surprise to the man who lay in the middle of the room on a mattress. That he was able to lie on his side now, turning carefully with Loris's help from his stomach was a plus, but he couldn't predict how long it would take to accomplish enough healing for him to turn to his back.

For now, he'd be content with what progress he'd made.

Before he could utter a protest at seeing the visitor, she was there, almost pushing Loris aside as she entered the room. "What have you done to my son, Loris? He's been working on a farm all his life and never got hurt, other than a splinter or two. Now, he's here with you and he almost gets burned to death."

"I'm a long way from dead, Mother," Connor said sourly. "And Loris had nothing to do with my being burned. *My* horses were in the barn and I got burned getting them out. Loris's cow died in the fire and we almost lost her draft horses. I don't need you here causing trouble. Please leave my wife and me alone."

"Wife? You call this creature your wife? I thought you had more sense than to marry this female, Connor. You could have had her in your bed without going through all the legalities. I thought surely you were smart enough to keep out of her clutches."

Connor laughed, a dry, humorless sound. "Quite the opposite. She tried to escape my clutches and I wouldn't let her. Now leave here and don't come back. Loris is quite capable of taking care of me."

For the next few weeks, Connor remained on the mattress in the parlor. Loris spent her nights on the couch, waking when he stirred, dosing him with his medicine, changing his bandages daily, and keeping him clean. She was exhausted, but happy with his healing process.

On the third week, a crew of neighbors showed up and tore down the remains of the barn. On the next Saturday almost twenty men and their families rode down the lane, on horses, in buggies and farm wagons to build a new barn for Connor and Loris.

The women carried bowls of food, fried chicken and roasted beef and pork. Potato salad and baked beans were in abundance, and the ladies took over Loris's kitchen while their husbands and teenaged sons began the barn raising.

Among the crew was Paul Logan, his sheriff's badge gleaming in the sunshine, his eyes alert as he viewed the wreckage of the barn once more, watching as the men swarmed over the mess like bees in a hive, cleaning up the burned wood and clearing the site for new walls.

He spoke to Loris and then Connor, offering his services for the day.

"There's not much going on in town," he said. "Nobody in jail and hardly anyone on the streets. I think most everybody is here, so I thought I'd lend a hand. Haven't had to pound any nails in a long time, but I don't think I've forgotten how."

"I appreciate your help, Sheriff," Connor said. "Any news about the fire? Any strangers around town?"

"I thought of that," Logan said, "and I've been asking around. There was one fella, looking for work, but not willing to give anyone an honest day's labor. I heard he used to live hereabouts. He got kicked off two different farms. Bob Hitchcock and Roy Wells both said he was totally worthless as a hired hand. I'm not sure where he went from there, but he doesn't seem to be visible now. I've got some ideas I'm working on, though."

"A stranger?" Connor asked, his attention caught.

The sheriff shrugged. "He looked kinda familiar to me, but I couldn't place him. So I reckon he might have been someone who lived in these parts years back. We're still keeping an eye out, but there doesn't seem to be any link between him and you."

The sheriff looked out toward the barn. "I think I'd better get out there and put in my time," he said. "I don't want to miss dinner." He looked at Loris and smiled. "Your kitchen smells downright delicious, ma'am."

The work progressed quickly, with the crew of men working in unison, their voices raised in laughter and teasing, even though they worked hard, as though this project would benefit themselves. Lending a hand to their neighbors and friends seemed to be a way of life, and Loris lifted a prayer of thanksgiving for the host of men and women who had come today to give their support to Connor.

Connor had insisted on being moved to the back porch, the better to watch the proceedings, and Loris helped him to the rocking chair she'd carried out for him. Her softest pillow was at his back and he took an extra dose of the pain medicine the doctor had left for him.

In fact, midway through the morning, the doctor showed up, driving his surrey with matching black horses, pulling to a stop with a flourish by the hitching rail. "Well, well. It surely looks like you're havin' a party," he said loudly. "How's the back?"

"Good enough for me to be out there lending a hand," Connor said, waving a hand toward Loris. "My wife is a watchdog. Won't let me do anything."

"Well, good for her. I'm glad to hear that one of you is following orders."

"When can I get back to work?" Connor asked.

"When Loris says your burns are healed up real good. We can't have you getting an infection or you'll be in a heap of trouble."

With a wave at the men who were in the process of raising the first wall of the new barn, the doctor headed in their direction, took off his coat and helped hold the wall firmly while three of the men pounded nails into place.

"I didn't think it would go this quickly," Loris said. "I can't believe all these people came out here to help us."

"You'll notice my father isn't among them," Connor said bitterly.

"Did you expect him to be?"

He was silent, and then shook his head. "I suppose not."

"Then you shouldn't be disappointed not to see him here."

"Well, that's one way of looking at it." He grinned up at Loris, and she thought it closely resembled his usual, cocky smile. "As long as you're here, I don't need anyone else, Loris. But I'll admit I'd give a lot to see him."

She sobered abruptly. "I wish my folks had shown up today."

Connor grasped her hand. "We have each other, sweetheart. And a whole slew of friends lending a hand."

The ladies in the kitchen were busily heating food and preparing for the influx of men who would devour it very shortly. The scent of brewing coffee reached the porch and Loris went in to pour Connor a cup. In the yard, four pairs of sawhorses had been set up, and planks placed over them, providing a place to set down the food and for some of the men to eat. Quilts dotted the grass, and the younger children were already vying for space in anticipation of the meal to come.

"You wanna ring that dinner bell, Loris?" The preacher's wife stood on the other side of the screened door and behind her, a dozen women were ready to carry out bowls and platters of food.

Loris pulled on the rope and the bell clanged loudly. It was apparently a welcome sound, for the men working on the barn who quickly finished up whatever task they were doing and headed for the watering trough to wash up. The older boys looked around for the girl of their choice, and soon several of them were paired up with one or another of the girls who'd been watching and cheering them on in their work.

The crowd of people stood around the tables and all eyes were on the preacher, who'd managed to get his share of blisters from lifting a hammer all morning. He raised his eyes to the blue sky above and uttered words of thanks for the meal and the ladies who had prepared it. Then they began to devour the food.

"I'll get you a plate," Loris told Connor. "A little of everything?"

"What did you fix?" he asked softly as she bent to kiss his forehead.

"A kettle of beans and the pies I baked yesterday."

"I'll have a piece of your pie and some beans and a piece of chicken."

"There's some cobbler that looks mighty tasty," she told him. "And Mrs. Carlson's potato salad is the best I've ever had."

"I like yours better," he said stubbornly.

"Then I'll make some for you tomorrow." The man was obstinate but she couldn't help but be pleased at his declaration. He ate every blessed thing she fixed for him, and usually asked for seconds. Somewhere, Connor had learned how to be a good husband.

And Loris was reaping the benefits.

By evening the barn was ready for use. The new wood would need paint—but that could wait.

For now, they had a barn, thanks to the neighbors who all wished Connor well as they left for home in the twilight.

Chapter Nine

Connor sat at the table, eating the promised potato salad.

"Where are you going?" He'd made his way to the kitchen for dinner, refusing to eat in a prone position any longer. Now he watched as Loris slid her feet into sturdy shoes and tied her apron about her waist.

"Out to paint the barn." Never slowing her movements, she grinned at him. "How was the potato salad?"

"You know it was wonderful. I ate three helpings." And then he sobered. "Loris, I don't want you on a ladder or anywhere you might get hurt. Wait until I can get out there and do it."

"The wood is raw and needs a coat of paint," she said firmly. "The man from the hardware store brought out twelve gallons this morning for us to begin with, and I assure you I know how to hold a paintbrush. I won't climb a ladder, either. I'll leave all the hard parts for you to finish."

"It needs to be done from the top down," he told her stubbornly.

"Well, our barn is not going to be done in the traditional

way. I'll paint whatever I can reach, and we'll go on from there. You can sit on the porch and watch if you like."

Connor muttered beneath his breath and rose from the table. There was no way on earth he could climb a ladder yet and the woman knew it. She was taking advantage of his situation, and he'd be doggoned if he'd let her have the last word.

"I'll bring a chair out and help," he said stubbornly. "I can paint sitting down."

"No." Her quick return left no room for doubt in his mind as to her feelings on the subject, and her frown emphasized the word. "Joe said he'd send two men over to help, and one of them can climb the ladder. Now, does that make you happy?"

"No." His own denial was as firm as hers had been. "I won't be happy till the sheriff catches whoever set the fire and burned the damn barn. I'll have to work at being a good sport about things until I can get up and do my chores and be a husband again."

She stood at the back door and looked at him. A smile lit her face as she scanned his long body, and then she walked to where he stood by the sink. Her arms circled his neck and she kissed his jaw, his cheek and chin and finally settled her lips against his. "You can start being a husband anytime you want to," she told him, whispering the words against his throat. "I was thinking that you might be getting lonely on that mattress all by yourself."

She knew what she was doing. He'd give her that much. Her kisses and the feel of her arms around his neck were enough to set his fire burning. His own arms circled her and he took her mouth with a desire that made her sigh. She shivered against him, and her arms clung tighter.

"You know how to make your wife happy, Connor. You can be my husband any day of the week."

"All right. Go on out and paint. But I'm going to be watching, and if I catch you even looking at that ladder, I'll swat you a good one."

"You'll have to catch me first," she teased, slipping from his embrace. The gallons of red paint were in the washroom and she picked one up in each hand and with a spanking-new brush tucked under her arm, she headed across the yard.

"You'll need a screwdriver to open the paint," he shouted after her, and was rewarded by her nod of agreement. "There's one in the shed."

"I'll get it." Settling the paint on the ground in front of the new structure, she backtracked to the toolshed and found the screwdriver where he'd left it just days ago.

Two sawhorses sat to one side of the barn door and Loris picked up a plank, clearly too heavy for her, Connor noted, and placed it atop the wooden structures. The paint cans were deposited there, and she worked to pry the lid from one of them.

Even as she struggled with it, and as Connor was about to leave the porch and go to her rescue, a horse and rider came across the pasture. It was Joe Benson, Connor noted with satisfaction. Maybe he'd get some support now.

"Whoa, ma'am. You shouldn't be doing that sort of thing. Let me have that screwdriver. I'll get you in business quicker than you can say—" He halted, a grin appearing on his face. "Well, pretty damn quick anyway."

"Thanks, Joe," Loris said with a thankful look. "I was afraid that Connor might come charging down from the porch in a few seconds if I didn't manage this right."

"Well, this is one job he can just supervise," Joe told her, entering the barn door. He came out with a piece of lumber in his hand, probably not more than an inch wide, and stirred the paint he'd opened. "This'll work just fine," he told her. "I'll get out the ladder from the toolshed and do the top, and you can work on the bottom."

"Thanks, Joe," Connor called from the porch. "I'm feeling a mite useless here, but Loris won't let me help."

"You married a smart lady," Joe said, flashing a wink at Loris. She was already dipping her brush into the paint, then reaching over her head to apply the red stuff in a slash of color.

"I think John from the hardware store brought along more than one brush, didn't he?"

Loris nodded. "I only needed one, but I'll be happy to go up and get you another from the washroom."

"Good idea, ma'am," Joe said with a grin.

It was a productive afternoon, even if Connor was edgy and out of sorts. He sat on the chair, Rusty by his side, and watched, noting the amount of paint Loris managed to get on her apron, wondering when she would tire enough to call it quits. But he waited in vain. She worked at the job for four hours and only halted when Joe begged off till the next day.

"I need to be getting home to do my chores," he said. "My two hired hands are busy with mending fences, and I told them I'd take care of the milking tonight."

"I can't thank you enough, Joe." Loris was truly grateful for the help, for her voice trembled as she set aside her brush and lifted the cover of the second gallon of paint, settling it in place before she tapped it down, sealing the can.

"I'm your neighbor, ma'am, and I'm smart enough to know that it could have been me who lost his barn. When you get a firebug in the area, you gotta be real careful. I want you to make good use of that dog I sent over. You'd better let him run at night. He'll bark good and loud, I guarantee you, and I'll warrant he'll scare off any scalawags."

"He's pretty protective, of me, especially, and we surely appreciate him. And you, too, Joe. I hope that you have some idea how much. He's turned into quite a watchdog and I feel safe with him at my heels." Rusty had made his way to her side and she reached down to pat his head.

"Well, I knew most any woman would like a pretty little pup like this one. I'm glad he's fit in well here."

"Thanks so much for helping with the painting today. I knew Connor'd worry if I didn't do as he asked."

"I'll be back tomorrow with my hired hands. Between the four of us, we should be able to put a big dent in your paint supply." He wiped his hands on a rag from his pocket and strolled toward the house. One hand was outstretched as he approached Connor and it was met by Connor's own palm.

"My thanks," he said. "Maybe I can give you a hand when you need one."

"I'll count on that," Joe told him. He turned then to Loris. "You just leave that paint where it is, ma'am, and we'll take up tomorrow where we left off. Put those brushes to soak in some turpentine till then. I think there's a gallon of it in your washroom."

"Yes, I will," Loris said, carrying the brushes with her as she made her way to the house, the dog at her heels.

"She's right. That dog knows who his mistress is, doesn't he? He's right fond of your wife."

"Aren't we all?" Connor's voice lit with pride as he watched Loris step into the house. "She's a real catch."

"Well, it's about suppertime," Joe said, reaching the hitching rail and untying his horse. "You folks have a nice evening, you hear? I'll see you tomorrow."

Connor followed Loris into the house, watching as she went to the washroom to put the brushes to soak. He pulled a chair from the table as she appeared in the kitchen doorway once more, and his words were more than a suggestion. "Sit down. You've done enough for one day."

"I need to put supper together." She looked at the stove regretfully. "But I'll admit I don't feel much like cooking."

He took her arm and lowered her into the chair. "If I can't find enough for us to eat, I'm a sorry excuse for a man, Loris. I've been sitting on that porch watching you work for the whole afternoon."

"I know you can fix something," she said. "I just worry about you. I'm supposed to be taking care of you. Not the other way around."

"Well, worry no more, sweetheart. I can get out plates and the leftover potato salad and ham from yesterday, and you can slice some bread. How's that?"

"Suits me," she told him. He'd put the breadboard in front of her and handed her the long knife. Now, he brought a loaf she'd baked yesterday and she unwrapped it and cut three slices. "Two enough for you?" she asked.

"How about you?" he wanted to know.

"I'm almost too tired to eat," she told him. "I didn't realize how weary I was until I sat down."

He set her plate and silverware before her and put the sliced bread on another plate. A pat of butter on the flowered dish appeared next, and then he brought the ham and the crock of potato salad from the pantry.

"I think we're ready. There's no milk, sweetheart. Will coffee do?" He lifted the pot from the back of the stove and hefted it. "It feels about half full from dinner."

"That's fine." She frowned, remembering the loss of her cow and the subsequent lack of milk. "I think I'll ask Joe to bring the new heifer over, first chance he gets."

Connor nodded agreeably and settled in his chair across from her. "I'd feel better if both of our fathers had found it in their hearts to help out with the barn raising," he said quietly. "I was hoping they might have second thoughts about us. I'll guarantee your folks know we're married."

"You're a dreamer," she told him. "Daddy will never come around, and neither will my mother."

The very next day, Loris found she was wrong when her father's buggy pulled up near the back door and her mother slid down from the seat. Brushing down her skirts and settling her hat securely on her head, Mrs. Peterson took a moment to look around as if she would paint a mental picture of her surroundings.

She made her way to the porch and climbed the steps. Loris stood at the door, her heart pounding in a quick staccato, her lungs expanding to contain enough air to supply her with the next breath, and watched her mother, aware of the exact moment when Minnie caught sight of her.

The flowers on her hat bobbled as the woman nodded in greeting. "Loris. I thought it was time for me to come visiting. May I come in?"

"Of course." It was all she could do to be reasonably polite, but Loris dragged up a smile and pinned it in place. "How have you been?"

"Better than you, from what I hear in town."

"It's been a troublesome time lately," Loris told her bluntly. "What with the fire and Connor being burned, we've been pretty busy." She waved her hand at the new barn. "As you can see, the neighbors and townsfolk banded together and built us a new one last Saturday. I've been busy painting, and our neighbor, Joe, came to help. His hired hands finished up the high spots and I've only the lower boards left to do."

Her mother took stock of the kitchen, her eyes seeming to approve what she saw, her look one of satisfaction. "I see you learned well while you were growing up, Loris. I certainly can't fault your housekeeping, and from the smell of that kettle on your stove, I'd say you were making chicken soup."

"You're right. It's one of Connor's favorites. He killed a young rooster for me this morning. I'll have the soup ready for his dinner."

Minnie looked toward the backyard. "Where is he?"

"Working with his horses out back. Probably in the pasture. He walks them every day, getting them used to a bit in their mouths, and then he saddles them and lays a bag of feed over the saddle for weight. When they're used to carrying a load, he'll climb on himself, and hopefully by that time, they'll be so used to him, they won't balk."

"He spends his days playing with horses?" Minnie sounded aghast at the idea, and Loris was hard pressed not to laugh aloud.

"I'd say he's doing a lot more than *playing* with his

horses," she said. "It's his livelihood, Mother. He makes a tidy sum from people in return for his training their animals. When he finishes with his own horses, they'll be sold and then he'll begin on another generation of colts and mares."

"It sounds like a foolish way to make a living, if you ask me. Why can't he get a job in the bank or the hardware store? Your father could have used him at the newspaper office."

"He's a farmer. You know he's been a farmer all his life and will always be one. I'm a farmer's wife, and a very happy one. It's strange you didn't have all these questions when I planned to marry Connor last year."

"I suppose I'd thought he'd get a good job when you got married. Instead, he's got you living in this place, working your fingers to the bone."

"Hardly, Mother. I have lots of flesh left on my fingers. I don't think you understand at all. We're happy here. I have a house to care for, and Connor has the property he needs for his animals. We cut over forty acres of hay twice this summer, had a good corn crop and my garden has given me enough vegetables to fill almost two hundred Mason jars. What more could I ask?"

"I'd hoped for more for you, Loris."

"Is that why you put me out of the house on a cold January night, when it was snowing to beat the band? So I'd have *more?*"

"No need for sarcasm, Loris. Your father and I are concerned about you."

"Since when? You had no qualms whatsoever about what happened to me that night. You didn't know if I'd freeze to death by the side of the road, or if I'd find shelter. The only person who cared about me was Connor."

"He felt guilty for not marrying you." Her mother was staunch in her avowal.

"How about you?" Loris asked. "Did you feel guilty? I'd say that's where the guilt lies. Right with you and my father. Connor did the right thing by me."

"Well, I can see I've wasted my time coming here to visit," Minnie told her sharply. "I'd thought we might have some sort of a reunion, maybe mend our fences."

"The only fence mending you're interested in is for me to tell you that you were right to kick me out of your house, and I'll never do that."

"Well, I'd say you landed on your feet." Minnie sniffed elegantly and rose from her chair. "I'm certainly glad that your grandparents don't know anything about all this. They'd be mortified."

"Why? Because I married a good man, and we're making a good life together?"

"You married a good man, did you? And how long did it take him to turn you into an honest woman?"

"I've always been an honest woman, Mother. Connor did nothing to change that."

"Those Webster boys are bad clear through. And bad blood will show every time. I never did like their mother. Peggy is not to be trusted. She's out to get you, Loris. You just watch your step."

With another sniff, Minnie sailed out the back door and unhitched her horse from the rail. She climbed into her buggy and was gone in moments.

Loris stood at the window, looking out at the empty yard, not hearing Connor's entrance as he came in the back door. He approached her and wrapped his arms around her, drawing her back against his body.

"Loris, I overheard what went on in here."

"Where were you?" she asked, leaning against him as if he were her shelter against the world. His arms held her securely, and his breath was warm against her cheek as he bent his head to kiss her from her temple to the firm outline of her chin.

"On the porch. I saw your mother come in the house and I headed up here to speak with her, but by the time I'd sorted out things, she was already giving you what-for and speaking her piece. She sailed out the back door and totally ignored me, in such a blamed hurry, she couldn't even lift a hand to wave goodbye."

Loris laughed. She couldn't help it. The thought of her mother waving goodbye to Connor in the midst of her snit was a sight she could not fathom. "She was really on her high horse, wasn't she? She was glad, though, that you finally made an honest woman out of me." Her voice was teasing as she quoted her mother's words.

"I loved your answer," Connor said. "You've always been an honest woman, and I thought to myself, 'ain't that the truth.' At least you made her stop and think."

"For some reason or another, she doesn't like your mother, Connor. It sounded almost as though she holds a grudge against her, didn't it?"

"I've about decided they make a good pair, the two of them," he said bitterly. "And I'll tell you one thing right now, Loris. Next time, I won't stand and listen. I'm afraid I'll join in the conversation and let her have it with both barrels."

"I think I held my own," Loris said quietly. "She doesn't frighten me."

He hugged her tighter. "I'm proud of you, Mrs. Webster. You're quite a lady."

On her next trip into town, Loris saw her father. They'd stopped by at the doctor's office to let him examine Connor's burns, then Loris had left him there and gone on to the general store. A number of townsfolk were inside, and she was greeted with waves and smiles. A number of women came up to her to ask about the barn. Loris found herself to be somewhat of a heroine when they found that she'd done a good share of the barn painting.

"We're doing fine, really," Loris said to the group around her. "We've missed having milk, what with the cow being gone, but Joe is bringing us a replacement late today, for the one that died in the fire."

"You should have let someone know. We'd have seen to it that somebody brought you some every day or so," the storekeeper said, feeling generous.

"We survived," she said brightly. "Here's my list. I'll just look around while you find the things I need."

She was busily investigating the display of yard goods and oilcloth on a counter near the back of the store when she felt a hush come over the flurry of talk and laughter that filled the big room. A man had come in the door, and Loris turned to see who had caused the pause in conversation.

It was her father. He looked weary, older than he had a few months ago, she thought, and his shoulders were bent low. She felt a pang of sorrow for the loss of his usual vitality and yet, could not bring herself to approach him, lest he shun her and embarrass her in front of half the town.

Then he spoke from directly behind her. "Hello, Loris."

Startled, she turned and looked up into his eyes. "Father. It's good to see you."

"Is it? Your mother said you wanted nothing to do with us. I can't blame you, child, but I just want you to know that I miss you." He drew out his handkerchief and, turning his back on the townsfolk behind him, wiped a tear that had fallen to slip down his cheek.

"We were wrong to put you out, Loris. I knew as soon as it happened that we should have worked things out. I was so afraid about what folks would think, I forgot about the harm we'd done you." He watched her, scanning her features and nodding.

"I wanted to come out to the barn raising, but your mother thought it wasn't a good idea."

"I wish you had."

"Well, if he'll let me, I'd like to give him a hand if he needs any help. I heard he was laid up after the fire. Is he doing all right now?"

"You can ask him yourself," she said. "He should be here from the doctor's office any minute now. We stopped by so the doc could look at his back and make sure it's healing well."

"Did you take care of him yourself? Or did you have help?" he asked her.

"I did without help. He's my husband, Father. What else would you have expected me to do? We've both learned how to cope with anything that comes along. I'd thought the barn fire might be the end of our farming days, and Connor feared not having a place for his animals, but when everyone came out and helped us, it was like a gift from heaven."

"Everyone but your family." Accusing himself with his own words, Loris's father looked away from her as if seeking absolution from an onlooker, but no one had heard his declaration. Only his daughter, and she answered in the only way she could.

"I understood why you didn't come along with the rest. Connor's folks didn't come either."

"I think you're being too understanding, Loris," her father said. "We should have been there, your mother and I. So should Connor's folks. You needed our support and you didn't get it."

"Well, when Mother came to see me last week, she didn't seem to hold that opinion. She seemed to feel that I was bad through and through and Connor was no better. She thought I could have done better, said she wanted *more* for me, whatever that means."

Alger Peterson listened to what his daughter had to say and then shook his head. Whether he was disputing her words or agreeing with her about her mother, Loris didn't know. And then he eased her mind. "Everyone in the county knows that Connor Webster is a good man. He's well-liked, sharp with horses, and he's got a good reputation for honesty and hard work. I don't know what more your mother wants for you."

"Why weren't you so reasonable when you made me leave home last January?"

"I was angry," Alger said quietly. "Your mother was upset, and I was angry. We should have done things differently."

"Well, you won't have to be ashamed any longer. The baby died. Connor and I buried him in the orchard. Your daughter is married and there are no embarrassing leftovers hanging around to remind folks that I was pregnant out of wedlock."

Her father cast his eyes downward. "I'm sorry that you lost your child, Loris. I'll admit I felt betrayed when you turned up pregnant by James, while all the time you were engaged to Connor, but things have worked out and the past is over and done with."

"You need to tell Connor that," she said. "If you'd come to help with the barn raising, he'd have been pleased. As it was, he hoped his own father would show up, and it hurt him badly that his family has disowned him because of him marrying me."

"They have no right to hold that against him. After all, he was betrothed to you last year. You'd have been married anyway by this time. If it hadn't been for James and his shenanigans, things wouldn't have happened the way they did."

Suddenly the door of the general store opened, and once more the crowd grew silent. Loris looked up directly into Connor's dark eyes, and recognized the look of anger he wore.

He walked to her, put his arm around her waist and lent his unspoken support should she need it. "Mr. Peterson." His greeting was far from cordial, but at least he hadn't snubbed her father, Loris thought with relief.

"Connor. I was just talking to Loris and apologizing for not showing up at the barn raising. I know you could have used another hand to help, but circumstances wouldn't allow me to be there. Loris tells me the barn is not totally painted yet. I'd like to come out and lend a hand if you'll let me."

"That's very generous of you, sir," Connor said, shooting a glance at Loris as if doubting his own hearing.

"Not generous at all. Only trying to make amends in some small way for how Loris's mother and I have behaved. I understand you were burned in the fire, and Loris took care of you."

"That's right," Connor said agreeably. "She's one fine nurse. I'm almost back to normal now, but she still won't let me work a full day."

"Well, if it's all right with you, Connor, I'd like to come out to your place tomorrow and spend the day. I'm sure you'll find enough for me to do."

"Thank you, sir. I'd appreciate the help. Loris is about run ragged what with tending my back and painting the barn, and then doing chores. We're having a new cow brought over tomorrow, and it would help if a man were there to get her settled."

Loris poked him in the ribs. The nerve of the man, thinking she couldn't get a cow into the pasture or a stall.

Connor shot her another look, and she suddenly understood. He was making certain her father felt needed.

They gathered up their supplies and Connor carried them out to the wagon. Loris put the small items in her basket and hung it over her arm. "I'll look forward to seeing you, Father," she said. "I don't suppose—"

"No," he said abruptly. "Your mother won't be with me. She's not even speaking to me, to tell you the truth. She knew I planned on seeing you, when I saw your wagon go by the house on your way into town. She knows how I feel, but she's already blamed this whole thing on me, Loris. Said it was my bullheadedness that sent you out into the snow last January. And maybe she's right. I just know that it's time to call a halt to things."

Apologizing to his daughter had been a big step for him. He was a proud man, and Loris knew that eating crow was not palatable to the man. But he'd done it, nicely, too. She felt a measure of pride herself at his uncharacteristic behavior.

Connor's arm around her waist reminded her that he was in a hurry to go, and she climbed up on the wagon seat, grasping his hand as he assisted her. Her skirts were settled around her and tucked beneath her bottom, lest the wind take them, and then she looked down at her father.

"We'll see you tomorrow. I hope you don't get in trouble at home, Father. I don't want to be the cause of problems between you and Mother."

"I can take care of myself, Loris," he said, touching his hat brim in a salute. "I'll be there."

After supper, Joe brought the cow over, the animal trailing behind him on a rope as he rode his saddle horse. She was a pretty little Holstein, black and white, with a smattering of dark freckles on her face.

"She's gonna be a good milker," Joe said. "Ought to give you all the cream you need for butter."

"I was looking for you tomorrow. Connor will stop by your place and settle up with you for her," Loris said as she took the lead rope and turned toward the new barn.

"You don't need to worry about that," Joe said quickly. "She's a present. My missus said anybody that works as hard as you and Connor do deserves a helping hand once in a while. I'm just doing what she tells me. I found a long time ago that if Wilma is happy, so am I."

"Now that sounds like a good bit of advice from a man who's been married for a lot of years," Connor said, from the porch where he'd been sitting on the swing with Loris when Joe rode into the yard.

"Well, it's worked for me for almost thirty years," Joe said with a grin. "My wife is an easy woman to live with, and I discovered that I was a big part of keeping her in a good humor."

"I wonder if it would work with Loris," Connor said with a laugh. "She's been giving me a hard time lately."

"She's been taking good care of you, son, and you'd better appreciate it."

Connor sent a look of tenderness in Loris's direction. "I'm as grateful as any man can be," he said. "She's one in a million."

And for those kind of words, Loris was more than willing to take on the milking of a cow every evening. It seemed that Connor was intent on following Joe's dictum. Keeping his wife happy seemed to be his intent, and she felt cherished by the idea of Connor spending his energy on the project.

In fact, she felt like a woman who loves and is loved in return.

Chapter Ten

The kitchen garden was a mass of dead tomato vines and rustling cornstalks from the sweet corn they'd enjoyed over the past weeks. Only a few stubborn tomatoes lingered on the vines, and after supper Loris picked the best ones to place on her kitchen windowsill, allowing them to ripen as they would. She'd carried a saltshaker out into the garden with her and now sat on the ground, looking over the last of the crop. One fully ripe specimen was perfectly shaped—the right size to fit into the palm of her hand.

She rubbed it gently against the bodice of her dress, inspected it for specks of dirt and then judged it edible. A bite proved her right and she sprinkled a little salt on the bright red interior she'd revealed. A second bite caused a small trickle of tomato juice to run down her chin and she swiped at it with her hand.

She looked up to see Connor standing at the end of the row, offering a challenge. "Come over here and I'll clean it off your chin for you." His eyes sent a message she welcomed.

"Come over here and I'll give you a bite," she teased. "You know, they called these things love apples a few years back."

"Well, you look good enough to love, sitting there in your garden, sweetheart. I think I may just keep you around."

"You'd better, mister. I'm going to be baking bread soon and if that isn't tempting enough, I thought I'd make sugar cookies, too."

"Looking at you is tempting enough. I don't need bread or cookies to keep me close to home."

She thought he was the handsomest man she'd ever seen. His dark hair hung over his forehead, making him seem young and vulnerable. The eyes that looked at her held a wealth of love that made her heart sing with joy, and his tall, strapping body lured her as a horse is tempted by a bit of apple or a carrot.

Only she was no mare, but a woman in love with the man who lived in her house, slept in her bed and made her life a pleasure. And yet there was a certain likeness between her situation and the mares in the barn. They were all in competition for the stud who had given them rounded bellies and the promise of new life.

The urge to be filled with Connor's child was an ever-present yearning deep in her soul. She knew well the joy of carrying a child, even though the last time had not come to fruition. Nevertheless, that baby had been a part of her and she ached again for the knowledge that a new life blossomed within her body.

It seemed that she would have to wait a while longer to have that dream fulfilled, for her body had not welcomed Connor's seed yet, and she mourned quietly when her monthly time arrived. He'd held her close that night and whispered his love in her ear, lending his warmth to her and massaging her back with a strong hand.

"You're disappointed, aren't you?" he'd asked softly.

"I want your child, Connor."

"It may be too soon for your body to handle it," he said. "I don't want you to have problems."

"Maybe next month," she'd said stubbornly, even as she vowed to give Connor a son or daughter of his own.

"We'll see," was his enigmatic answer.

The Holstein cow took to the new barn well, giving an abundance of milk that evening. More, in fact, than Loris had expected, given the young age of the animal. Putting her out to pasture ensured a good diet of grass, for the weather had brought a late greening to the land.

In the morning her father came to help with the painting, and Loris found herself enjoying his company, even more so than she ever had when she was living at home. He told her tales of his boyhood and the early years of his marriage to her mother, and then his eyes lost their gleam for a moment and he seemed cast into a mood that signified sadness.

Loris hesitated a moment and then asked for his confidence. "What is it, Father? Is something wrong?"

"I'm thinking back to when our babies died, and wondering if there is something passed down from mother to child to account for your baby's death."

"You lost a baby? Before I was born?"

"Several," Alger said quietly. "Your mother couldn't seem to carry beyond the seventh month, and we buried three in the churchyard."

"Why didn't I know about it?" She felt bereft at the

thought of her own siblings being buried and she wasn't given the opportunity to visit their graves.

"We were so happy when you were born, I suppose we thought things had finally begun to go our way, and there was no point in making you feel…like a replacement for the children we'd lost."

"I don't think I'd have thought that," Loris said, a deep sense of grief making her yearn to hold her father close and somehow comfort him. Perhaps this had stood between her parents for years, each blaming the other for something neither could have foreseen.

"Well, we wanted you to be happy, Loris. We wanted you to have a perfect life, with all the good things we'd planned to give our children. Maybe we were a little overprotective, and maybe we expected too much of you sometimes, but you seemed to be our only chance to have the family we'd always wanted."

"And then I disappointed you dreadfully when I came home and told you I was going to have a child."

"Yes, we were heartsore about it, and I lost my temper. Your mother was hurt that you'd strayed from the rules of behavior set up for you."

"I appreciate you telling me all this," Loris said. "It helps me understand you and Mother better, gives me something to think about."

"I hope I didn't discourage you, Loris. About having more children, I mean. The chances of you and your mother having the same problem is unlikely, but I spoke before thinking." He looked upset, as if his tongue had run away without his permission and now he was ruing the consequences.

"I've often wished that the baby we had was still

alive, Father. I can't say I know how you and Mother felt, but I certainly have a good idea. I didn't know such pain existed in this world. I felt that my heart would surely break apart in my chest."

"Funny." Alger laughed, a short bitter sound. "Your mother said almost the same thing once. Said her chest hurt as though she could feel her heart breaking to bits."

He picked up his paintbrush and dipped it into the half-full can of red paint. "I'd better get back to this job, or we'll never get done with the other side of the barn today."

He was tireless in his painting, pausing only to talk to her as thoughts came to mind, and Loris was pleased by the rapport they established over two paintbrushes and a gallon of paint. If only her mother could bring herself to open up and be more of a friend instead of judging her daughter. Perhaps, someday.

They stopped for dinner, and Loris was surprised at the meal Connor had prepared. "If you'll make some biscuits, we'll be all set," he told her as she and her father came in at noontime. "I thought we'd have something easy, so I made breakfast for dinner. Is that all right?"

"Fine with me," Alger said quickly. "Is that sausage I smell cooking?"

"I added some flour and milk and butter, the way I've seen Loris do it, and the gravy turned out pretty good," Connor said, with just a touch of pride. "I guess just about anybody can scramble eggs, and we always have plenty. Our hens are laying real good."

"You've got yourself a prize here, Loris," her father said with a smile.

"Don't I know it," she beamed. "And I didn't even

know he'd been watching me make gravy. There's no excuse for him now. I'll let him practice all he wants to."

"Don't push it, sweetheart," Connor said, dishing up the sausage gravy and eggs into bowls on the table. "In a few days I'll be out there working my horses and finishing the barn and you'll be back in here, up to your pretty little neck in cooking and baking. I've got my mouth all set for apple pies."

"Let me know when you want some apples and I'll bring some out to you, Loris," her father said. "My apple tree is loaded this year."

"We've got some already, too," she answered, "and the peaches are beyond ripe. I need to be canning them before they go bad."

"Maybe your mother can come out and give you a hand. She's a fine hand at preserving food."

"I'll go out in the orchard tomorrow and pick what I can reach from the ground," Loris said. "I've got enough Mason jars to do a bushel of them for starts."

They ate their meal, Connor smiling as Loris paid him wild compliments on his culinary skills. "I'll let you lend a hand with supper tonight," she said graciously.

"Don't get carried away, love. I only do this when the mood strikes me." He stood and cleared the table, piling the dishes in the sink, and wiping off the oilcloth.

"I'll give it another hour, and then I'll have to get back home," Alger said as they went out the back door. "I hate to leave in the middle of the job, but I've got chores to tend to, and this week's paper to go over tonight."

"I can't tell you how glad I am that you came out," Loris said, feeling a new surge of ambition as they approached the barn. She looked up at the fresh coat of paint beneath the eaves, where her father had painted from the top of the ladder. "I hope you aren't totally washed out. I'm afraid you worked awfully hard today."

"It was worth it to see this barn looking good. Let's see if we can finish up this side, then when Joe and his men come over you'll only have a second coat to put on the front."

They worked quickly, and before the sun had shifted beyond the roofline of the house, they had completed their task. Loris took the brushes to soak and Alger closed the paint cans and tapped the lids in place, then carried them into the washroom.

The peaches were ripe and juicy and Connor sat at the kitchen table, slipping the skins from them almost faster than Loris could scald them in the big kettle and bring them to him. She cut them in half then, pitted them and placed them in jars, ready for the canning kettle. It was a job that required much time and effort, but together they managed to fill almost thirty quart jars with peach halves before noon.

"I think we need to celebrate," Connor said, leaning back in his chair and counting the jars that were arrayed on the kitchen cabinet. "Another day like this and we'll have a good supply for the winter, won't we?"

"Shall we go to town?" Loris asked, her face pensive as if she plotted something he might not agree to.

"Anything special you want at the general store?" he asked.

"No. I thought we might take a bushel of peaches in for my folks. They don't have a peach tree in the yard, and my father is real fond of them. I'll never be able to put up all the crop here; there's just too many getting ripe at one time. In fact, I thought we might see if Joe's wife wants some, too. They've been awfully good to us."

"Now, that's a winner of an idea, if I ever heard one," Connor told her. "I've been trying to come up with an idea, something we might do for them."

"Maybe they have peach trees. But I don't remember seeing any when the trees blossomed in the spring. I know they have apples."

"I'll harness the horses and bring the wagon out into the orchard," Connor told her. "We'll pick from the wagon bed, and reach the higher ones that way. I'll warrant it won't take long to fill two bushel baskets."

Loris stood and cleared the kitchen table. Only their coffee cups remained, for she'd cleaned up after breakfast. But Connor had enjoyed his morning coffee for several hours as he slipped the skins off almost two bushels of peaches. The kettles were washed and put into the pantry, and Connor went out to the barn to tend to the horses and wagon.

By the time she was ready, Connor had already driven the big vehicle out to the orchard, and was standing in its bed, the bushel baskets at his feet, busily choosing and picking the peaches that were the ripest. Loris climbed up into the wagon and was almost lost in the low hanging branches.

It was cool, with a westerly breeze and the ripe fruit smelled like autumn to her. A feeling of total contentment swept over her and she sighed happily. To think that only last January she'd thought her life was ruined and happiness would elude her grasp forever.

Now she worked side by side with the man she loved

and found her life to be filled with joy and the happiness of a good marriage. Surely she had paid the price for her failures in the past and God would grant her the pleasure of giving birth to a child for Connor within the next year.

Her heart seemed to be lifting toward heaven as she stood within the embrace of the peach tree, her silent prayer winging its way, as the yearning for the fulfillment of motherhood filled her being. That the joy of bearing and delivering a live child might be hers.

They worked together, silently for the most part, but with an energy and pride in their work. Connor picked a large peach, one that seemed to be the perfect specimen, and presented it to Loris.

"Have a bite, sweetheart. Isn't this one a beauty?"

She accepted it from his hand and bit into the soft skin, relishing the sweet fruit and smiling her thanks. He took it from her then, and ate several bites before he returned it to her hand. "Umm…juicy, isn't it?" he said, and she nodded her agreement.

"I wonder how your lips would taste right now." The question was spoken in a teasing voice, but the kiss he took from her was tantalizing, a blending of mouths that lit the fire of passion.

He pulled her to the wagon floor and held her close in his arms. The sides of the vehicle were high enough to protect them should anyone approach, and only the sun, filtering through the tree above them was witness to the caresses he offered to her welcoming flesh.

She found herself tugging at Connor's shirt, then helping him as he undid the buttons on her dress. They shed what clothing came between their yearning bodies and then when her breasts pressed firmly against his chest, when his manhood was snugly captured in the valley between her thighs, he sighed and nestled his nose and mouth into the bend of her shoulder, just beneath her ear.

"You smell so good, sweetheart. You're so soft and perfect."

She held him carefully, aware of the tenderness of his back, and kissed him wherever she could find a bit of flesh to bless with the fruity taste of her lips. His groan of passion told her he was almost beyond the point of no return, that they would consummate their love here and now, and she was swept away by the realization that this man needed her with every fiber of his being.

He was hungry for her, needed the fulfillment only her body could bring him. She curved against him, opening to him, urging his entry, lifting her hips, the better to take him within her body.

Connor's hands roamed against her sides, then he lifted from her and found the curves and hollows that pleased his touch, and took his time, giving her the pleasure his clever fingers and hot kisses could provide to her hungry body.

His possession of her was quick, his body demanding a response she gave gladly. As though all that had transpired over the past few days had led to this moment, they came together as a man and woman, in love and tenderness, and were transformed into the blending of soul and body that had been ordained from the beginning of time.

They lay there, almost hidden by the lush fruit, the heavy branches and the sound of bees flying from their hives to the trees and back again. The sun still shone, perhaps a bit brighter now, Loris thought. The breeze still blew, the branches above them swaying in time to the rhythm of the wind. Yet, time seemed to stand still. For just those few moments, she felt that she and Connor were alone and their lives had been forever changed.

She touched his face with her index finger, tracing the line of his jaw, his eyebrow, then his mouth, and her words were soft and spoke of the solemn moments that had been theirs to share.

"I think we just made a baby, Connor. I pray we did, anyway. If love is the reason for children being conceived, for families being formed, then our love surely is enough to give life to a child today."

He kissed her as though he could not taste her enough, as though his lips hungered for her, and his hands framed her face. "You're my wife, Loris. If we've made a child today, I'll be a happy man. If not, I'll still be a blessed man, knowing that I have you in my life."

She felt hot tears fall from her eyes and burn their way to her temples and into her hair. "I didn't know you could say such beautiful things to me. I love you so much, Connor. I can't begin to express it to you."

"You don't have to say a word, sweetheart. Everything you do is for me, for us, and I appreciate your tenderness and your loving care of me."

"You're my whole life," she whispered, lifting to kiss him again and again.

He held her, rolling to his side, keeping her close in his embrace, and then he chuckled softly. "I think we'd better get ourselves put together, Loris, or we'll never make it to town today."

She grumbled beneath her breath. "I was hoping you'd forgotten our plans for the trip."

"Not a chance, honey. We'll have our supper at the hotel restaurant to celebrate, once we've dropped off the peaches at your folks' house, and at Joe's place."

"We're going to eat in a restaurant?" It was a rare treat to eat someone else's cooking.

"Of course we are. I have to take my wife out once in a while, don't I?"

"Well, if I'm going to be seen in public, I'd better get myself in shape for company. I'll need to get washed up and change my clothes."

Connor stood and pulled her to her feet, then climbed over the wagon seat and gave her a hand as she sat beside him. "Isn't this handy?" he asked with a grin. "I knew we'd make good use of this wagon today."

A half hour was all Loris needed, and she found Connor a clean shirt and trousers to put on, deeming his others only fit for the wash basket. It was well past noon when they set out, each of them content with a bowl of peaches for dinner, thinking of the meal they would order in a few hours.

The stop at Joe's farm was quick, his wife, a dark-haired lady named Wilma, happy for the gift of fruit. "We don't have a peach tree to our name," she said cheerfully. "I'll get these put into jars in no time."

"If you want more, come on over and pick them," Loris said happily. "We've got a lot more still on the trees, and I can only put up another couple of bushels."

They set a time for Wilma to visit, and Loris was happy at the thought of neighboring with her. Sharing a cup of tea and a cookie was an ideal way to get to know another woman, and Wilma seemed to be a friendly sort.

They stopped at her parents' home for a longer spell, with Loris going to the front door to knock and await admittance. Her mother opened the door and her mouth opened with surprise. "What are you doing here?" she asked bluntly. And then she looked beyond Loris to where Connor sat atop the wagon seat. "Did you come to visit? Your father isn't here right now."

"I came to see you, Mother," Loris said. "I brought you some peaches. I didn't know if you'd gotten any yet, and I thought I'd share mine with you. Our trees are heavy with fruit, and I've already canned a goodly supply, and dropped some off at our neighbor's house. Would you like a bushel?"

"Well, I suppose that would be nice," Minnie said slowly. "I've got a whole shelf full of Mason jars I haven't filled yet. Do you need some apples?"

"Father offered some for me to make pies when he was out helping me paint," Loris said. "I'd be happy to take enough home for some applesauce and a few pies."

"We'll go out back and fill your basket, if Connor wants to bring it in the house for me to empty first. I can put the peaches in a couple of big bread pans. I'll probably need to put them up today or tomorrow."

"They're not dead ripe, but pretty close," Loris told her. "Will you need help?"

"No, I can handle it, but if you want more apples so you can put up applesauce, I'll have your father help me pick you some more and he can bring them out to you."

It seemed that this would be a friendly visit, Loris thought as Connor carried the bushel basket in the house. Her mother was reserved but friendly, and she lent a hand picking apples enough to fill the basket.

The house seemed smaller, than she remembered, as if distance had somehow made it shrink to a size she could more readily cope with. No longer did the ceilings seem so high, the doorways so wide, the rooms so chill and forbidding. It had not been an entirely happy home, she realized now. Now that she shared a home with Connor, where their lives were filled with love and laughter and the joy of working together to build a lifetime.

They left as her mother was preparing supper, Loris whispering the news of Connor's treat in her ear as she hugged her mother goodbye. "He's taking me to supper at the hotel. We're celebrating, but I'm not sure what."

And then she thought of their private celebration in the wagon earlier, and she felt a blush climb her cheeks. Her mother laughed and patted her on the back. "I imagine you have lots to celebrate, Loris, living with a man like Connor. He's a handsome scamp, isn't he?"

"You don't know how wonderful he is, Mother. He's so good to me, and I'm happy with him."

"I can see that," Minnie said softly. "Things have worked out well for you. I can only hope that you have smooth sailing now. I fear I spoke too harshly about him. I was wrong."

An ominous chill came over Loris as her mother spoke those words, and she shivered, as if the future might not be as smooth as her mother hoped.

She was quiet as they rode toward the hotel, and Connor put his arm around her. "Are you all right?" he asked. "You've been in another world since we left your folks' house."

"Just thinking," she said, unwilling to put a damper on his mood. "What shall we have for supper?"

"Whatever the special is, probably," he said. "It's always good. Sometimes chicken, other times roast beef or steak, or pork cutlets. The desserts are something special, too. Eclairs and pies and cakes." He smiled down at her and winked. "Not as good as yours, of course, but pretty tasty for a restaurant."

"How many restaurants have you been to?" she asked.

"Just this one and a couple of others when I was out of town picking up horses to train."

"You haven't traveled since we've been married," she mused. "Will you have to?"

"Never know," Connor told her. "Once in a while someone wants me to pick up a horse, and I usually take the train and put the animal in the stock car to travel. Quicker than riding and a lot less tiring."

They pulled up the wagon at the hotel and Connor found a place for his horse to be hitched. "We won't be long. We'll just leave it here," he said. "This is for hotel guests anyway."

Loris took his arm and let him usher her up the steps to the double doors of the building. They were heavy, the glass beveled and cut into a pattern of leaves and flowers. Loris halted before them to better appreciate the designs. Connor opened one door and she entered ahead of him, then waited for his arm to guide her toward the wide doorway that led to the dining room.

White-covered tables filled the room, over half of

them occupied, with white-aproned girls bustling here and there, serving their customers and carrying plates and pitchers of water. A woman approached them and smiled, asking if they had a preference as to where they would sit. Loris shook her head, in awe of the place, willing to follow wherever the hostess led.

Their table was near a window and they sat down, Connor holding her chair as if he were in a fine establishment in the big city, and she were someone of importance. She told him of her thoughts as he sat down across from her, and he laughed softly.

"You are important, Loris. You're the most important person in my life." He looked at the sheet of paper the hostess had handed him, and then shared it with Loris. "See, they have two specials tonight. Fried chicken and dumplings and ham with sweet potatoes. Does either of them appeal to you?"

"Why don't we order one of each and then share them?" she asked quietly, as if uncertain that such a thing could be done.

"Sounds good to me," he said, raising his hand to alert the waitress that they were ready to order. He asked the girl for two coffees, and then looked at Loris expectantly. "Anything else, sweetheart?"

She blushed at his endearment, aware that the young woman who served them had been looking at Connor as if he were a delicious sweetmeat. "That'll be fine," she said, wishing for a glass of milk but unwilling to change his order.

"Would you like some milk, too?" he asked, as if he had read her mind.

She nodded, meeting his gaze with a melting glance.

"You always seem to know ahead of time what I'd like," she told him, driving home the message to the waitress that he was a man already taken.

They ate well, sharing the two plates and laughing together as they compared notes on the food. Loris thought it perfect, Connor insisting that the fried chicken was not nearly as crispy or tender inside as what he'd eaten at home. Loris was pleased at his compliments. Their dessert was a cream cake, freshly baked, the white layers separated by a filling of whipped cream and then topped with more of the same.

"I'm too full to move," Loris sighed. She thought she might have to loosen her clothing before she got home, and when Connor helped her from her chair, she had the urge to put her head on his shoulder and go to sleep. She did just that as the wagon headed down the road back towards their farm.

The wagon rolled past the Simpson place until it reached their own lane, leading to the house. Then Connor brushed the wisps of hair from her face and whispered her name. "Loris, wake up. We're home."

She stirred and snuggled closer to him, as if unwilling to desert the dreams that had occupied her during the trip. She opened her eyes, tilting her head, the better to look into his face, and he was treated to a joyous look that transformed her from a pretty girl to a beautiful woman. *His* beautiful woman.

For the rest of the night, he let her know in ways she could not mistake, that he considered her just that. Beautiful, loving and all that was good in his life. He possessed her, gave her assurances that happiness was theirs to share, that they would find contentment in the home they had formed together.

And when she slept, it was with the deeply seated knowledge that Connor had, on this day, given her a child.

Chapter Eleven

"Mrs. Webster, do you know of anyone who might want to harm your son and his wife?" Paul Logan sat on his horse and faced the woman who had come out on her porch to greet him.

Peggy Webster was tall and spare, gray-haired and gimlet-eyed, a woman who presented an appearance guaranteed to repel any friendly advances. The sheriff was no fool, and thought it wise to stay in his saddle and conduct this conversation from his high vantage point.

"Are you accusing me of something?" Her voice was shrill, her tone sharp and her attitude that of a woman who had been insulted. And well she might feel that way, the sheriff not having prefaced his inquiry with any sort of conversation that might be considered passing the time of day.

"No, ma'am," the sheriff said quickly. "We're just trying to find out who set the fire that injured your son and burned his barn almost to the ground."

"Well, I don't know anything about it, I'm sure," she

answered. "I'm not responsible in any way for their troubles. They brought them all on themselves."

"What do you mean by that?" His forehead creased as though truly puzzled by her words.

"That woman coerced my son into marriage and made a fool of him, carrying his brother's child and then trying to pass it off as Connor's."

"I heard in town that Connor knew what he was doing when he married her. He seems quite happy with Loris, now that you mention it. And he certainly has no use for his brother, not that I blame him, the way James walked away from his responsibilities."

"What do you know about it?" Peggy asked sharply. "My boys were close as two peas in a pod until that girl started trouble between them. She's to blame for everything that's gone wrong for Connor."

"She didn't set the fire, ma'am," he said quietly. "But someone did. And I'm going to find out who did it and why, if it's the last thing I do."

"Well, you won't find anything out by coming out here and asking questions. I don't know anything about them. In fact, I resent the fact that you've wasted my time with your shenanigans."

"Shenanigans. That's an interesting word to describe my duties as a law officer, ma'am. Someone had it in for Loris Webster, and we're investigating every person who meets that description."

He lifted his reins and turned his horse in a tight half circle, then rode from her sight quickly. As if he wanted to be rid of her presence.

Peggy Webster stood on the porch and watched Sheriff Logan ride away, her mind focusing on the man who had so badly botched the job of ridding the world of Loris's place in Connor's life.

It was time to light a fire under Howie Murdoch, see to it that he did the job quickly, before the sheriff stuck his nose too deeply into things.

Peggy took off her apron and found her sunbonnet. The mare was easy enough to hitch to the buggy, and when her husband came out of the barn to see what was going on, she had already put the bit in the mare's mouth and tied the reins to the buggy.

"Where you goin'?" he asked bluntly. "What about my dinner?"

"I've got an errand to run. I'll be back within the hour. If you're starving to death, the soup is almost done cooking. You can have a bowl while you're waiting."

"And who's supposed to dish it up and get things ready for dinner?" he asked.

Peggy shot him a disgusted look. "If you don't know how to put a ladle of soup into a bowl, you deserve to starve to death." With a brisk nod of her head, she climbed into the buggy and snapped the reins over the mare's back, sending the vehicle rolling down the lane and out onto the road.

She found him at his camp, about halfway to town, in a grove of trees. He looked up in concern as the buggy approached through the trees. "What you doin' here?" he asked curtly.

"I came to let you know that I want something done. That woman has turned my son against me, and I want her out of the picture. Permanently."

Murdoch nodded slowly and then bent to locate his gun and holster from his saddlebag.

* * *

Loris lit a match and set the bit of newspaper on fire. It was the bottom layer of a carefully arranged pile of kindling and firewood, topped by the dried weeds and tomato vines from the garden. She stepped back as the fire flared to life and the kindling caught the flame, sending it upward to where the dry vegetation awaited burning.

The potato vines were next, the potatoes having been dug last week and stored in the cellar, and Loris shook any remaining dirt from them and tossed them on the pyre. It was a good feeling, this cleaning up the garden, preparing it for next spring, when she would once again plant crops for her kitchen.

She'd loved this job at home, helping her mother to plant and weed, then finally pick the produce that grew with abundance in her garden patch. Now Loris had her own home, her own garden and a husband to share the rewards with.

"Don't let that fire catch your skirt," Connor said from the porch. He was resting from doing the chores, and Loris had bid him sit in the rocking chair while she did the final task of working the soil and burning the bits and pieces left from the summer.

"I won't," she said. "I've done this before."

"I can see that. You're an old hand at this business of being a farmer's wife."

"I'm a fast learner," she said, teasing him as she bent to pick up her pitchfork and then turned back to the house. Just as she stood up, a shot rang out and Connor could only watch in horror as Loris crumpled to the ground, a red patch blossoming against her left side, blood staining her clothing.

He leaped from the chair and was off the porch in mere seconds, kneeling by her side, turning her carefully to her back, and then tearing off his own shirt, folding it, and then placing the wad of fabric against the place where blood flowed.

He couldn't leave her alone to ride for help and he feared he couldn't carry her into the house. And yet, there seemed to be no choice. He slid his arms under her knees and shoulders and lifted her with care. No matter that the pain in his back corresponded with the strain of using muscles he'd been pampering for weeks. All that mattered was getting Loris inside and away from any more danger.

He'd barely gotten to the porch when a man rode up the lane, hailing him with a shout. "Connor. Wait up. I need to see you." It was the sheriff, and Connor blessed whatever powers had sent him here today.

"What's going on?" Paul asked as he slid from his horse and jumped to the porch, taking in the blood that still flowed from Loris's side to stain Connor's clothing.

"Someone shot her. I didn't see anybody, but it came from out beyond the pasture. Sounded like a rifle to me."

"Who on earth would want to harm a woman out here minding her own business?" Paul asked helplessly. He took Loris's inert body from Connor's arms and nodded at the screen door. "Open up the door and I'll carry her in."

The sofa in the parlor was long enough to hold her and it was there Paul placed her, then bent low to look beneath the padding on her side. Connor had wedged it inside her dress, tearing the seam to make room for it, and Paul shook his head.

"I don't want to take this off until we have a towel or something else to replace it. And then I think we'll need to get the doctor from town."

Connor went to the kitchen, searched out a stack of clean towels in the washroom and returned. He folded one and gave it to the sheriff. "Will this work?"

In reply, Paul took the pressure pad from Loris's side and watched as the blood ran from the wound. He tore her dress farther and made room for the towel to cover the area, then looked up at Connor.

"You want to hold this in place or go to town for the doctor?"

Connor was torn. But the idea of leaving Loris for even a minute was not to be considered. "I'll stay here," he said sharply. "You go."

He knelt beside her and bent to her. "Loris? Can you hear me?"

A murmur passed her lips and she opened her eyes, then allowed them to drift closed. "Hurts," she said softly, and Connor winced.

"I know it does, sweetheart. But we're going to have the doctor here in no time and he'll fix you up as good as new."

"Don't push," she said, wincing as he applied pressure on the towel.

"I have to hold it firmly, so the bleeding will stop. Or at least stay under control," he told her. "I know it hurts, but I can't help it."

"Where's the medicine the doctor left for you when you were burned?" the sheriff asked. "Any of it left?"

Connor's head came up and he nodded, approving the idea. "In the pantry, in a bottle on the right. It's marked with my name."

"I'll get it before I go and we'll dose her with it."

"It won't hurt her, will it?" Not for the world would Connor jeopardize his wife by dosing her with the same bottle of medicine that had made him so sleepy and groggy.

"It'll make her feel a whole lot better, if I know anything about it," Paul said. "She needs to be asleep when the doctor gets here, and this is the best way I know of to accomplish that. He'll have to get that bullet out."

"All right." Connor was happy to let the sheriff take charge and let him make the decision, because he was anxious for him to leave and the doctor to arrive.

In less than an hour both men rode up to the porch, and Connor breathed a sigh of relief.

The afternoon went by slowly, Connor sitting by Loris's side, holding her in place as the doctor located the bullet. It had cracked a rib and lodged there, the doctor said, and Loris was lucky it hadn't been a few inches closer to her heart.

"Luck had nothing to do with it, Doc," Conner said bluntly. "Loris is a good woman and it wasn't her time to go. She's got a guardian angel looking out for her."

"I won't argue that. Stranger things have happened. Loris is going to be fine. I suspect whoever shot her wasn't aiming to wound. I think he just missed his target a little."

Connor relived the moment in his mind as he told the sheriff what had happened. "She was bent over in the garden, picking up her tools and when she stood up the shot rang out and she dropped where she stood."

"Sounds like he was aiming for her head, maybe. He wasn't playing games, that's for sure." Sheriff Logan stood in the doorway and offered a final word. "I'm going on a manhunt, Connor. If I see or hear anything, I'll be back, and I want you to keep a weather eye out for anybody hangin' around in the area."

"Will do, Sheriff. Much obliged for all your help." Connor shook his hand, then went into the house to tend to Loris.

It was early in the evening when the sheriff returned, but Connor had barely noticed the passing of time, so caught up was he in Loris's condition.

"I've got news," Paul said, as he walked in the back door. He'd knocked, then opened the screen door before Connor could move from his post next to the couch in the parlor.

"Come on in here," Connor called out. "Loris is just starting to rouse. I think it's about time to give her another dose of the medicine Doc left."

"She may want to hear this first," Paul said, walking across the threshold into the parlor. He took a seat near the door and propped his elbows on his knees, folding his hands as he leaned forward.

"I went back and forth over the area out back, and I found where our friend stood when he fired his shot. The ground was trampled, his horse had left a deposit there, and there was a shell casing in the grass."

"Any ideas?" Connor asked.

"Maybe. I saw a camp almost hidden beyond a grove

of trees on my way back to town. The coals were still warm in the fire pit, and someone had left the remains of breakfast lying around. It looks to me like he'll return there, what with the odds and ends he left behind."

"Are there any strangers in town?"

"A couple of cowhands looking for work, a man looking to open a bakery, and on the lookout for a space to build. Other than that, I haven't seen anyone I didn't recognize. But that doesn't mean anything. I doubt if our man is about to expose himself."

"But why would a perfect stranger want to hurt Loris?" Connor's query gave away his bafflement. He looked down at his wife and anger rose up within him. "I'd like to get my hands on him, whoever he is."

"I'll do the chasing. I want you to stay here and take care of your wife," Paul told him sternly. "I think someone may have hired the dude anyway."

"Any ideas?"

Paul paused and glanced at Loris, whose eyelids were fluttering, a sure sign she was aware of the conversation. "I don't want to tell you what's going on in my mind, Connor. I can't throw stones at anyone without some sort of proof. And right now, I don't have any."

"Who would want to hurt her?" Connor repeated his question, and Paul's eyes darkened as he stood up and adjusted his holster against his thigh.

"Use your head, Connor," he said tightly. "Who do you know with a grudge against Loris? This whole thing, the barn fire and now the shot that wounded her, is far from accidental. I think we have a hired criminal doing someone else's dirty work."

Connor felt a chill pass through his body. And before

his face rose the likeness of his mother. But would she be so dead set on erasing Loris from his life as to do such a thing? He shook his head. "I can't believe she'd do this," he said quietly. "But there isn't anyone else with a grudge against Loris. At least no one I can think of. She's even made peace with her folks."

"Well, someone is desperate to eliminate Loris from your life, Connor. I think the barn fire was to scare her off, maybe cause her to leave here, which in turn would send you back home to your folks. When that didn't work, the next best thing was to get rid of her permanently."

"I think I'd better take a ride," Connor said. "I may have some family business to tend to."

"You'd better have someone here to guard your wife, if you do that," Paul said. "If it were me, I wouldn't leave her alone. I think she's still in danger."

"What if I tell my folks that Loris was killed?" Connor asked. "They have no way of knowing differently."

"What would you accomplish?"

"Maybe it would get rid of the gunman. And I could take care of her in peace while she recuperates. We'd have to let Doc know, so he wouldn't noise it around town that there's a problem out here."

Paul shook his head. "I think you'd be stirring up a hornet's nest, Connor. Your folks would probably expect you to come home, and if you didn't, they'd be suspicious."

"I don't think my father knows anything about all this," Connor told him. "He's as honest as the day is long. My mother's the one with the hang-up about James and me. She's sure that James will come home to stay if I make peace with him. And the only way she can see that happening is if Loris is out of the picture."

Loris struggled to sit up, groaning at the pain in her side. Connor pressed her back against the pillow and shushed her. "Don't move, sweetheart. You'll start bleeding again."

"I've been nothing but trouble to you from the very beginning, Connor. I should leave. In fact, I'll warrant my folks will let me come home."

"No." Spoken in a firm, concise tone, Connor's reply left no room for doubt as to his opinion. "You're not leaving me, Loris. You're my wife and we'll work through this together."

"Well, I'm headin' back to town," Paul told them. "I'd say you need to stay off your feet and get your strength back, ma'am. And you'd better keep your shotgun or rifle handy, Connor. I'll stop by Joe's place and tell him what's been going on. If you have trouble, shoot in the air three times. He'll hear it and come a-runnin' lickity-split if I know anything about it."

"I've got good locks on the doors and windows," Connor said, "and I'll put off going anywhere for a day or so. If you find anything, let us know."

Early the next morning the back door was rattled by a knock that sent Connor searching for his trousers. Snatching up his shirt from the chair next to the bed, he bent low over Loris and whispered in her ear. "You stay right here and don't move," he said gruffly. "I'll see who it is and then come back upstairs. I've got my shotgun right here, so don't worry about anything."

She nodded her agreement, and Connor headed from the room and down the stairs, barefoot, but armed with his loaded long gun.

The back door rattled in its hinges as a fist pounded

again, and Connor was hard pressed not to shout out a warning. Instead, he opened the door far enough to see outdoors, and then swung it wide.

"James. What the hell are you doing here?"

His brother walked into the kitchen, letting the screen door slam behind himself. "Is Loris all right? I stopped at Joe's place and he said she'd been shot yesterday."

"She was in the garden and a gunman shot from out back, a rifle from the looks of things," Connor told him. "He missed her head, which was probably where he was aiming. She'd been crouched in the garden and stood up just as the shot was fired. It hit her in the side."

James's face was pale, as if shocked by the news. "What does Doc say? Will she be all right? Where is she?"

"Upstairs. I wanted her in her own bed, instead of on the sofa in the parlor. In fact, I'll carry her down in a few minutes and put her in the rocking chair by the window. So long as she can't be seen from outdoors, she'll be safe."

"Who the hell would want to hurt Loris?" James asked, his voice rough as if he held back a wealth of emotion.

"I've got a good idea," Connor told him. "You been home yet? I thought you were in Missouri."

James shook his head. "I rode into town and thought to come out here first. I wanted to see you. And work was slow on the ranch I'm working."

"What for?" Connor didn't have it in him to welcome his brother with open arms.

"We need to talk," James said bluntly. "I've had a hard time living with myself. You're my brother, Connor, and I want things to be right between us. If I can be of any help to you, I'm at your disposal. "

"That's the best news I've had in a month of Sundays,"

Connor told him. "It sure beats the mess we've been in here, lately. You heard about the fire, didn't you?"

"Yeah, someone in town told me, and then Joe filled in the details. How are your burns?"

"I'm about healed up. Loris took care of me, and Doc came out here several times. And now we've got this mess going on."

"Spill it, Connor. What are you thinking? You must have some ideas going around in that head of yours."

"Why don't you sit down and have some coffee first. Last night's leftovers are pretty strong, I imagine, but I'll make a new pot in just a minute or two. I'll start breakfast and then carry Loris down here."

James took his brother up on his offer and sat at the table, seeming more comfortable since he'd been invited to stay for breakfast. He sipped at the mug of coffee Connor brought him and then settled back in his chair as Connor headed for his bedroom to let Loris know what was going on.

"James is here?" Her voice rose as she repeated Connor's news. "Whatever for?"

"He apparently heard about our bad news, and he seems to be interested in getting to the bottom of things."

"You really think he'll help us?" She sounded dubious, and rightly so, given James's behavior in the past.

"He apologized to you before he left here, Loris. I think he's maybe turned over a new leaf. At least I have to give him a chance. He's my brother."

She nodded and slid carefully to the edge of the bed, waiting till Connor gave her his hand before she tried to stand. Her legs were wobbly, and Connor held her full weight against himself as he reached for her robe.

"Here, put this on and I'll carry you down," he told her. Even as she demanded that she be allowed to walk, once her robe was tied in place, he picked her up, shushing her neatly with the one threat that he knew would work. "Hold still, Loris, so I don't hurt my back rassling with you." Lifting her higher against his chest, he made his way from the bedroom and down the stairs.

James rose as they entered the kitchen. "You need a pillow or anything?" he asked Connor.

"Yeah, get one off the sofa for her to sit on, will you?" Holding Loris in his arms was beginning to tire him, and Connor turned her carefully, lest he hurt her side, and then allowed her feet to rest on the floor. She swayed before him and James came back in the kitchen just in time to place the pillow on the seat of the rocker before she sat down.

"I'll get you the footstool," he said quickly, and left the room, returning in moments with the tapestry-covered stool from the parlor.

Connor bent to lift her feet, resting them there, and laughed as he recognized that she was barefoot. "I'd better get you a throw to keep your feet warm," he said, but Loris had other ideas, it seemed.

"It's plenty warm in here, Connor. You must have built a huge fire in the cookstove." She looked at him with a grin. "What's for breakfast?"

"Well, if James will go out to the henhouse and see how many eggs there are, we'll mix up a batch of scrambled eggs to go with the sausage I'm about to fry."

Taking the hint to heart, James picked up a crock from the kitchen buffet and sailed out the back door, a wide grin on his face.

"He's looking pretty pleased with himself," Loris said quietly.

"I hope you don't mind, I asked him to stay for breakfast, Loris." He lowered his voice and bent down to speak to her. "He said he wants to make things right with me, and he'd like to help catch the person responsible for our problems."

"And you said?…" she asked, already knowing his reply.

"That was when I asked him to stay for breakfast," Connor told her. "I think he got the message. I don't want any more hard feelings. We've got too many years ahead of us to live to let problems fester between us. He's my only brother, Loris."

"And mine, too," she answered, reaching up to touch Connor's cheek. "Does he have any ideas?"

"We haven't talked that much yet, but I suspect we're on the same track. Our minds have always seemed to think alike."

"Where's my cash? I did what you wanted."

"What do you mean? What did you do?" Peggy Webster looked up at Murdoch who'd waved her down on her way to the chicken coop. He'd been behind the corn crib and out of sight of the barn where her husband was working. Now she watched him as he demanded his money.

"Is Loris gone?"

"Depends on how you mean that, I suspect," he said. "She took a bullet and her husband carried her in the house. She wasn't moving when he picked her up. I suspect it hit her right where I aimed it."

"And then what happened?"

"Well, the sheriff arrived just as your son was takin' his wife inside, and I vamoosed. I didn't want to be hangin' around in case the lawman decided to look around."

"And did he? Did he know where the shot came from?" Peggy felt exultant at the news, yet there were no guarantees that the job had been a success. Only time would tell. She'd have to ride into town and see if anyone had heard about Loris being shot.

"The sheriff rode out to where I'd been hiding beyond the pasture and I skedaddled when he came in my direction."

"Did he see you? I wouldn't want him to recognize you."

"Naw, I was on the edge of the woods by then and I just got my horse and rode off. I went into town and talked to some folks in front of the general store, kinda coverin' my tracks. I asked about a job as a hired hand at one of the ranches, seeing as how the owner had hung a sign in the store, sayin' he needed two new ranch hands. But I'm about ready to hightail it outta here. Never did like this town."

"What about your campsite? Did you gather your belongings and clean up the place? I don't want the sheriff to find you've been squatting out there in the woods."

"I'm gonna find a new place to sleep later today," he told her. "If that rancher wants me to work for him, I'll go there. If not, I'm headin' out as soon as you pay me what you owe me."

"I'm not paying you one red cent until I know that Loris has left town. That was the deal and I'm not changing my mind."

Saliva spewed from his mouth as he cursed at her. "I'm beginnin' to think I shot the wrong woman."

"You listen to me," Peggy said curtly. "I've written everything down that's gone on, and if anything happens to me, they'll be on your trail in a hurry, Howie. There's folks in town who'd remember what a troublemaker you were."

"I doubt anyone would even care if anything happened to you," the man said mockingly.

"Get on out of here," Peggy said quietly. "I hear my husband out in the barn. He's gonna want his dinner right quick, and you'd better make tracks."

"You just get that money together, you hear?"

"Get your horse and leave. I'm going to the barn to keep him busy for a couple of minutes. When you see me go in there, just climb on that horse of yours and ride out of here."

She walked from the chicken coop toward the barn, and as she entered the wide doorway, she heard the sound of a horse's low whinny behind her.

"Peggy? Is that you?" From the depths of the building, Amos called her name and she hurried to where he was working in the tack room. She stood in the doorway, watching him repair a bridle.

"Yeah, it's me. I'm gonna fix your dinner now. Come on in the house when you get that finished."

"Sure wish I had one of our boys here to help with this," he said. "Takes too much time away from my other work, messin' with odds and ends like this."

"Maybe James will come back," she said hopefully.

"And maybe the sun will forget to rise in the morning," he said, with a note of sarcasm.

"Stranger things have happened," Peggy told him. "The boy knows he can come home if he wants to."

"He's got some fence-mendin' to do first, I'd say. He needs to set things right with his brother."

"His brother is the one who made Jamie leave, don't forget," she said cuttingly.

"Nobody made him leave, woman," her husband told her harshly. "He made a mess and left Connor to clean it up. I think you've forgotten the whole story. Connor's the one who's taken up the slack for James. And doing a good job at it, too, from what I hear."

"He's betrayed us by taking up with that girl, and marrying her to boot."

"That's what James should have done. At least Connor saw his duty and did it. Don't be blaming the girl for James leadin' her on. He's a scamp from way back. And it took all of this to make me see it."

"Well, he's my son, and if he wants to come home, I say, let him."

Her husband shook his head, finished up his work in the tack room, then joined his wife on her walk back to the house.

Chapter Twelve

❧

"**I**'m going to go home and stay there for a while," James announced after breakfast, as if he'd made a momentous decision. And so it was, because going back to live with his parents would put James right back in the situation he'd left behind months ago. His father and mother would pamper him, cover up his mistakes with mention of his youth, and he would be right back in a position of being the younger, favored son.

But during the past year, James had changed, Connor realized. He was no longer the spoiled boy he had been the day he rode off to Missouri for a job on a ranch.

"Did you have a tough time in Missouri?" Connor queried.

James grinned at him from across the table and nodded. "I learned how to take orders as well as give them. Worked my tail off herding cattle and branding steers. It made for an interesting life, that's for sure. I met a young woman there, the ranch owner's daughter and learned how to ignore an outright invitation from the fairer sex."

With a quick grin in Loris's direction, he ducked his

head. "I've made too many mistakes with women to be messin' around with any more of them. I decided I needed to grow up a bit before I started courting one, and that meant keepin' my nose to the grindstone and behaving myself."

He looked pensive as he leaned back in his chair. "I guess the main thing I found out was that family ties are strong. Even with Mother and Dad treating me like I had a halo and wings, I managed to get in a peck of trouble, and then ran off when I couldn't face up to it. They were good to me, but I wasn't made to face my responsibilities, not since I was just a kid."

He shot a look at Connor. "They were different with you. And I decided I'd rather have them treat me the way they did you, with respect, and a lot of demands that made you come up to snuff."

Connor looked quickly at Loris, and then admitted a truth he'd kept to himself for too long. "I have to admit I missed you, James. We used to be real brothers, both of us on the same side, looking out for each other. I don't know when it all started to go wrong, but I'd like to think we could salvage that old friendship."

"Well, that sounds good to me," James offered.

"Wish you'd been around for the barn raising," Loris said with feeling. "We'd have been able to use another hand, even though the men did a wonderful job of it."

"Even though none of our own families showed up to help," Connor added dryly.

James glowered. There was no other word for the dark, angry look he shot in Connor's direction. "I'm ashamed that Mother and Dad didn't pitch in and help." He looked at Loris then. "And your folks, too, Loris. They ought to all be ashamed of themselves. That's what I mean about family ties, Connor. You stick with your own, through thick and thin, no matter what the circumstances."

"Well, it's good to know I can call on you if our rifleman comes calling again. I don't look for him to be shooting anywhere around here in a hurry, now that he knows we're after him, but he may try something else. If he wasn't the one who set the barn on fire, I'll eat my hat."

"The thing is," James said slowly, "I can't imagine that anyone around here would want to harm you and Loris. Maybe he's a hired gun."

"I've thought of that, but you won't like my suspicions."

"You don't really think that Mother would go to those lengths, do you?" James asked, his voice dubious.

"Yeah. I'm afraid she would. She blames Loris for your going away. And in one way, she's got that right. You might have gone, anyway, but all the trouble that came along speeded up your leaving."

"Maybe," James allowed. "Maybe if I go home for a while, she'll quit her trouble-making, if she *is* the one who's behind all this."

"And maybe you can spot something or someone that will give us a clue while you're there. At least you'd know if some stranger was hanging around."

"That settles it. I'll ride over right now and see how the wind is blowing. If she's in a good mood, I'll talk to her about coming back home, and then I'll talk to Dad and see how he feels. Whether or not I stay, I'll be seeing you again right shortly." James rose from his chair and approached his brother, standing before him as if he were at a loss as to what to do next.

Connor reached for him and hugged him, expressing without words exactly how he felt about finding peace with James. Loris thought she saw a tear making its way down James's cheek, and had to swallow hard to keep back her own salty drops. It was worth it to her to forget the past and move on into the future with Connor, just to know that the brothers had come to an understanding, that they were once more on the same side.

James left in moments, and Connor came to where Loris sat in the rocking chair, kneeling before her and then sitting on the floor to place his head in her lap. She ruffled his hair with one hand, then bent low to kiss his cheek. With that encouragement, he turned his head to one side and she placed her lips softly against his forehead, then the corner of his mouth.

He rose again to his knees and reached for her, his long arms encircling her waist, drawing her to the edge of the rocking chair as he whispered his love against her skin. She held him fast, relishing the feel of strong muscles across his back, his beard, not yet having been acquainted with a razor this morning, and the crisp, dark hair that clung closely to his head.

They were so much alike sometimes, but it was easy to realize how very different Connor and James really were, she thought. James was the scamp, the easy-win-easy-lose scalawag, and Connor was levelheaded and responsible. And why two brothers should be so different was a puzzle she stood no chance of solving. But to her benefit, she'd married Connor instead of her baby's father, and for that fact, she was truly grateful.

Before her was that man, who chose to look after her, to give her his love and protection. "I love you,

Connor," she whispered, and was pleased when he circled her waist in long arms that easily met at her back.

"You're the most important person in my life, Loris," he told her. "Don't ever doubt that. I'd turn away from everyone else who ever mattered to me, in order to keep you by my side."

"That won't ever be necessary," she said easily. "I want you to be on good terms with your parents, and especially your brother. The love you have for them doesn't take away from what you feel for me."

He grinned and kissed the tip of her nose. "How did you ever get so smart, so young? Some folks never learn that in the whole of their lives."

"Some days I don't feel especially smart," she said quietly. "Like now, when I'm filled with doubts, wondering what will happen next, if someone is after me, wanting to be rid of me."

"Well, with James going home, we'll have a set of eyes and ears there to watch for just that very thing," Connor told her. "If my mother is up to anything, it has to be apparent to someone on the lookout for it. And trust me, James will be keeping his eyes open for anything out of the ordinary."

"If your parents let him move back in."

Connor sounded confident as he replied to her dubious remark. "They will. I haven't any doubt about that."

"Of course you can come back home." Peggy Webster's eyes held a shimmer of tears as she welcomed her younger son into the kitchen of the old farmhouse. He'd made his petition from the back porch, standing in the open doorway, and then his mother had pulled him into the house, where she hugged him tightly.

"I've taken a better job at the ranch where I've been working, but the fella I'm replacing won't be leaving for a couple of months, so I told the owner that I'd be back in November. In the meantime, I figured I could give Pa a hand here and help him get things in shape for winter."

"I declare, James, I think you've grown," his mother said with a laugh. "But you surely haven't gained any weight. Did they feed you good while you were up there in Missouri?"

"Yeah. I ate like there was no tomorrow, but I worked it off. I'm skinnier, not taller. When you don't have family with you, no brother to watch your back, you're open to all sorts of stuff. Like jealous cowhands and drunken men on Saturday night."

"Why would anyone be jealous of you?" Peggy asked, peering up into her son's eyes.

"Maybe 'cause I'm so cute?" His nose wrinkled as he laughed, and then his voice took on a serious tone. "I was pretty young for the job I had to handle, Mother. And, I hope you won't think I'm blowing my own horn when I tell you I did a damn good job at it. Kept the men busy working, and the boss happy. You can't do much better than that."

"I suspect you're right, son," she said, her pride visible in the hand she lifted to smooth back his hair. "I always knew you were born to be a leader."

"Not as good a man as Connor, though. Maybe he'll teach me a bit about being the sort of fella he is while I'm home." His brow furrowed and he smiled down at his mother. "I've pulled a lot of stupid stunts, you know, and the last one could have been a total disaster if Connor hadn't cleaned up behind me."

"It was all that woman's fault, James. Loris Peterson is a tramp, and when she couldn't get you to marry her, she settled for Connor."

"Well, they seem pretty happy to me for a couple who were forced into this marriage. I've never seen Connor look so pleased with himself."

"She's got him hoodwinked," Peggy said with a sour look, branding Loris as worthless. "One of these days he'll wake up, and it'll be too late to get out of this fix. You mark my words, she's a peck of trouble."

"I'm afraid I can't agree with you on this, Mother. Loris was sinned against, and I was in the wrong, totally. She didn't seduce me. It was quite the opposite, in fact. I chased her until she gave in to me, and—"

Peggy held her hands over her ears. "I don't want to hear this sort of talk, James. Loris may have you and Connor both at her beck and call, but I've got her number, and she's done all the damage she's going to do to my family."

James shot her a look of inquiry. "Is that a threat? If so, you're walking on thin ice. Connor would die before he let anything happen to Loris. And I'd be right there to take his place if it came to that."

"You'd marry the girl?"

"I should have married her months ago. In fact, if I'd had my head screwed on right, I would have." James's face reddened as he faced his mother. "Right now, she's happy as a clam with the choice she made, and I'm willing to settle for being her brother. One of these days someone will come along for me. And until then, I'll just work and wait and keep my nose clean."

"She's not worthy of either of you." Her own face was turning crimson as Peggy stalked across the kitchen. "She'll come to a bad end, you watch and see if she doesn't."

James stood taller, his shoulders back, his jaw set. "Watch what you say, Mother. If it ever comes to light that you've done anything to hurt Loris, you'll be in a heap of trouble. And not just from your family, but the law. Connor would see you in jail before he'd let you give Loris any grief."

A noise on the back porch drew their attention in the kitchen, and they turned to the screened back door. The man who stood on the other side looked like a thundercloud as he jerked the door open and stomped into the house.

"What sort of foolishness have you been up to?" his father said, his frown directed at his wife. And then he looked at James. "You plannin' on puttin' your ma in jail, sonny?"

"If she hurts Connor's wife any more than she already has, she's in a heap of trouble, Pa."

Peggy stiffened and her blush reappeared. "Who says I've done anything to hurt her? You haven't any proof, James."

He looked at her sadly and shook his head. "You've just incriminated yourself, Mother. I don't know how you managed it, or who you hired, but the fact remains that it was your doing that got that barn burned down and then got Loris wounded."

"Loris wounded?" His father growled the words. and James turned to him.

"Where you been, Pa? Hiding under a rock somewhere? Everyone in town knows about the gunman who shot Loris."

"Didn't kill her, did he? Do they know who he is? And what makes you think your mother had anything to do with it?" The queries came fast and furious, aimed at James with anger.

"Open your eyes, Pa," he said tightly. "Everyone knows how Ma feels about Connor and Loris getting married. She hasn't made any secret about her hatred for the woman, and if you'd just stop and think a minute you'd realize that no one else hereabouts is carrying a grudge against Loris."

"Well, that doesn't point the finger at your ma, as far as I'm concerned," his father answered, stalking to where his wife stood and looking down at her. "Did you have anything to do with the attacks on Loris and on her barn?"

Her head moved from side to side as Peggy Webster silently swore her innocence.

"There, now. Does that satisfy you?" Turning to James, his father shouted the question and James only smiled.

"Surely you didn't think she'd admit it, did you?"

Peggy again claimed her innocence. "I had nothing to do with that woman getting her just deserts. I just hope she gets run out of town before this is done."

"Well, don't count on it, Ma," James said. "Connor has sworn to kill anyone who touches Loris or does anything to harm her. You'd better watch your back." He turned from his parents and stomped through the doorway and out into the yard. His horse waited there and he leapt on the animal's back in one quick motion, hauling up the reins and turning his mount to ride from the home where he'd been raised. The home he now found to be a place he could not stay.

On the porch, his parents watched and his mother's eyes were dry as she scowled at her son's back and folded her arms across her chest. "He'll find out one day," she said bitterly. "He was planning on staying till we mentioned Connor and Loris. One day he'll be back asking us to take him in."

Her husband looked at her darkly. "Don't count on it. He's madder than a wet hen, and he's gonna hold a grudge against you for a long time, Peg. I just can't understand why you'd do such a thing."

Without a pause, he jumped from the porch and headed back to his barn, his long legs carrying him rapidly. Behind him, Peggy Webster glared at her husband, the man who had just patently accused her of attempted murder. Her jaw hardened as she vowed revenge, and her words were bitter.

"I'll get you for this, Loris. Just wait."

"I can't stay at home, Connor. I'm not sure what I'm gonna do, but I know that being in the same house with our mother is never going to be in my future." James looked like he'd just lost his last friend, and Connor couldn't help but feel a pang of sorrow for the man.

"I'd let you stay here, but it wouldn't look right, James. We'd know that everything was on the up and up, but the whole town would be talking about you staying with Loris and me."

"I wouldn't ask that of you. If there was a chance of finding the man who caused all your trouble with the barn fire and shooting Loris, I'd camp out in the woods,

but I suspect he may be well on his way out of here."
He looked thoughtful for a minute and then his face
brightened, as if a sudden revelation had struck.

"That might not be a bad idea, you know. I could set
up camp out beyond your pasture, in the woods just the
other side of the hayfield, and just lie low for a while.
Or maybe stay out in the barn. It might just work, and
at least I'd be able to help you keep an eye on things
here." He paused and hung his head as if the words he
were about to speak were difficult for him to wrap his
tongue around.

"If someone hurts Loris again, I'll feel in some odd
way that it's my fault, Connor. I'm at the bottom of all
your problems, what with me abandoning her to you,
and then not doing what I should have done. If I'd stayed
at home, our mother might not have acted so crazy." He
looked up at his brother. "I'm convinced she's conniving against Loris. She hates her with a passion, and I'm
really worried she'll harm your wife. I couldn't stand
that, Connor. I know I've long since lost any right to care
about Loris, but I still can't help but acknowledge her
in some way as a woman who means more to me than
I can tell you.

"At this point, she's my sister, and I'll look out for
her safety."

"I know your motives are honest," Connor said
slowly. "And I'm not altogether opposed to you keeping a lookout for us. So long as no one else knows about
it, we'll be ahead of the game. Sort of get a jump on this
man if he shows up again."

"That's my thought," James said.

The brothers were on the back porch, under cover of

dark skies and hidden in the shadow of the house. The lights were out, Loris already abed, and Connor felt a stab of real concern as he looked into the darkness beyond his barn. Even now someone could be making his way toward them, and he and James would be protected only by the dubious shelter of night.

"Why don't you come on in for tonight and use the sofa in the parlor?" Connor asked quietly. "We'll work things out in the morning and get you set up."

"I'd as soon stay in the barn, I think. I can bed down there and be able to listen for any strange noises, maybe keep an eye out the back door. I think I can see across the pasture to the woods from there."

"I hate to send you out to the barn alone, James. If you go to sleep and someone creeps up on you…"

"It ain't gonna happen." His confidence showed in the quick grin he shot Connor's way, and James looked pleased with himself. "I've grown up a lot in the past eight months and I know how to take care of myself. Your little brother's a man now, Connor."

"I know that. But you're even more precious to me now than ever. You were my best friend for a lot of years, James, and now you're standing at my back, putting yourself on the line for me and mine."

"I'm glad things are working out for us," James said. "I want you and Loris to know that I'll do anything I have to, in order to keep the both of you safe and secure here."

"Well, let's go on out to the barn and get you set up there," Connor said, keeping his voice firm with difficulty. He felt emotions for his brother swelling up inside him. There was a lot to be said for family ties, and he and Loris would ever be grateful for James's help.

"Just give me a quilt to cover the hay and I'll stack up a pile by the back barn door. There's no reason for you to expose yourself. I doubt you can be seen here on the porch."

"All right. Hold tight and I'll be right back."

With careful steps, Connor went up the stairs to the closet in the hall where Loris kept the extra bedding. A dark quilt was on the top of the pile, and he pulled it from its place and draped it over his arm.

"What's going on?" Loris stood in the bedroom doorway, a pale shadow in the night, her long gown almost touching the floor. "Where are you going with that quilt, Connor? You're not planning on sleeping downstairs?"

"No, sweetheart. James is going to set up in the barn tonight, and I'm taking this down to him. I'll be right back."

He hurried down the stairs and opened the back door. James took the quilt from him and murmured a word of thanks. "Shut the door, Connor. You'd better lock it, too. And make sure your front door is secure."

With long strides, he set off across the yard, then opened the barn door almost silently before he slipped inside and pulled it closed behind him. Connor closed and locked the door, then did as James had told him, and checked the door at the front of the house. Seldom used, it still boasted a lock that was in pristine condition, and Connor set it securely, feeling a surge of anger as he did so.

No one in this county ever locked a door. Things were considered safe hereabouts, and he resented the fact that his home was in jeopardy, his wife exposed to danger.

Loris stood to one side of the bedroom window when he opened the door, expecting to find her in bed. She turned to him, her slender form barely discernible in the shadows. "I just saw James go into the barn," she said quietly. "Will he be safe there?"

"I think he's more concerned about our well-being than his own, honey. My brother has made some big strides lately. It seems we have a ready-made guardian angel out there."

Loris crossed the room to him and wrapped her arms around his waist, leaning her head against his chest. "I'm so glad you and James have made peace. I hated the idea that I'd come between you."

"He doesn't feel that way, Loris. And neither do I. You're the one that's suffered this whole time. James wants us to be safe and happy. Maybe he thinks it will make up a little for his wrongdoing."

He lifted her in his arms then and deposited her in the middle of the bed, then stripped his clothing off to join her there. They clung to each other on the mattress, the sheet pulled to their waists, whispering words meant to soothe and comfort each other.

Loris sighed and fought sleep. It seemed she should stay awake, maybe help James keep watch. If she could just hold her eyes open and let Connor sleep, she would. If the dog heard anything from out back or in the barn, he'd set up an alarm right off, she knew. The warm weather had persuaded him to stay outdoors at night lately, and she was happy to have him running loose.

Maybe he'd join James in the barn, she thought, yawning widely. And beside her, she heard Connor chuckle softly.

"Just close your eyes, sweetheart," he whispered. "James is a big boy. You don't have to lie awake worrying about him."

"I know," she murmured, even as her eyes closed and her breathing slowed. Soon she was asleep.

Chapter Thirteen

"**D**id you sleep at all last night? Anything happening out back?"

"Everything was quiet," James said in reply to his brother's questions. "I didn't get a lot of sleep, though, just waiting for the least little noise. I was sure there'd be action of some sort. But no dice."

James had come in for breakfast early and sat at the table as Connor poured two cups of coffee. Now, he yawned and stretched. "I just may grab a catnap for myself in the house this morning," he said. "Or are you going to be working inside the barn? If so I can give you a hand and then snooze out there."

"I've got horses to tend to first off," Connor said. "Two of them need shoes, and I thought I'd set up my forge out in front of the barn and take care of that. Then I'm going to put a saddle on that pretty little buckskin gelding later on. It might prove interesting," he said, laughing as he considered the idea. "That fella has more than his share of spunk, but if I'm real lucky, I won't land on my rump."

"You could make good money if you set yourself up

as a farrier, Connor. You'd have folks coming here from miles around. Jay Turnbull has more than he can handle at the livery stable. He's been turning away business right and left, I heard."

"I've thought of that, more than once," Connor admitted. "Might even do it, if I need some extra cash. Right now, my time is pretty well taken up with the horses I've already got out back. I'm getting four of them ready for sale, and two are already spoken for once I have them broken to saddle."

"I never thought my brother would be so successful," James said. His grin was wide as he picked up his coffee and sipped at it.

"To tell the truth, I've got you to thank for a good share of my success lately," Connor told him. "When I used the money you left for Loris for the back taxes on this place, it gave us a home, plus a spot to set up my stable and training arena. I'm thankful for your help."

"You had it coming," James said quietly. "You've made this a thriving place. From the looks of it, you'll have hay to sell this fall, won't you?"

"Maybe a little. We lost an awful lot of the crop when the barn burned. But, you never know. There's still the last cutting to take care of."

From the kitchen doorway, Loris cleared her throat, demanding their attention.

"Did you plan on letting me sleep all day?" she asked her husband, looking around the kitchen. "I noticed you haven't started breakfast yet. I'm tired of lying around and I feel almost good as new this morning. Aren't you boys hungry?"

Connor held out a hand in her direction and clasped

her fingers in his as she stepped to his side. "We were waiting for you, sweetheart. Do you feel up to cooking? No one else can cook eggs like you. In fact, I haven't gathered them yet this morning. How about if James and I go out and do the chores right quick and let you be in charge of the kitchen for a while?"

"I'm glad I'm good for something around here," she said, as she went to the pantry to find her apron. "How about biscuits and gravy to go with your eggs?"

Both men looked properly appreciative of the idea, and in mere moments she was left alone to put together the first meal of the day.

The buckskin gelding proved to be amenable to the saddle, only fighting the bit in his mouth for a matter of minutes, before he trotted placidly around the perimeter of the corral, Connor astride his back.

"I keep waiting for him to toss you off," James said from the back door of the barn. "You lucked out this time."

"I've spent a lot of hours getting him to this point," Connor said. "He carried a burlap bag of oats for several days, tossed over his saddle. Tried to get it loose, bucked and carried on for a good ten minutes before he decided it wasn't going anywhere. I'd been making up to him, babying him and giving him treats, and I think he considers me his friend by now. I wasn't too surprised to have him show off so nicely."

"You've got a real knack with horses, Connor. There's no disputing that. No wonder you've got a list of prospective customers a mile long."

"Not quite that long, but certainly enough folks lined up to keep me busy for a while." Grinning, Connor slid from the gelding and led the horse to the barn. He tied him to the back door and took his saddle off, placing it on a sawhorse. Then his curry comb and a well-worn piece of rough blanket were used to clean and dry the animal before Connor walked him.

The gelding nosed at him greedily, and Connor laughed as he pulled a bit of apple from his pocket and fed it to the gentle giant. "He's a tall one, isn't he?" He stood back and eyed the gelding. "Mr. Ryan is going to like the looks of him. He's getting him for his boy's sixteenth birthday."

"I've been lookin' at that pretty little black mare you've got out on the far side of the pasture," James said. "She's tall, a good size for a man, I'd say. Any chance of me buying her from you?"

"You'll have to fight with Loris to get that one." Connor laughed. Pride seemed to fill him as he looked across to where the mare in question tossed her head and whinnied, as if she knew she was the subject of discussion. "She's got her staked out as her own, I fear. I could have gotten a dandy price for her, but I can't do that to Loris. She doesn't ask for much, and I can spare one horse if it'll make her happy."

"Does she ride?" James looked surprised at the thought, leaning on the corral fence, eyeing the horses in the pasture. "There's a smaller gelding there that looks more Loris's size."

"She rides," Connor said, his pride evident once more. "She decided since horses were my business, she'd better be a part of it. Bought herself a pair of britches and a boy's shirt and climbed aboard that black mare. For whatever reason, she never once got bounced off. I worried that she might get some bruises, but the mare took to her like an old friend. Loris brought her apples and carrots out every day, till the mare literally eats out of her hand. She comes running when Loris slams the screen door."

"That's called spoiling a horse rotten," James said, his grin approving of Loris's actions. "No wonder the critter doesn't give her any trouble. She doesn't want to mess up the double-cross she's runnin'."

The buckskin butted Connor with his nose, nickering softly, and in return, Connor spoke softly in the animal's ear, rubbing between the wide, dark eyes with his knuckles.

"When will your buyer pick him up?" James came closer and took a turn at using the curry comb, the animal lowering his head obligingly as James approached.

"A couple of weeks now," Connor said. "I've got to work with him for a while."

"I don't have to leave for Missouri for a few weeks," James told him. "Why don't I stay here in the barn and work for you till then? I might just learn something."

Connor felt a surge of pleasure at his brother's words. "You can kill two birds with one stone that way," he said. "You'll be on hand in case of trouble and you'll be able to take some of the load from me. I'll put it about that you're living in the barn, and maybe that fact alone will give us a little protection. Maybe I'll have another man come and stay, too. I could use help with cutting the hay."

"I'll knock together a couple of cots for us if you like," James said. "You've got enough spare lumber out here to do it, and if Loris can spare another quilt, we'll be all set."

"I think there's some decent mattresses in the attic,"

Connor told him. "I'll take a look. And in the meantime, I'll let folks know that I've got two new hands staying here. No one will think much of it, especially with you sleeping in the barn. I think it'll work," he said finally, and offered James his hand to seal the bargain.

Together, the brothers put in a full day's work, and by the time supper was on the table the barn had taken on the looks of a bunkhouse. With two beds set up, two feather pillows at their heads and a decent mattress covering each of them, it was more appealing than the hayloft, James thought cheerfully.

Connor's trip to a neighboring farm netted him Ray Cromwell, a young man who'd worked for him doing haying and odd jobs around the place over the past few months, and the idea of a permanent job appealed mightily to the youth. He showed up in time for supper, apologizing for coming at mealtime, but Loris simply got out another plate and set of silverware, setting him up opposite James at the table.

They discussed what work would be done, and Connor asked his new hand to take a turn at watch during the night.

"I don't have any problem with that," Ray said quickly. "My pa was pretty shook up when y'all had the fire in the barn. He said it could have been any one of us faced with the job of rebuilding. I'll be glad to help stand guard."

Connor doubted that anyone else in the area had been in danger from the man setting their barns ablaze, but he wisely kept his mouth shut. Perhaps just the suggestion that they were guarding against any further problems was enough explanation for Ray. Knowing that

James was not alone in the barn gave Connor additional peace of mind, too.

"We're just making do for supper," Loris told the new hand, as she set bowls and platters on the table. "I made scalloped potatoes with ham leftover from dinner. But the beans from the garden are fresh and the apple-sauce was just cooked yesterday. I think it's enough to survive on for the evening."

"It looks like a feast to me," Ray said cheerfully. "My ma has been laid up lately with a case of the grippe, and Pa and me and the little ones have been makin' do in the kitchen. She's feelin' better now, and Pa said it was okay for me to leave, that they'd be fine."

"Maybe we should send a meal over there tomorrow, to lend a hand," Loris said. "I know I surely appreciated it when folks brought casseroles out here while I was abed."

"If you feel up to fixing it, I'll take it over before noon tomorrow," Connor offered. "I need to take a quick trip to town anyway." He shot a glance at James, not mentioning aloud his plan to pass the word around that there were now two men staying on the place.

"Sounds like a good plan to me," James said. "Maybe we oughta see if one of the young'uns at Ray's house would like to come and help Loris out for a few days. Might give her a break, and some company to talk to while we're out back or in the fields."

"Cora would like that, I know," Ray said. "She's a good hand at following orders and doin' housework. Helps Ma out real well. If she comes here, the other girls can lend a hand at home and take a turn at doing Cora's chores. It'd be like a holiday for her. She'd like you, Miss Loris."

Loris blushed at his words. "I wouldn't expect a lot

of her, just running up and down the stairs for me, to save me steps. And she could help with meals and the chickens. That's usually my job, feeding and gathering eggs. Connor has been doing double duty for a while now. He needs a break."

"I'm not overworked," Connor said, protesting his wife's words. "And if Cora can lend a hand so Loris can recuperate at a slower pace, I'd appreciate it."

So it was settled, and when Connor set off the following morning, he carried with him a potato casserole, with more of the ham and a good measure of cheese on top for the Cromwell family, and the promise that he would bring Cora back with him if her parents agreed.

"Cora is tickled pink to have her own bedroom," Loris said. The swing was moving slowly, Connor's foot pushing the floor to keep it in motion. The sun had set and the two men in the barn could be heard laughing together.

Connor had snatched Loris's hand and taken her to the swing, right in the midst of doing the dishes. With a promise that he would lend a hand later on with the chore, he held her in the circle of his arms, as she perched on his lap.

"I'd rather share mine with you," he whispered in her ear. "There's a lot to be said for having a pretty woman in my bed, I've found."

"Well, Cora is a bit young for that sort of thing," Loris told him sternly. "The girl is only fourteen years old. Though she acts more like a woman than girl. It must come from working at home, helping her mother keep things going. She knows how to do most everything in a house, even the cooking."

"You don't mind having her in the kitchen, do you?" Connor asked. "I wasn't about to change cooks. I sorta like the way you put meals together."

Loris shot him an arch glance. "I've noticed. It's a wonder you don't gain weight, with the food you manage to put away. Between you and James, you make it a challenge to come up with new meals. At home, my mother used to tell me what we were fixing for supper or Sunday dinner, and I just did what she told me to. Now, it's all up to me, and I keep trying to think of the things I enjoyed eating at home."

"Well, if your mother is half the cook you are, I don't doubt your father comes home for supper every night."

"Hmm…I notice you show up every time I ring the dinner bell. Either you're awfully hungry, or I'm doing something right." She attempted a grin, reveling in his words of praise.

He snuggled her closer, biting at her ear and teasing her with his nuzzling there. "You're nice to have around, Loris. I never thought being married would be such fun. I'm glad we tied the knot. Aren't you?"

She nodded, turning her face to press her lips to his. "I feel like I have the best of everything, Connor, and I wonder if I appreciate it as I should. With you and James being brothers again and my having you for a husband, I'm one lucky woman. If it weren't for my sore ribs I'd be good as new. And I will be soon," she said firmly.

"When I was a child, I used to play house with my friends, but we didn't have enough sense to recognize that a husband came along with the deal," she mused softly. "We just pretended to cook and set the table with my play dishes. We raided my father's garden for peas and green beans, and the raspberries when they ripened. I ate raw vegetables by the ton. We fed our dolls at the table and even had my mother's washroom all to ourselves, every day but Monday."

"I wish I'd known you then," Connor said. "I'll bet you were a pistol."

"Not any more than I am now," she said.

"Yeah," he said, grinning widely. "That's what I mean."

She poked her fingers in his ribs and taunted him, nibbling at his neck with small biting kisses. "I'll teach you to call me names," she said, laughing as she spoke.

"Did I ever tell you I like you just the way you are, Mrs. Webster? You can poke at me all you want, so long as you keep up the kissing part."

"Well, I'm not a pistol," she said with a pout. "I don't even know what that means."

"Oh, yeah, you are," he countered. "The very best kind." He leaned into the curve of her shoulder and nosed at the neckline of her dress, at the same time releasing the top two buttons with his hand. "You're the woman who shares my bed and turns my nights into a dream come true."

"You make me sound like a…like a hussy," she said, trying hard not to laugh, and finally not succeeding.

He caught the sound of her giggles in a simple, age-old fashion, smothering her merriment with his lips, persuading her to his will readily. And when he stood to his feet and picked her up in his arms to carry her, she merely wrapped her arms around his neck and leaned her head against his shoulder.

He closed the back door by the simple measure of leaning against it until the latch clicked, and then made his way in the darkness, up the stairs and into their bedroom. Standing her on the floor, he reached back for the door to their sanctuary and closed it quietly, setting the latch with an audible click.

"Now, young lady, we'll see just what sort of a pistol you've turned out to be," he said solemnly, his fingers busy with the rest of the buttons on her dress, opening it wide until his nimble touch persuaded it to fall to the floor. Her vest was next, then her drawers and petticoat. "I'll be careful, Loris. Just let me love you."

She was silent, watchful and trembling as he made short work of her clothing and then began on his own. Her hands lifted to clutch at his and her words halted his progress.

"Let me do it, Connor. I want to undress you."

He allowed it, giving her leave to lower his trousers and drawers, until they lay in disarray, hiding his stockings and boots. She unbuttoned his shirt and slid it from him, tossing it aside carelessly, then motioned at the bed.

"Sit down there and I'll finish the job," she said in a low, seductive voice, and he did as she asked, as if he were stunned by her aggressive behavior.

She tugged at his boots, but he soon took over, pulling his stockings off, sliding his feet from the legs of his trousers, then looked down to where she knelt between his legs, looking up at him. The room was almost in total darkness, but for the faint light of the stars and moon outside, but her features were discernible to him.

"I love you, Connor," she whispered, laying her head

against his thigh, her hands rising to touch the length of his arousal, fondling it and rubbing the taut skin in the way he liked best.

He lifted her then, stretched out on the bed and pulled her down to cover him, as he spread his legs to give her room. Skin touched skin, his rough with the abundance of dark hair he wore on his chest, hers soft and silken, her breasts flattening against him.

She wiggled to find a comfortable spot and he laughed softly. "You'd better lie still, sweetheart, or you'll be in a heap of trouble up there."

She lifted her head and he saw the flash of her teeth as she grinned at him. "I like that sort of trouble," she whispered, rising to sit astride his body. But he turned her carefully to lie beneath him. "You're not ready for this yet," he said, guiding himself until his swollen member found a home in the depths of her warmth. She shifted against him and he groaned. "Lie still, Loris. Let me do this my way." He lifted, shifting his weight from her.

And then he showered upon her his reasons for loving and cherishing his wife, his words soft and encouraging as they found their pleasure together. He whispered of her beauty, the soft comfort of her body that welcomed him, and the passion that carried them to a blessed fulfillment of their love.

It was a solemn time of communion, yet a joyous blending of bodies and hearts, and they slept with the sure and certain knowledge that their life together was truly one of love and passion and need for each other, the purity of this act of marriage ever bringing them to a deeper commitment and unity of spirit.

* * *

James and Ray rapidly formed a friendship that seemed to feed on their living in such close quarters. Their meals were taken in the house, their jokes were almost nonstop, and their admiration for Loris was obvious.

"I'm not a child," Loris protested after James had lent his opinion to her upcoming trip to town.

"He only said it wasn't wise for you to go alone," Connor told her, smiling at her show of pique.

"Surely I'm old enough to make that decision on my own," she sputtered. "I'm only going to get supplies. And Cora will make dinner."

"And surely James and I are aware of the danger you'd be putting yourself in should you take the buggy by yourself. You'd be a sitting duck, Loris. I'll change my shirt and go with you. Just wait for me and I'll harness the mare."

"I know how to put the harness on a horse," she said, glaring at him.

"I know you do. But there's no sense in you getting your dress dirty out in the barn." He went to the back porch and called for Ray. When the young man appeared in the barn door, Connor made his wishes known, that the buggy be readied for a trip to town, and received a quick nod and wave of Ray's hand in reply.

"Now see. Wasn't that easy?" Connor asked, heading inside, finding a neatly folded shirt on the clothes basket, where Loris had placed the ironing as she completed it. He took off the one he'd worn to do the chores and replaced it with the one in his hand, tucking it into his trousers neatly.

"All right," Loris complied grudgingly. "I'll let you take me to town. Just don't expect me to always be so easygoing. Once this bandage is off and the binding gone, I'll be as ornery as ever."

"I believe you," he said, winking at her with an arrogance she recognized. She relished his care of her, no matter that it got her dander up on occasion. She was feeling a bit complacent these days, she realized, with the men looking out for her, and things going along well.

It wouldn't do to relax totally, lest another attack catch them unaware.

Connor held the reins, the horse trotting placidly before the buggy, a rifle propped by his side, his alert eyes scanning their surroundings as they traveled. At the edge of town, he drew the mare to a stop and handed the reins to Loris.

"Sit right here and wait for me. I want to check something," he said. Without another word, he stepped down from the buggy and walked into a small clearing just inside a grove of trees. She saw the pale shadow of his shirt as he walked past items on the ground, watched as he bent to examine something, and then felt a sense of relief as he returned to the buggy, a frown riding his face.

"What did you find?" she asked.

"Someone's been camping out here. Not in the last few days, from the looks of it, but fairly recently. Left the remains of a campfire and some bones from a rabbit, looks like. I have to wonder if it was the man we're watching for."

"I wonder where he went from here," Loris said, looking around as if she might spot him.

"Probably long gone," Connor told her, climbing back into the buggy. "But I'm going to ask around. He's a big one, from the size of his footprints, and his horse has an odd shoe on one hoof. It's different from the other three. Looks like a part is broken off, making it crooked. I'm surprised he hasn't replaced it already."

"Well, if we see tracks out back of the pasture, we'll have to take note, and see if they match these."

"He'll be wise to steer clear of our place," Connor said gruffly. "If I spot anyone lurking around where they shouldn't be, I'm afraid I'll shoot first and ask questions later on."

Loris shivered. Connor was a peaceable man, not given to violence, yet his words sounded a warning that rang true. He'd protect his own against any intruder, and thankfully, his brother would stand behind him.

They traveled into town and Loris went into the general store. Connor dropped her off, lifting her from the buggy, and told her he'd be back to pick her up shortly.

"I'm going to see the sheriff," he said before she had a chance to ask. "I won't be long."

The store was far from busy and Loris was able to sort through the available merchandise to find the foodstuffs she needed. A bolt of fabric caught her eye and she fingered the selvage thoughtfully as she imagined new curtains at the kitchen windows made from the checkered material.

"Buy it if you want it," Connor said from behind her, his hand at her waist. "What will you make from it?"

"New curtains. We don't really need them. The old ones will do, I suppose, but it would look cheerful, wouldn't it?"

Without another word, Connor lifted the bolt of yellow-and-white checked fabric and carried it to the counter, then turned back to Loris, who had followed him apace. "How much do you need?"

She narrowed her eyes, envisioning the windows she wanted to cover. Two of them, with curtains to the sill level, a topping for each and ties to hold them back midway down. "About eight yards should do it. I'll have enough left over for an apron, too."

"How about some new dresses?" Connor asked. "You can buy them ready-made if you want to."

"Not right now," she told him. "Maybe in a couple of months." Then she turned away to instruct the store owner. "I'll need a new spool of thread, too," she said, "and a couple of rings to sew on the tie-backs."

Within ten minutes, they'd gathered up their essentials and a few luxuries Connor had chosen and made their way to the double doors of the store. She carried the light bundle with her fabric in it, and Connor had a large box of groceries.

The back of the buggy was equipped to handle the box, once he tied it in place, and Loris was lifted to the seat, where she held her bundle in her lap, her mind already picturing the kitchen with its new curtains.

"I hope we have enough vinegar to wash the windows," she said thoughtfully. "I'll bet Cora knows how."

"Shall I go back in and get some?" Connor sat beside her and waited for her response. "Was there any left over when you put up the pickles last week?"

She shook her head. "No." And then quickly changed her mind. "Yes, there is. I remember now that there was a new bottle in the pantry. I didn't use it all."

"All right." He picked up the reins and urged his mare into motion.

"What did the sheriff have to say?" she asked.

"He said he'd take a ride out later this afternoon and look the campsite over. I doubt he'll find any more than I did, but at least he'll see things firsthand. In the meantime, I'll let James and Ray know what to look for."

The three men rode across the pasture and out the back gate later that afternoon. From the porch, Loris watched them, noting their pace slowing as they neared the woods. They looked down, as if searching the ground they traveled and then all three dismounted and bent low to examine something.

After riding a bit further they headed back toward the house, still intent on their surroundings. She watched as they unsaddled their horses and led them into the barn, carrying their tack in one hand, as if the heavy saddles weighed little. And for a moment, she envied men their strength. Women were softer, not so strong, unable to lift great loads or carry the weight that a man might find light.

But with all of that, she reveled in the knowledge that being a woman gave her the power to bear children, a joy a man could never know, even though he might share in the months of pregnancy with his wife. As Connor would share with her in the months to come.

She smiled, a secret sort of triumph curving her lips as her hands rested, widespread, measuring the width of her flat stomach.

Chapter Fourteen

Alger Peterson accepted the cup of coffee from his daughter's hand and bent to kiss her cheek. "I wasn't sure I'd be welcome," he said. "But I've wanted to come out ever since you were shot. I'm glad to see you, Loris."

"Of course you're welcome, Pa. Anytime you want to visit." She waved at a kitchen chair and watched as he settled at the table, then sat down across from him. "I'm healing real well, Doc says," she told him. "I'd hoped maybe Mother would come out one day."

"She'll be all right, Loris. It just takes her a bit more time to accept things as they are. On the other hand, I'm right pleased with the way Connor's taken hold here and made himself a thriving business. He's going to be a good husband for you."

"He already is," she said. "And I'm counting on him to be a good father, too."

"I hope that comes to pass for you," Alger said. "You deserve a family."

"Pa, I'm going to have a family, maybe sooner than you realize."

His look sharpened and he sat erect in his chair. "What are you tellin' me, girl?"

"I think I'm going to give Connor a child. In about seven months, if I've got it figured right."

"What does Connor say about it?"

Loris bent her head and considered the tablecloth, then spoke quietly. "I haven't told him yet. I know he'll be worried, and he has enough on his plate right now to take care of."

"Well, give him the right to add you to his list, Loris. The man deserves to know, maybe keep an eye on you."

"I know. I've been hoping to talk about it to Mother—" She lifted her head and felt her father's silent disapproval. "I'll tell him, Pa."

"Tell him what?" Connor stood outside the screen door, peering into the kitchen. "And who are you going to tell?"

"Come on in, son," Alger said. "You're in for a surprise."

Connor shot Loris a questioning look as he opened the door. "Is Loris finally going to tell me she's pregnant?" he asked, and then moved quickly toward her as she burst into tears. "Honey, what's wrong?" he asked, kneeling beside her chair and wrapping his long arms around her. "Are you all right?"

Her head fell to rest against his as she shook her head. "This isn't how I'd planned to tell you." She lifted her face and glared at him. "How did you know? Why didn't you say anything?"

"I'm a man, sweetheart, but I'm not stupid. I can figure things out pretty good for myself. I thought when you wanted me to be in on your secret, you'd tell me."

"I wanted to be sure, first," she said, her voice a wail of distress.

"Well, *I'm* sure, if that's any comfort," he told her. "You've been acting like a banty hen lately, all set to scold everybody in sight, your feathers all in an uproar."

"I have not," she said sharply, denying his assertion. "I'm always easy to get along with."

"You're a pistol, Loris. I told you that the other day, remember?"

The look she offered him promised revenge, but her father broke into the conversation with an attempt at reason.

"Well, I, for one, think this is a dandy bit of news. Your mother will be pleased as punch, Loris, and I'm bustin' to tell her. I believe I'll head for home and give her something to smile about. I'll bet this will light a fire under her. She'll be out here to see you lickity-split."

He drank down the last of his coffee and leaned across the table to snatch up Loris's hand. "You take care of yourself, you hear now? Don't be doing too much."

"Yes, Pa, I know. And I'm sure Connor will wrap me in cotton batting and tote me around on a pillow."

Connor stood up and pulled her to her feet, hugging her carefully. "Well, you're not too far off on that, sweetheart. It's for sure I'll take good care of you." He looked across the table at Alger. "I hope you know that, sir."

"Never doubted it for a minute," Loris's father said. "I'll come out and lend a hand if you get too bogged down with work, Connor. I know you've got James and a new hired hand working here, but I'll warrant you could use someone else some days to fill in the gaps."

"I'll probably need a couple more men by this time

next year," Connor said. "If things go as I plan, I'm going to buy a few head of cattle and see what develops. I'd like to raise some Black Angus here."

"Good money in beef," Alger said quickly. "You'd have folks lined up, wanting to buy their meat from you."

"If you don't keep them around too long, they can be a profitable venture," Connor said. "I figure our pasture is lush and heavy, so it shouldn't cost too much to feed them. Hopefully, we'll just sit back and watch them grow."

"Is that all there is to it?" Loris asked innocently.

The two men laughed. "Not quite," Alger told her, "but with the branding and cutting and probably breeding, Connor will be able to use some help. Might as well be ready for the future."

"I thought you loved working with your horses," she said, frowning as she thought of Connor abandoning his thriving business.

"I do. And I'll still have my mares and the stud, and probably I'll always be training for others, but it doesn't hurt to stick an extra iron in the fire," he said.

Alger offered his hand, and Connor accepted it, shaking it firmly. "Let me know if you need me, son. I'll be available. I've about decided to close up my business, anyway. I've got a buyer for the newspaper. I'd rather be involved with yours, I think. It'll give me more of a chance to see my daughter."

Loris beamed at him. "You're always welcome here, Pa. I hope you know that."

"Now, let's have a little talk, just the two of us," Connor said briskly as his father in law rode down the lane, heading for town. Loris stood beside him at the door, and he turned her in his embrace to face him. She lifted her chin and darted a quick glance at his stern visage.

"Are you mad at me?"

He shook his head. "No, just wondering how long you were going to make me wait for your news."

"I wanted to be sure," she said haltingly. "I was worried that maybe I was wrong."

"I've been pretty sure for a week or so now," he told her.

"How did you know?" she asked.

"The same way you did, I suspect," he said readily. "You've been available to me on a regular basis for the past two months, haven't made me stay on my side of the bed for a long time now."

"I never did that," she protested. "I always sleep with your arms around me."

"Just a manner of speaking, honey," he said with a smile. "I've caught you lookin' kinda green a couple of mornings, too. Like you weren't really in the mood for cookin' breakfast."

"That's about how I felt a few times," she admitted. "But I don't care. It'll be worth anything to have a baby of our own, won't it?"

"Having a baby with you will make me feel like the luckiest man in the world, Loris. I didn't mean to scold you for not saying anything to me. I knew you were probably waiting for the right time to spring it on me."

She laughed up at him, her hands rising to cup his face, drawing it down within her reach, kissing him gently. "I love you, Connor Webster. We're going to have a beautiful child. Boy or girl, it'll be a welcomed baby."

He held her tightly, his mouth moving against hers.

"I love you, Loris. You and our baby, too." And then he was silent, offering her the comfort of his kiss, his hands warm and caressing against her body.

Howie Murdoch rode up to the farmhouse and looked in all directions before he dismounted. The back door opened and Peggy Webster stepped onto the porch. "What are you doing here?" she asked, her frown focused on him as he approached her.

"I want half of my money up front," he said gruffly. "It might be too dangerous to hang around after the fact, so I'd like to be certain of at least fifty dollars."

"You haven't done anything yet," Peggy said.

"Oh, yeah, I have," he told her. "I've made life miserable for the both of them, and the woman is still walking around like a wounded bird. I doubt she's feeling very comfortable in any way, shape or form. Those men don't let her out of their sight, and getting near enough to make her a target is proving to be a problem."

"Well, don't let them catch you at it," Peggy told him. "I don't want you involving me in this."

"You're in it up to your scrawny neck, lady," Murdoch said harshly. "Now give me my fifty dollars or I'll be pushin' you for the full amount."

"I'm not giving you anything till you show some results. Get Loris out of town and I'll come up with the whole amount."

"Don't make me mad," her cohort said bluntly. "I'm callin' the shots here."

"It's my money that's going in your pocket," she reminded him.

"I haven't seen the color of your cash yet," he said.

"For all I know, you may be double-crossin' me. You could be plotting to turn me in to the law, and get out of paying me altogether."

From the barn, her husband's voice could be heard. "Who's up there at the house, Peggy? One of the boys come home?"

"No," she shouted back. "Just a fella wanting directions."

The barn door slid open and her husband stepped out into the sunshine. "What do you think you're doing here, stranger? If you want something, come on out here. Don't be bothering my woman." And then he frowned and stepped closer. "Wait a minute. I know you. You're no stranger around these parts, even if you haven't been around for a while."

The man turned to face Amos Webster, his belligerence apparent in his stance and the harsh expression on his face. "Don't be interfering with me, mister. This ain't none of your business, anyway. This is between Mrs. Webster and me."

At Peggy's look of fright, her husband came toward the house. "What kind of a mess are you tangled up in, Peg? What's this fella doing here?"

"Nothing," she answered quickly. "I told you. He's just asking directions."

"Don't try to pull the wool over my eyes, Peg. I suspect he's up to no good." And then as Peggy shook her head mutinously, he came closer. "Is this your hired gun, Peg? This the man you found to help you get rid of Connor's wife?"

Amos's right hand fumbled a bit as he sought to draw the pistol he wore at his side.

Murdoch beat him to it and drew his pistol, halting his target in his tracks. "You see too much, Webster," he said.

"Go on back to the barn," Peggy told her husband. "This isn't your concern."

Amos's pistol was free now from its holster. "I'd say anything that goes on here is my concern. You tell your friend to hightail it out of here, Peg. I won't let you be involved in this kind of trouble any longer."

"You don't have much to say about it," the gunman said. "Don't come any closer, or I'll start by putting you six feet under."

"Don't threaten me on my own property," Mr. Webster said. His face reddened and his gun rose, and then a shot rang out and he fell to the ground, blood blossoming on his shirtfront like a bouquet of red flowers.

For a moment there was only the sound of a horse neighing in the barn and the cackle of hens in the coop. And then Peggy moved, leaping from the porch to the gravel path below. "Amos! Amos!" She turned to Murdoch and shrieked her pain aloud.

"You've killed my husband," she shouted, raising her fist to the gunman. "Get out of here, you worthless piece of—"

"I'm gone, lady. But I'll be back for my money, you just wait and see. And you'd better have it for me, or I'll let your sons know just what you've been up to."

Peggy covered her face with her hands and then dropped them to look down at her husband again. She watched through her tears as the man she'd hired rode off, then went to kneel over the man she'd killed. For even though it hadn't been her finger on the trigger, she would have sworn she felt the warmth of her husband's lifeblood on her hands, even as his hands turned cold within her grasp.

"My father is dead." Connor stood in the kitchen doorway and his face was drawn, his eyes holding a wealth of sorrow as he broke the news to Loris.

"What happened?" she asked, stunned by his words. "How did you find out?"

"The sheriff just came by and told James and me about it. Ma rode into town and said that some fella stopped at the house and got in an argument with Pa and shot him."

"Why on earth would anyone do that?" Loris crossed the kitchen floor to wrap her arms around Connor.

He leaned into her and his head dropped to rest against hers. "I don't know, honey. James hasn't any idea, either. And the sheriff said that my mother is too upset to be reasonable about it. Just keeps crying and carrying on. I think we'd better go over there, both James and me."

"I'd say that would be best," she told him. "She probably needs you, and there'll be the funeral to take care of, and all the to-do that goes with it."

"Do you want to come along?" he asked. "I really don't want to leave you here by yourself."

"I'll be fine," she told him. "I've got a lot to do today, starting with the washing. By the time I get that done, you'll probably be back. Besides, Ray will be out back, won't he? And I've got Cora in the house."

"Let me fill your washtub for you," he said. "I can do that much before I go." With a bucket in each hand, he went to the cookstove and dipped hot water from the reservoir into the empty pails, then transferred it to her metal washtub. Two buckets of cold water from the sink half filled her rinse tub, and by the time James walked up to the porch, leading two horses, Connor was ready to leave.

"Bring your dirty clothes up before you go and I'll wash them with Connor's," she told him. "Might as well get them all done at one time."

James nodded agreeably and trotted back to the barn, returning quickly with a bundle tucked under his arm. "Thanks, Loris," he said. "I appreciate it."

Using a scrub board was a hard job, but until a better way of getting clothes clean was brought to her attention, Loris decided she might as well get at the task and get it over with. Cora showed up in mere minutes, scolding Loris like a mother hen, and then took over.

A buggy pulled into the yard as Cora picked up the first basket to carry out for hanging on the line she'd strung between the trees and porch. Her load was heavy and she welcomed the chance to set the burden down at the edge of the back porch and greet Loris's company.

Her neighbor, Wilma Benson, stood beside her buggy. "I thought I'd check on you, see how things were going here," she said cheerfully. "How are you healing?" She eyed the basket of wet clothes. "Why don't I give Cora a hand hanging those and then we can sit down and talk?"

Welcoming the offer, Loris nodded and Wilma helped Cora lift the clean, wet clothing from the porch,

carrying the basket to rest beneath the clothesline. Together they emptied it within five minutes, the wind
catching the clothes and causing them to billow in the
breeze.

The two women found cups in the kitchen and Cora
made them a pot of tea, a luxury Loris seldom in-
dulged in, since Connor preferred his coffee. Once it
was brewed, Wilma led the way to the porch, and they
settled in the swing together. "Now tell me all the
news," she said, "starting with what happened to Connor's father, and then I want to know about your bullet wound."

"How did you find out about Amos?" Loris asked,
stunned to know that the news had spread so rapidly.

"The sheriff stopped by to talk to Joe. He said they
were suspicious that Peggy Webster knew more about
the whole thing than she was telling. I'm not sure what
he meant, but Joe seemed to agree. He said Peggy has
been acting real odd lately. Said the folks in town
thought she was having a hard time with both of her
boys being gone."

"I don't know any more than you do," Loris said.
"Connor and James have gone over there to check on her
and help make arrangements for their father's funeral."

"Well, I'm glad I stopped over then," Wilma said.
"Maybe I can organize some women to make food for
a funeral dinner. I'll go into town, probably in the morning, and see who'd like to help. But first, let's get your
wash done and hung."

"You don't need to be working here," Loris protested.
"I'll bet you've got work enough of your own to keep
you busy."

Wilma shook her head. "Not much. And I've been wanting to spend some time with you. Get to know you better."

"I appreciate that," Loris said. "I've needed someone to neighbor with. I've got Cora now, but she's a child."

"Good girl though, ain't she? She's been her mama's right arm for a couple of years now. Heard that her mama had the grippe pretty bad, but she's doin' better these days."

"Cora goes home every few days to give a hand over there," Loris said. "I don't have enough here to really keep her busy." She looked up as the girl came out the back door. Loris smiled. She was tall for her age and too pretty to remain unmarried for long. "She must be sorely missed at home, but well appreciated here."

"Hi, Miss Loris. I've got everything done upstairs, and I dusted the parlor. Would it be all right if I go home for a while to help my ma? Josie don't cook very good yet, and Ma is feeling kinda bad. Ray went over last night, and he told me she was in bed before dark."

"You go ahead, Cora. If you want to stay there for supper, it'll be just fine. Are you going to ride one of the horses?"

"Yes, ma'am. Mr. Connor said I could take the little brown gelding any time I wanted to. He's real gentle, and I can ride him without a saddle." She smiled at Wilma, and nodded a greeting, then turned to leave. "Will you be all right?" she asked, walking backward across the yard.

"I'll be fine," Loris told her. "Run along. Tell your ma I said hello."

* * *

It was late afternoon before Wilma climbed into her buggy and headed home. Her wave was jaunty, and she left with a promise to return soon. Loris viewed the pile of clothes she'd brought in from the line, sorting through them, separating Connor's from James's shirts and pants, and folding her own small things.

With both arms full, she climbed the stairs to her bedroom and put the stacks away in the bureau they shared, her side aching from the effort. The bed looked welcoming to her and she sat on the edge of the mattress, yawning widely, then leaned back with her head on the pillow and relaxed.

Connor should be coming in any minute, she thought, and the stew she'd cooked was simmering on the back of the stove. He and James would be hungry unless their mother had fed them, and she doubted if the woman had enough wits about her to cook a meal. She probably should have sent something along with Connor for Peggy to eat.

If Wilma went into town tomorrow and rounded up the women to cook for the funeral dinner, it would give Peggy enough to eat for a week. Despite the sorrow that was enclosing Connor and James, she couldn't help but enjoy the time she'd spent with Wilma. Talking to another woman for a change was a wonder. Cora didn't really count, being not much more than a child at fourteen. And as she thought of the girl, she heard the back door slam shut.

"Cora? Is that you?" she called.

"Ma'am?" There was a frantic tone to her voice and Loris felt a pang of fear. As Cora neared the stairway she called out again. "I just got back, Miss Loris, and when I was putting the horse in the barn—" she seemed to run out of breath and her voice trailed off. Then her footsteps pounded on the stairs and she burst into the bedroom.

"There's a fella out back, riding across the pasture. I never seen him before, but I didn't like the looks of him."

Loris's feet hit the floor and she crossed the room to the window, from which she could see the barn and beyond. The stranger was riding a pale horse, slouched in the saddle, carrying a long gun, a rifle from the looks of it.

"Is Ray in the barn?" she asked Cora.

"No, ma'am, he's not. He went on home when I did, and he ain't back yet. Should be here most any time though."

"Run down and lock the back door," Loris told the girl. "I don't know who that man is, but we can't be too careful. I'll find Connor's shotgun. He keeps it up here under the bed. I think he took his rifle with him, but I know how to shoot the shotgun."

"Yes, ma'am," Cora said quickly, leaving the room to clatter down the stairway and into the kitchen. Loris heard the door shut, waited for the thud when the bar fell into place, and breathed a sigh of relief.

Turning back to the window, she scanned the pasture for the man, and found him gone. Probably into the barn, she decided. But what he was doing there was a puzzle. If he wanted to steal a horse, there were six already in the pasture. He didn't have to go hunting for another one.

And then she saw Connor and James riding up the lane from the town road. It wound its way around the back and for about three hundred yards they were out of her sight on the other side of the house. From the barn, the man who'd apparently entered the back door through the corral slid open the wide door, at the front of the barn, and was now visible from her vantage point.

She knelt on the floor and braced the shotgun on the windowsill. If she shot it off, it would be enough to warn Connor of trouble. She pointed it toward the barn and pulled the trigger. First one, then the other. Two loud explosions rocked her, and her shoulder stung from the force of the shells leaving the gun.

The man in the doorway of the barn staggered a bit, then looked her way and lifted his own gun. His rifle aimed at her as she knelt before the window. And then, from the lane, men's voices shouted and Connor and James rode hell-bent toward the gunman.

Confused by the two men who rode toward him, guns lifted in his direction, he backed from the door and vanished into the depths of the barn.

"Loris?" Connor halted his horse halfway across the yard. "Are you all right?"

"I'm fine," she called back from the window. "I knew you'd be ready for trouble if I fired the shotgun."

Connor looked up at her. "Where's Cora?"

"I'm right here, Miss Loris," the girl said from behind her.

"She's all right," Loris called out the window. "She's with me."

Connor jumped from his horse and headed for the house, James right behind him. Their heavy boots clumped loudly on the stairs as they made their way to the bedroom, and Loris was still kneeling at the window when they came across the threshold.

Connor scooped her up, holding her against his chest and she felt the heavy thump of his heartbeat against her. His breathing was labored and he bent low to press his face to hers. "I was scared out of my wits," he whispered. "Loris, I was so frightened that something had happened to you."

"I'm all right," she managed to murmur, her own heartbeat pounding in her throat.

James lifted Cora from the floor, where she'd huddled behind Loris. Unsteady, she clung to him. "You're all right, Cora. Loris had the gun. She wouldn't have let anything happen to you."

"She was brave," Loris said, recalling the girl's actions. "She ran downstairs and dropped the bar over the back door." And then she looked up at Connor. "How did you get in the house?"

"Kitchen window," he said shortly. "I knocked out the screen and climbed through. But I doubt the gunman could have done that. He's quite a good-sized fella."

"Did you see where he went?" Loris asked. "I know he was in the barn, but I didn't see him leave."

"He hightailed it out the back and rode across the pasture to the woods," James said. "I should have followed him, but Connor and I were both frantic to get in and make sure you girls were all right."

Cora preened a bit at the inclusion with Loris. "We were fine," she chirped.

"Well, at least we've seen him, and I'm positive he was at Pa's place when he was killed. We'll catch him now," Connor said.

Loris was placed on the edge of the bed and she

smoothed back her hair and straightened her skirt. "He was at your folks' place?" she repeated. "How do you know it was him?"

"Remember the hoofprint I told you about?" Connor asked, and at his wife's nod, he went on. "The sheriff noticed them first. All over the yard, in front of the house and barn. I'll lay money that we'll find the same set of hoofprints out behind our barn in the corral."

"Well, I'm ready for a cup of tea," Loris said, rising unsteadily. Connor took her arm and led her to the door, then out into the hallway and down the stairs to the kitchen.

"If you'll sit down at the table, I'll fix it for you," he told her.

"I'll do it," Cora said, taking the kettle to the sink and pumping water into it. Placing it on the front of the stove, she left it to heat, then rinsed out the teapot and found a cup and saucer for Loris.

"My ma always likes tea when she's not feeling good or something upsets her," she said confidingly to Loris. "You just sit still and let me take care of you."

"Well, so long as you're in the mood to wait on folks, how about a cup of coffee?" Connor asked.

"Yeah, I'll have one, too." James pulled out a chair and sat down as Cora poured the hot coffee that had been left on the back of the stove since dinnertime. Strong and black, it was welcomed by both men.

"We've had an eventful day, brother," James said to Connor as he picked up his cup. The strain of their loss showed more on James, Loris thought. His face was drawn, his eyes reddened, and though he tried to present a normal facade, he was obviously shaken by his father's death.

Connor put his own cup down and reached across the table to take his brother's hand. "We'll make it," he said firmly. "Pa would want us to go on with our lives, Jamie."

Loris looked up in surprise, at the nickname Connor had used for his brother.

"You haven't called me that in a lot of years." James smiled, a slow movement of his lips reaching his eyes, softening their dark blue depths. "I think I like it."

"What are your plans?" Loris asked. "Did you decide on the funeral?"

Connor nodded. "It'll be tomorrow. The undertaker came out and got Pa, and he'll have things ready at the cemetery in the afternoon."

"Wilma said she was going to talk to the ladies in town about fixing dinner. Will your mother want it at the farmhouse? Or should we plan something in town?"

"She'll feel better in her own home," James said quickly. "I'm going to send a wire to her sister, Hazel, down near Dallas, and see if she can come up and stay with her for a while. I think she needs another woman there."

"Sounds like a good idea," Loris said. "Is she all right?"

"Yeah," Connor told her. "One of the neighbor ladies came in and will stay with her tonight. They'll take her to town for the funeral, and we'll meet them there at two o'clock in the afternoon."

"I suspect that Wilma will find out all the plans when she goes into town. I'll leave it to her to tend to the food. But maybe one of you could ride over later on and let her know to have the ladies carry things out to the farm."

"I'll go," James said quickly. "Connor had better stay here with you."

"But first of all, I'm going out back to check out that horse's hoofprints." With that, Connor pushed his coffee aside and headed for the door, James on his heels.

"I'll be going along to Joe's place," James said, and then tossed Loris a look. "I'll want to talk to Wilma as soon as we check things out in back."

They walked together across the yard, their heads tilted toward each other as they spoke together. In less than five minutes, Loris saw James heading out of the barn, watched as he lifted himself deftly into his saddle and then set off to the neighboring farm. Conner walked back toward the house, his face grim.

"Just what we thought," he said as he came in the door. "The same horse, and without a doubt, the same man." He sat down at the table again and picked up his cooled coffee. "Something's kinda rotten about this whole thing," he said. "I'm afraid my mother is involved deeper than she wants us to know."

"Don't accuse her yet, Connor," Loris said firmly. "It will work out, I know it. Right now she'll be grieving for her husband."

"Maybe so," he said, his demeanor enigmatic. "Maybe so."

Chapter Fifteen

The funeral service for Amos Webster was brief, a simple graveside ritual, with most of the townspeople gathered around the open grave. They sang several hymns, listened to the pastor of the small church read from his Bible, and then several men stepped forward to speak a few words about their deceased friend and neighbor.

Extolled in death as a hardworking man, given the title of friend by those who knew him, and mourned by his sons, Loris thought it strange that his wife should stand dry-eyed as though she were in a trance. Perhaps it was the way she could best handle the grief that had to be tearing through her mind. To lose a husband was a tragic event, even if the couple weren't as close as they might have been.

And according to Connor, his parents' marriage had not been ideal. His mother had always ruled the roost. The three men who lived there with her had bowed to her dominance, rather than argue. It hadn't seemed worth the hassle to fight with her, but once he'd learned to speak his mind, Connor had known it was time to leave and live a life of his own.

He told Loris that it had been a godsend for him to have found her the day after her parents had forced her to leave home. If he hadn't, he still might be chafing at his mother's domination of her family and their home. "I'll bet she made life a living hell for my father after both James and I were gone. And now I'm having a hard time believing that she's really mourning for him." His words resounded in her mind as Loris watched the woman who was her mother-in-law.

Peggy Webster wiped her eyes with a handkerchief edged in black, even though there were no tears in sight. The white hankie, the only bright spot in her surroundings, caught Loris's eye, and she watched as it was stuffed into the pocket of the woman's dress.

All in black, as befitted the widow she was, Peggy was the recipient of the sympathy of women from the neighboring farms, all of whom knew the struggle she would face living alone and trying to keep her husband's farm going. No doubt, she would expect James to come back and take over for his father, and Loris felt a pang of sympathy for him, thinking of the choice he must make.

Beside her, Connor was unmoving, his head bent, his thoughts his own. She reached for his hand, and he slipped her arm through his, holding her against his side.

At last the service was completed, the mourners tossing flowers into the open grave after the coffin was lowered to its waiting spot in the earth. Then two men picked up shovels and began to fill the hole that would be Able Webster's final resting place.

The ride to the Webster farm was not long, and it was traveled in silence as Connor and Loris rode in their buggy. James had chosen to travel with his mother, apparently feeling an obligation to do so. The house was ready for the crowd that gathered, and the dining room table was laden with a tempting assortment of food.

"Best looking offering I've ever seen here," Connor murmured in Loris's ear as they entered the room. "My mother was no great cook."

Loris gave him a sharp jab with her elbow and shushed him. "Behave yourself," she muttered. "For just one day, be nice to her."

"I've tried for years to do that," he said quietly. "It didn't work."

Loris couldn't have told anyone what she ate that afternoon, only that Connor fixed a plate for her and she consumed less than half of the food he'd brought her. He took her plate, placed it atop his own and managed to plow through her leftovers.

"I was hungry," he said, scraping the last of the potato salad on his fork.

"I noticed." Loris smiled. "You'd think I never fed you at home. You and James both."

That she had been the recipient of several dark looks from Peggy Webster had not surprised her. The woman had made no secret of her hatred of Connor's wife, and Loris expected nothing better from her. Even her parting shot as they left the farmhouse was designed to cause pain.

"I hope you're satisfied, young woman," Peggy said. "I'm all alone now, and you've managed to snag both of my sons."

"That's enough, Mother," Connor said sharply. "You're wrong and you know it. In fact, I'm wondering—"

"No, Connor," Loris said quickly, interrupting his words, fearful that he might make an accusation in front of the townspeople. She knew his thoughts, knew his suspicions, and even though she shared some of them, she was unwilling to make them public property. It was bad enough that Peggy's sons suspected her of plotting to harm her daughter-in-law. There was no point in dragging the whole town in on it.

Connor pressed his lips together and took Loris by the arm, thanking the young minister as he left the house. Several men came up to them as they walked toward their buggy, expressing their sympathy and their own doubts about the killing.

"We'll probably never know the whole story," Connor said to one man, a close neighbor. "Seems strange that a man should show up out of nowhere and do such a thing."

"Sounds mighty suspicious to me," the neighbor retorted. "I can't imagine your father being involved in any sort of criminal dealings, Connor. He was honest through and through."

"I know he was," Connor said firmly. "I never doubted that—or him."

"Well, he was proud of you, son," another man said, reaching to shake Connor's hand. "You've done right well for yourself. And you've sure got a pretty wife."

"I think so, too," Connor told him, looking down at Loris.

The ride home was filled with Connor's memories of his father, each of them brought to light as if Connor had decided to recall his childhood and young adulthood. He spoke of Christmases when he, James and his father went out to get a tree. He mentioned the first time he'd held his own gun, his father giving him detailed instructions on its use.

He told Loris of chopping wood, learning the proper way to handle an ax, finding himself on the business end of a hammer as he helped build stalls and attached barbed wire to fence posts.

"It's no wonder you can do so many things without even thinking about it," Loris said finally. "He gave you a complete education, taught you how to be a man, didn't he?"

"Yeah, I'd say so. Jamie was his pet, his baby, but I was the firstborn, and he gave me a certain amount of respect that Jamie never received from him. It formed a barrier between me and my brother."

"Did James recognize it?"

"He mentioned it before he left, that he knew our father respected me. The kid had never been given a chance to show his stuff. Mother had always treated him like her baby, and he went along with it, got all the spoiling."

"He expected the same treatment from everyone else, too." Loris thought of the young girls in town, how they'd flocked around the handsome youth, falling under his spell and being added to his list of conquests. She, too, had been in their midst.

"I think going away to Missouri was the best thing for him," Connor said. "He's grown up a bit. I like him now, and when he left, he wasn't worth the powder it would take to blow him away."

"Will he leave again?" Loris asked.

"He's planning on it," Connor told her. "In a few weeks."

The buggy rolled up into their yard, the horse coming to a halt before the hitching rail. Connor jumped down and lifted Loris from the seat. He held her closely against himself, his face buried in her hair, as if he inhaled her essence and was comforted.

"Are you all right?" she asked, aware of the faint trembling that gripped him.

"I'll be fine, honey. Let me put this horse away and get the buggy under the lean-to and I'll be right in. I can do chores in a little while."

"All right," she said, making her way to the house. As she opened the back door, another farm wagon pulled up at the side of the house and Cora got down, running toward her.

"My pa brought me home, ma'am. I was at the cemetery with the rest of my kin, and I told him I wanted to come back here, so he brought me. Is that all right?"

Loris held out her hand. "Of course it is, Cora. This is where you live. At least until you decide you want to go back to your parents' house."

"I like it here, Miss Loris," the girl said firmly. "And my pa says they're doing pretty good there. He said my mother's getting better, she even fixed them all breakfast this morning."

"That's good news," Loris said, pleased that the burden of tending to her family's needs had been lifted from the girl's young shoulders. "Just don't let me overwork you here, Cora. You haven't had it easy for a young woman."

"I don't mind working, ma'am," she said. "And if you need me when the baby comes, I'll stay on and help out."

Loris looked at her sharply. "How did you know about the baby? I haven't said anything to anyone but Connor and my father."

"My ma's had six young'uns since I was born, Miss Loris. I saw her bein' sick and feeling tired, and I knew when she was about give out with her swollen feet and aching back. I know all about what women go through when they have babies. And I know the look of a female who's nesting."

Loris laughed. "Is that what you call it? Nesting?"

"Sure is," Cora answered. "Just like a broody hen, fixin' up a place to lay her eggs and hatch them out. You'll see. Before long, you'll be cleanin' and scrubbin' and makin' things for the baby to wear, and pretty soon you'll be poppin' out of your clothes again, and Mr. Connor will have to buy you some new dresses to wear."

Loris shook her head. "I have a few dresses that will fit me for a while. But I'm glad you're here to keep track of me and look after things. I'm an amateur at this whole thing, you know. I've had one baby, but I can hardly remember the months passing. I was so unhappy, and then so busy being a bride and taking care of a new husband, I didn't pay a lot of attention to what was really going on with my body. Except for enjoying the fact that I was having a baby, I never really knew what was normal and what wasn't."

"Well, it's a good thing I'm here, then." Cora fluffed her hair a bit and went to the sink to wash her hands. "Why don't you just sit down now, Miss Loris, and let me fix you some tea. I'm thinking you won't want much to eat after that spread at Mrs. Webster's place, but tea always hits the spot, my mama used to say."

Connor came in the back door as Loris's tea was poured and she turned to him. "Do you know that bringing Cora here was one of the smartest things we've ever done?"

Not knowing what brought on Loris's enthusiasm, Connor was wise enough to agree with his wife, nodding his head and including both females in his approval. "She sure is a spot of sunshine," he agreed. "I'm glad she's made it her business to take care of you, Loris."

Cora brought sugar and cream to the table, obviously enjoying the compliments coming her way. She found a cup for Connor and poured him the last of the coffee in the big pot, then sat down at the table.

"James will be along shortly," Connor said. "He stayed for a while to talk to some folks he hadn't seen lately."

"Well, I, for one, am about ready for bed," Loris said, sipping at her tea, stifling a yawn as she looked outdoors where the sun had disappeared beneath the western horizon. Bands of golden- and pink-hued clouds had settled in the dark blue of the sky, following the sun to its rest, and she stood, walking to the window, the better to see the beauty of twilight coming on.

Connor came to stand behind her. "My father will never again look up at the sky and see the stars and moon," he murmured. "I can't believe he's gone, Loris. And I won't rest until I find out what really happened to him."

A pall hung over them for several days, and Loris tried to think of some way to brighten Connor's life. She watched him go about his chores, noted the lack of enthusiasm for his animals, and mourned the days gone by, when their lives were filled with laughter and the knowledge of everything being right in their world.

Now he fretted over his mother, worrying that she wasn't able to do the work at the farm, wondering if she would sell it, or try to keep it running. James seemed to be on the same track as his brother. Between them they made several trips to the farm to check things out, and both came back with aggravation clear on their faces.

"She's as stubborn as ever," Connor said.

"Am I still the rotten apple in the barrel?" Loris asked. "Do you think I'll ever be able to win her approval?"

"I thought maybe knowing you were going to have a baby might help, so I told her about it," Connor said, "but she didn't seem to care. Just nodded and said she hoped things would go well this time."

"There's no pleasing the woman. First she wants the girl out of the way, then she blames me for her husband's stupidity, and now she's acting like a loony." His litany of anger aimed at Peggy Webster, Howie Murdoch sat next to his campfire, vowing that he would earn his money in the next few days and then leave for greener pastures. The Webster girl was pretty well protected by her menfolk, but he'd catch her alone outdoors and put a bullet in her if it was the last thing he ever did.

And then let the old lady try to wiggle out of her bargain. He'd take that house apart if need be, and someway he'd get his money out of her, with maybe a little extra thrown in for interest. He'd been living on promises long enough. He put out the fire, tossing the contents of his coffeepot on the smoldering ashes, and stood up. In moments his horse was saddled, the bit in his mouth, and he set off for the woods behind Connor Webster's place.

He'd found a tree near the edge of the grove behind Connor's pasture, one with large branches, easy to climb and with a comfortable arrangement that supported his back while he watched the house and awaited his opportunity. He'd have to set up there every day for a while, maybe, in order to get a chance at the woman, but it would be worth it.

He climbed the tree easily, after having tied his horse deeper in the woods. His view of the house and the backyard was clear and unfettered by branches, those that had been in his way now lying on the ground where he'd dropped them.

The back door opened and the young girl they had working there came outside, a basket over her arm. Damn. The Webster woman had always gathered the eggs. Now it looked like she had somebody else doing her work for her. He watched as the girl, barely more than a child, went in the henhouse and came out with her basket laden.

She put it on the ground and took a measure of grain from the barrel beside the chicken yard and tossed it through the fence to the cackling hens who gathered there for their morning's feeding. A bucket of water from the well was poured into the trough provided next to the fence, extending into the backyard, making it simple to feed and water the birds without entering the enclosure itself. Then as he watched, the girl went back in the house.

In a few minutes, the door opened again and Loris came out to hang some towels on the clothesline stretched across the porch. He cursed his timing, knowing he should have been ready for her appearance, should have held his rifle in a good position to fire. And then he settled back to wait.

He watched as the two brothers went from barn to house, thinking gleefully that they both made perfect targets should he decide to finish them off as he had their old man. But that wasn't in the bargain. Only the woman would earn him the cash money he had coming. Maybe he'd come back and shoot the brothers after he had his hundred dollars. Kind of like a bonus for the old lady. He could just see her fury if he killed her sons.

Finally, the men left the house again and went back to the barn, reappearing out the back door of the structure, heading through the corral and into the pasture where half a dozen young horses romped. Connor held a rope and selected one of the group, tossing his loop accurately and bringing the young mare before him. He tied the length of rope to her halter and led her in a series of training maneuvers, designed to ready her for the saddle and the weight of a man on her back.

Bringing her into the corral, he tossed a blanket on her back, then offered her the weight of a light saddle. She balked a bit, but Connor took her halter and seemed to be speaking to her, and she quieted, allowing him to tighten the cinch. Again, he led her around, and then seemed to surprise her with a heavy bag of oats tossed across her saddle. She sidestepped, but he persisted, and soon she was trotting at the end of his lead rope, making a circle around him.

"Fool man plays with those horses all day instead of being out earning a living," the watcher muttered, feeling more than a rush of envy toward the man who was known as the top horse trainer in the area.

And then he saw a flash of color at the house, watched as the screen door opened and Loris Webster stepped onto the porch. She shaded her eyes with her uplifted hand and scanned the horizon, perhaps looking for her husband.

"It'll be the last time you look for him," the man said, lifting his rifle and propping it against a sturdy branch. He took aim, his scope pinpointing her chest, just below her left shoulder…and pulled the trigger, just as Loris bent to pick up something from the porch. She was knocked from her feet by the bullet that hit her and fell to the wide boards beneath her feet. He couldn't tell if he'd missed his target or not, with the fool woman ducking when she did.

But the explosion was enough to wake the dead, the gunman thought gleefully, and sat back to watch the results of his single shot. Connor and James came full tilt from the barn door, heading for the house at a full run. The young girl came out the door and dropped to the floor beside the fallen woman and touched her face, then lifted a bloody hand.

He hadn't aimed at her head, but at her heart, and the sight of blood pooling beneath her head startled him. No matter. A head shot would do the trick.

He climbed down from the tree, rounded up his horse and rode through the woods to the main road leading to town. He'd get a room at the hotel and then go out to see the old lady and get his loot. He could afford a dollar for a hotel room once the old lady paid him the hundred dollars she owed him.

* * *

"Miss Loris. Oh, Miss Loris, look at me," Cora sobbed loudly, wiping her bloody hand distractedly on her dress. "Mr. Connor, come quick," she called, even as the two men reached the porch and leaped to its surface.

"Where is she shot?" James asked, looking behind him, out past the pasture where the shot had originated. The sound could not be mistaken, a rifle bullet fired from beyond the right side of the pasture, probably in the stand of trees.

"Her head," Connor said shortly. "Looks like just a graze. I can't imagine why he missed his target."

"Well, thank the good Lord he did," James said fervently. "Is she out cold? Should we get her in the house?"

"Yeah, hold the door open, Cora, and I'll carry her in. James, you go for the doctor, and I'll see what I can do for this wound."

Cora held the door, then ran to find a basin and hot water. A clean towel over her shoulder, she followed the path Connor had taken with Loris, into the parlor, where he'd placed her on the sofa, then slipped her shoes from her feet. A knitted throw over the back of the sofa was covering her, lest she be cold, and Connor was kneeling by her side.

"This is twice he's shot you," he growled beneath his breath. "And I couldn't manage to do anything about it either time. But I swear to you, Loris, as God is my judge, the man won't get away with this."

Cora watched, wide-eyed, holding the basin, then finally placing it on the floor next to Connor. He looked up at her and nodded his thanks, then dampened the towel and began wiping his wife's face, soaking up the blood that had finally begun to congeal on the side of her head. It was a shallow wound, but she was still unconscious, and he worried that she might not rouse.

And then he thought of the baby she carried and his heart sank within him. If she should lose the child, she would be bereft. And Loris bearing that kind of sorrow again was more than he wanted to consider.

His towel rinsed in the basin, he watched as Cora took it away and reappeared in moments with clean water for his use. He washed Loris's head again, then sent Cora for a clean, dry towel to hold against the wound. The girl complied without hesitation and Connor folded the fabric and held it tightly, knowing the blood had almost stopped flowing.

He bent low over Loris, kissing her cheek, her forehead, uncaring of the specks of blood he'd missed, only concerned that his wife should live, that their child should survive this attack. Beside him, Cora dropped her hand to his shoulder and murmured words of encouragement.

"She's gonna be all right. I've seen worse than this before, Mr. Connor. The bullet looks like it only grazed her, just enough to knock her cold. She's better off this way, anyhow—she's not feeling any pain. And I'll guarantee you she's gonna have one mighty headache when she does wake up."

"Thanks, Cora. I know you're right, but I sure wish the doctor would get here. We've already gotten her through one bullet wound, and I swore she'd never suffer so again."

"Well, don't be blaming yourself for this," Cora

said. "She said you was tryin' to wrap her in cotton batting, but that don't always work, you know. She had to step out the door sometimes, and besides, if a fella was after her, he'd have found a way somehow to take aim at her."

"I'm sure glad his aim was off this time, too," Connor said, remembering the doctor's words when Loris had been wounded the first time. The bullet had only missed her heart by inches, and again the unknown gunman had somehow missed his intended target, for Connor knew without a doubt that he had aimed to kill. And that thought made him sick with fear for the woman who lay before him.

James must have ridden like the wind and found the doctor without any problem, Connor decided, when the two men came in the house. Relieved at the appearance of the doctor, Connor stood and held out his hand.

"I'm sure glad you were available," he said.

"What's going on out here?" the doctor asked. "I just got her healed up from the last time, and here we are again."

"Well, we'll soon find out who's at the bottom of these attacks," James said firmly. "I'm about to leave right now and start tracking the fella."

"I'll be following right shortly," Connor told him. "As soon as the doc tells me Loris will be all right here with Cora, I'll saddle up and be right behind you."

James nodded, casting one long last look at Loris and then left the room. The back door banged shut and the doctor knelt by the sofa. "I can tell you right now, she's probably going to be fine in a week or so, Connor. Unless she's wounded somewhere else, other than this graze on her head, she's in decent shape. You've already done about all you can do. I'll put some salve on the thing and bandage it up, and plan on coming out here tomorrow to check on her."

He bent low over Loris, listening to her heartbeat, checking her eyes and shaking his head slowly. "She may have a little concussion from this. You'll have to keep her on her back for a few days, make her stay in bed and behave herself. No shenanigans, either. You got that, son?" He looked up at Connor, a speaking glance, and was given a nod of agreement in turn.

"One more thing, Doc," he said quietly. "She's gonna have a baby. Will this hurt him?"

With a slow shake of his head, the medical man gave his opinion. And then added for good measure, "I doubt it. The bullet didn't harm any vital organs, and unless Loris has already been having trouble, this shouldn't cause her to lose it. No guarantees, but that's my opinion."

Connor dropped his head, his eyes closing as he offered thanksgiving for his wife's close escape from death. And for the news that his child would probably be safe and secure within Loris's healthy body.

The doctor spoke more cheerfully. "Now, let this young lady sit here and keep an eye on things, and you go look for your man, Connor. We need to get to the bottom of this whole mess. First your pa, and now this. There's someone out there who needs to pay for all this trouble."

Connor nodded and stood, then bent low once more to kiss Loris on the forehead. "Keep a close eye on her, Cora," he said. "I won't be too long, I hope."

* * *

The trail was easy enough to follow, the tree bark scraped where someone had climbed into a pocket above his head, Connor noted. And a bit farther in the woods was evidence of a horse that had been tied in one place for more than a few minutes. A horse that had three hoofprints that were similar, and one that fit the pattern he had expected to find.

James was evidently hot on the man's trail, and Connor had no trouble following the path he'd left behind. It led all the way to town, where Connor caught up with him. It was there they saw the horse they sought, tied in front of the hotel. The brothers both went across the street to the sheriff's office and, leaving their own horses out front, went into the single room where the town's lawman did his business.

"Well, what's goin' on out to your place, Connor? I heard that James came to town to get the doctor. You got some kind of sickness out there?"

"No, something even worse," Connor said harshly. "Someone shot Loris again. Twice is too many times, Sheriff. James and I followed the man to town and his horse is over in front of the hotel right now."

The sheriff rose from his desk and peered out the window. "I don't see a horse over there," he said. "Must have ridden off in the last minute or so."

"Damn." Connor, not given to cursing, found himself searching for enough words to express his anger. "Let's go, James."

"Now hold on here a minute," the sheriff said. "I'll go with you."

"You can follow us," James said. "We're gone."

"I want to check in the hotel first," Connor said. "It'll only take a minute." He led his horse across the street and handed the reins to James, who was at his side, then walked through the doors of the establishment, approaching the desk.

"Yessir, Mr. Webster. What can I do for you?" the young clerk asked.

"Who was the fella who just left here?"

The clerk frowned. "I'm not supposed to give you that information, but I reckon it won't hurt anything. I don't know who he is, but his name is Howie Murdoch. A stranger hereabouts, I guess. He took a room and said he'd be back later on. He'd better be back. Hasn't paid for the room yet."

Connor thought for a moment. "His name is Murdoch?" At the clerk's nod of agreement, Connor's eyes narrowed. "There used to be a family lived not far from our place by that name. The old man was a rascal, my pa always said. He'd do anything for a five-dollar gold piece, up to and including robbery. Like the night he raided the church when they were having a strawberry festival out back, and he stole the offerings from Sunday."

Connor remembered vividly the occasion. "He got caught, too. Spent some time in a cell for that one. If he's the man I'm looking for, I wouldn't put anything past him."

"I thought the name rang a bell with me, but I wasn't sure," the clerk said.

"Well, you trot yourself across the street and tell the sheriff what you just told me, son. Tell him I've gone after the man."

"Yessir," the clerk said dutifully. "I'll do that."

James was ready to ride, and when Connor lifted himself into his saddle, he could only follow his brother, the younger man already three hundred feet ahead of him. He caught up readily enough and told James what he'd found out, bringing a scowl to his brother's face.

"That fella that used to live down the road about a mile when we were kids? Is that who we're looking to find?" he asked gruffly. "He was always in trouble of one kind or another, wasn't he? In fact, I remember how glad Pa was when the family moved away. I wonder what brought him back here?"

"We may never know for sure, but I'd be willing to bet that Ma hired him. She was determined to get rid of Loris, one way or another."

"But not Pa," James said quietly. "I don't think that was a part of the deal."

"You're no doubt right. She wouldn't have done anything to hurt him. Used to yell a lot and make his life miserable sometimes, but I don't think she'd have let anything happen to him if she could help it."

"Well, it sounds like things got out of hand, doesn't it?" James said as a statement of fact.

"Yeah, I'd say so," Connor agreed.

They followed the tracks past the edge of town, and within minutes, the knowledge of where they were heading made itself known to both of them. "He's headin' for Ma's farm," James said, shooting a look at Connor, as if seeking agreement of his theory.

"Sure looks that way, doesn't it?"

* * *

The farmhouse was quiet when Murdoch rode up to the back porch, and he waited impatiently until the door opened and Peggy appeared on the threshold.

"Haven't you caused enough trouble?" she asked harshly, glaring at him. "Killing my man was way beyond what you were hired to do."

"He got in the way. He was threatening me, Miz Webster. You heard him yourself. It was self-defense."

"He wasn't any kind of gunman, Murdoch, and you know it."

"Well, the woman wasn't either, and you won't be cryin' about it when I tell you I got her in my sights and pulled the trigger."

"Loris?" Peggy looked stunned. "You shot Loris again?"

"Ain't that what you hired me for to begin with?" he asked. "I did what you wanted and I come to collect my hundred dollars."

"How do I know you're telling the truth?" she asked bitterly. "You haven't any proof."

"You just take a ride over there, or into town and you'll find out," he said.

"And leave you here to rob me blind while I'm gone?" she asked. "I don't think I'm quite that stupid."

From around the corner of the house James's voice sounded, loud and clear. "You were stupid enough to hire this gunman to begin with, Ma. He's killed our father and tried twice to murder Loris, not to mention burning down Connor's barn and causing him to be laid up for weeks."

He stepped around the corner, Connor at his heels,

and pointed his pistol at Murdoch. "I'd say you've done about enough damage, Murdoch."

"What are you talkin' about? I ain't done nuthin'," the man shouted, glaring in turn at the two men and then back at Peg. "Yer ma is the one who dreamed everything up. Just ask her."

Connor looked up at Peg then as she opened her mouth to speak. "Did you really hire Murdoch to kill my wife?"

"No, not to kill her. I just wanted her frightened away, so she'd leave town and you'd come back home where you belonged."

"I would have crawled in the grave with her rather than go home to you."

"She's dead now anyhow," Murdoch said with satisfaction.

"That's where you're wrong," James told him. "She has a scalp wound, just a graze, and she'll be fine in a week or so, according to the doctor."

"I saw her fall," Howie Murdoch said, spewing the words in anger.

"She fell, all right, but you missed your target." Connor pulled his own gun from its holster and approached the man who had killed his father. "Now you're going into town to see the sheriff." He looked at his mother. "Do you want to come along and let him know what happened out here, Ma? It might be easier if you tell the sheriff yourself instead of him coming out here to get you."

"I'll go along," she said, her voice tired, her shoulders slumping as if she had aged twenty years in the past few minutes. "I'm sorry for what I did to you and Loris, Connor. I had no right to cause trouble for the girl. I should have left the two of you alone and taken care of things here instead of wishing for things I couldn't have. I knew it was wrong, but I was just so angry at her."

"Ma," James began, his voice low and filled with pain. "She didn't do anything to hurt you. I was the one at fault, not Loris. She could have been the daughter you never had, if you'd only given her a chance."

"Maybe so," Peg said sadly. "It's too late now."

"It's never too late for some things," Connor said, thankful for James and his words, acknowledging his own fault in the matter.

"Now, get on your horse, Murdoch," Connor said. "We're going to town. James, hitch up Ma's buggy so she can come along. You can tie your gelding on the back and drive her in."

"Right," James said quickly. "I won't be but a few minutes, Ma."

Howie Murdoch climbed into his saddle and glanced once more at the gun pointed at him. "We'd make this a whole lot easier if I just took off and made you shoot me," he said with a laugh.

"I don't think so," Connor told him, snatching up Murdoch's reins and leading his horse to the side of the house where his own mount was waiting. "Ma's seen enough blood in her backyard to do her for a lifetime. As filthy a piece of scum as you are, I won't dirty up her ground with you. The sheriff will know what to do."

And he did, placing Howie in a cell, searching him for weapons first to guarantee that he'd be free of trouble to his jailers. "He'll last till the judge shows up," he told Connor. "I wouldn't have believed it was him if the fella from the hotel hadn't told me who you were after. I'm glad we've finally got this whole thing cleared up.

And I'll run your mother on home after we've had a little talk, boys."

Connor nodded and bent to kiss his mother's cheek. "I'll be by later," he said, and stepped back for James to say his goodbyes. The brothers left together, riding down the middle of the street, heading for home.

Chapter Sixteen

"What will happen to her?" Loris felt torn between wanting to help Connor's mother and banishing her from their lives. She was without words to tell Connor and James how she felt. One minute she cared a great deal, the next moment she was filled with anger at the conniving woman who'd carried on against her.

Not just Loris, but the sons she'd borne and raised, the family she might have surrounded herself with, had she only opened her eyes to see the truth of things. And now Peggy Webster was in a cell in the county jail, waiting for the judge to come and pronounce his sentence upon her. For there would be no trial. She had admitted her guilt, not only to her sons, but to the sheriff. There would be no turning back.

"What will happen?" Conner repeated Loris's query. "What do you think, James?" he asked. "You've been away from home and seen how things go in other places. What will the judge do to our mother?"

James looked stricken. "I've been trying not to judge her myself, and I keep coming up with the facts. They all point to her guilt, to a woman who deliberately put her son and his wife in peril. Do you realize how close both of you came to losing your lives?"

Connor nodded. "Especially Loris. She was the target all three times Murdoch caused trouble. At Ma's instigation. I can't just sweep that under the rug. I love Ma, but Loris is my wife and my first allegiance is to her, no matter what." Connor turned to Loris. "If I think you're in danger from her, then I'd say put her away somewhere."

"And do you think I am? Do you *really* think so, Connor? Or are you speaking from the memory of what has already happened to me. Will she ever repeat her actions? Can she be trusted now? And could you be happy, knowing your mother was locked away somewhere?"

"Could you?" he asked. "If it were your mother, could you?"

"My mother put me out in the snow," she reminded him. "I might not have lived through the night if I hadn't found shelter."

"Damn," James said vehemently. "That it was *my* fault."

"My mother made a choice. Her judgment was against me, not you. And my father led the attack. If I had died, would I have wanted her to spend the rest of her life in jail? I don't think so. I'd have to balance her actions that night against all the years of care she gave me, the upbringing I had in a loving home, and a set of parents who truly cared about me."

"Until you made a mistake," James said. "And then they turned their backs on you."

"I'm sure my mother would have suffered for the rest

of her life, remembering what she might have done that night. The same way your mother will suffer the rest of her life, knowing she caused her husband's death and harmed her own son."

"You have a forgiving spirit, Loris," Connor said quietly. "I'm hopeful you would judge me in the same way, should I ever make mistakes in the future, that might bring harm or great hurt to you."

"It's because I love you, Connor. I feel that way about your mother because the Bible says we must forgive those who do evil against us. And I believe that."

"Will you talk to the judge?"

He looked hopeful, and she could not let him worry longer. "Of course, I will, Connor. I'll do whatever I can to help her."

"Don't ask me to go back and live with her," James said, his eyes full of wrath. "She might as well have pulled the trigger that killed my father, and I can't forgive her for that."

"I didn't figure you'd go back to the farm," Connor said. "I thought you'd be off to Missouri in a few weeks."

"You've got that right," James said, his jaw firm, his hands clenched atop the table. "I'll make sure you're all set for winter here, Connor. We'll get the hay taken care of and the stalls finished up. If those Black Angus get here before I leave, I'll help with a lean-to out back for shelter for them. A place to hold their feed, so you won't have to drive clear across the acreage to feed them all winter."

"No, I'll keep them close to the barn, at least for the first year or so," Connor said. "I should have six cows carrying calves, eight heifers and a young bull showing up any day now. The heifers will be ready to breed in the spring, and we should have six young calves about the same time."

"This is gonna be a busy place," Loris said. "Is Ray going to stay on and work for you, Connor?"

"Yeah," he said, "and I'll need to find someone else to fill in the gap once James is gone." He looked at her with a smile curving his lips. "You aren't going to be much help rounding up cattle for the next few months."

"But just think of the project I'll be working on for you," she said with a smile.

James was silent, and for a moment, Loris felt for him. One day he would find a woman to love. She suspected he would never be truly happy until he was married with a home of his own.

"Prepare yourself for a lot of coddling in the next months," Connor told her. "You for sure won't be working out in the barn. In fact, gathering eggs is about as strenuous as your work is going to get. You've got Cora here to dust and sweep, and do the heavy chores."

"Just hold on, mister," Loris said. "I'm not an invalid. I'm just pregnant, and on top of that, I'm a strong woman, healthy and capable. You won't be tying me down to a life of leisure. I won't have it."

"Did I tell you she's got a stubborn streak?" Connor said to James, and the two men laughed.

Loris fumed and turned to the stove. "Well, since I'm not allowed to work around here, I'll just forget the supper I was putting together for both of you. I'm sure Cora and I can find something to fill us up without me straining myself stirring and slicing and doing all those things that go into the making of a meal."

"I didn't say you couldn't *cook*, Loris."

She glared at Connor, turned on her heel, and swept from the kitchen. The stairs seemed long as she climbed, and she found that the hallway was dark, although the doorknob on her bedroom door gleamed dully. Opening the door, she stepped into her bedroom, then slid to the floor in a heap.

Her tears overflowed, and she felt a deep sense of shame. The sound of heavy footsteps outside her door, coming from the stairway, caught her ear and she sat up, wiping her nose on the dish towel she'd thrown over her shoulder. Connor came in the room, almost tripping over her as she sprawled inelegantly in front of him.

"Loris. Are you all right?" He knelt beside her. "Did you fall?" And as her head shook in a negative reply, he lifted her to her knees beside him. "You're crying," he said, his words soft, his hands tender against her skin.

"You don't usually shed tears unless something has really upset you, Loris. Was it my stupid remarks? I didn't mean to make you angry. I just don't want you to be doing too much. And I know that cooking is a hard job. I wouldn't begin to try it, and I appreciate what you do in the kitchen."

He halted his long monologue and lifted her chin, the better to see her face. "Loris? Aren't you going to answer me? I don't know how to fix things unless I know what's broken."

She turned her head away and sniffed, then lifted the dish towel to her nose again.

"Here, use my handkerchief," he said. "Don't wipe your nose on the towel."

"I'll wipe my nose on anything I please," she said

smartly. "I do the laundry, in case you've forgotten. I can wipe my nose on anything I want to."

"I know that," he said, stifling a smile as best he could. Watching his mouth twitch was the final straw, and she jerked away from him.

"Just leave me alone," she said. "You don't have to fuss over me or treat me like a child. I'll take care of myself, just see if I don't. I've even been thinking about using another room to sleep in, so I won't disturb you with my tossing and turning."

"Now there," he said harshly, "is where you're wrong. You will not take care of everything by yourself, nor will you do whatever you please. You'll allow me to pamper you, let Cora wait on you and clean up the messes around here, and then you'll climb into my bed every night."

"Since when are you in charge of whatever I do?"

"Since the day you promised to love, honor and obey me. Or have you forgotten?"

"No, but I've decided that speaking that word was a big mistake."

"Well, you said it, before God Almighty and witnesses, and you're going to stick to the bargain we made together. Like it or not."

Then, as if he regretted his words, he pulled her close. "I love you, Loris. I hope you know that."

She kissed his cheek, his throat, his lips and whispered against his ear, soft words of love that pleased him. He lifted her to the bed and pulled up the quilt. And then, as if she were knocked insensible, she was asleep. Her mouth opened a bit, releasing soft sounds that told him of her slumber, and he held her close.

* * *

The judge met with Peggy Webster's family in the jailhouse, asking each of them questions that were designed to decide on her future. The morning train had brought a visitor to town, a woman greeted with exuberance by Connor and James both. Their aunt, Peg's sister Hazel, arrived, bag and baggage, and primed to stay for a while.

She wanted to have a say in the proceedings before the judge and both boys were in favor of hearing what she had to say. Peggy was happy to see her sister, and was obviously already making plans to share her home with her.

Connor spoke before the judge first, telling of his mother's care of her family for all his growing-up years. James was next, giving examples of Peggy looking after the boys, helping with schoolwork and keeping them in clean clothing. They both told of the love and concern their parents felt for each other, and the loving home they had grown up in.

And then it was Loris's turn, and she sat quietly before the judge. "What is your opinion of this whole thing?" he asked her.

"I'll tell you what I told the boys," she said. "Their mama made mistakes aplenty, but she loved her family and wanted the best for her sons and her husband. She can't be faulted for that. She was wrong to do what she did, but maybe her mind was not working as it should have been. She was unhappy and missed her sons, and she needed someone to blame. That someone was me, and it didn't help matters when I married Connor and caused friction between the two boys."

"What could you have done differently?" the judge asked.

Loris shook her head. "I don't know. I honestly don't know. But what I do know is that I'll be forever guilty if she goes to jail because of me, because I loved her son and married him. I caused trouble between a mother and her sons, and I don't know what I would have done if I had been Peggy Webster."

"Thank you, young lady," the judge said, clearing his throat loudly. "I'll talk to Mrs. Webster's sister now, and the rest of you can listen in if you like."

Hazel sat in a chair and arranged her hands nicely in her lap. "Peg and I go back a long way," she said. "We never got along too well when we were young, but after we both married and moved from home, we made things right between us, and now we've turned the corner and we're pretty good friends. I think I could live with her, and between the two of us we could handle things at the farm. Or else, if she wants to, we can go back to my place in Texas and live there. I closed the house up for this trip, but it's easy enough to go back and turn the key in the lock if we want to."

"I think, Miss Hazel, you may have solved the problem we have here."

He rose and opened the door that led to the rest of the jail and Peggy stood facing him. "Come on in, Mrs. Webster," he said. "Did you hear the evidence your sons and Connor's wife have given me? And your sister?"

"Yes, I have," she whispered. "And I think Loris is a generous woman, taking the blame for my sins. I was wrong to try to harm her, and I'm sorry. I wish it wasn't too late to start all over again, but I know I'll be punished for my wrongdoing."

"It may not be too late for you," the judge said, peering at her through his spectacles. "I think I'm going to put you on probation, especially since Loris and Connor aren't going to press any charges against you. I'm going to send you to Texas with your sister Hazel, to live there for an undetermined length of time. You'll be answerable to the sheriff in her town on a weekly basis for a few months, and I'll check up on you every month, by having the sheriff send me a wire and tell me how things are going with you. Until such time as you and your sister leave here, I expect you to accept Connor's wife and treat her well."

Peggy Webster looked stunned, her eyes reddened, her face swollen from the tears she'd shed over the past few days. "I've mourned my husband, Judge, and I've wept bitter tears over my actions. If I have the chance to make things right, I want to do just that," she said. "And if going home with Hazel is your decision for me, then I'll do it, if she's agreeable."

"You have the chance to turn your life around, ma'am," the judge said. "Just use it wisely. I'll notify the sheriff in Hazel's town that you'll be there, and it'll be up to you to report to him weekly."

"Yes, sir," Peg said quietly. "I'll do that."

"Well, I'm more than agreeable to taking her home with me," Hazel said. "The boys can do what they want with the farm here, I suppose."

"I'll sign it over to them and they can sell it," Peg said. "It would have been theirs anyway, once I'm gone." And as if she were relieved to have things settled, she hugged her sister and shook hands with the judge.

The sun was shining brightly when she walked from the jailhouse and met her sons on the sidewalk. Loris stood between them and it was to her that Peggy went. She touched her daughter-in-law's hand and held it to her lips. "Thank you, Loris," she said. "Thank you for forgiving me. I want to be friends with you. Do you think that can ever happen?"

"My child will need a second grandma, besides my mama," Loris said. "One is never enough, you know. I think we'll get along fine, ma'am. And when you've gone, I'll write to you and we can keep in touch."

Peggy released her and turned to her boys in turn, touching their faces with her fingertips and asking their pardon for the evil she had done. Connor and James were not as forgiving as Loris, but they were in agreement that she should go home and make ready to move. It was agreed that they stop at the town lawyer's office and let her sign away her rights to the farm and the acreage that surrounded it. It was a major decision for her to make, but she seemed ready to do as she'd agreed.

James offered to take her home, since her horses and chickens and the cow needed to be tended by dark. He'd gone over daily to look after things while Peg was in the jailhouse. Now she would begin arrangements to sell the livestock and begin packing.

It was full dark by the time Connor and Loris arrived home, the lights in the house ablaze, Cora not liking to be in the dark. They went in quietly, lest she be asleep, but found her, instead, in the kitchen keeping supper warm for them. James arrived while they were eating, and Cora pulled another plate from the warming oven for him.

Chores were done, the horse put up for the night, and Loris and Cora sent off to bed, before the brothers sat down at the table to talk.

"I won't be here much longer, Connor."

"I figured about two more weeks," Connor said. "You don't have to leave on our account, you know."

"I made a promise to my boss in Missouri. Told him I'd be back to finish out the year. I don't know what I'll do after that, but I've got a mighty yearning to go to Texas. We'll see what happens. Whatever I decide, I'll let you know."

"All right. I'll miss you, you know," Connor said. "You'll always be my best friend, Jamie. You'll always be Loris's brother. I hope you know that."

"You're a forgiving kind of guy," James said with a laugh. "You must have been reading Loris's Bible."

"Once in a while," Connor told him agreeably. "I hear it read in church on Sundays, you know."

"I'm going over to see Ma in the morning," James said. "I need to give her a hand getting things organized before I leave."

"All right. We'll do fine. Most everything is done out back and I've got two men coming before the end of the week to pick up horses. Business is good, James. I'll hate having you miss the Black Angus when they show up."

"You'll do well, Connor. Beef is a good business to get into."

"If I need you…"

"If you need me, I'll be here," James said staunchly.

"Thanks, brother."

Connor stood and waved toward the back door. "Morning comes early," he said.

"Yeah," James said, "and you've got a pretty little wife waiting for you upstairs."

"You got that right." Connor's eyes twinkled as he closed the door behind his brother and turned to make his way up the stairs. It was time to look after Loris, to take care of her and their soon-to-be-born child.

Epilogue

"**Y**ou've got a beautiful baby girl, Connor," the doctor said, his grin a mile wide. Beside him stood Loris's mother, anxious to hold her first grandchild. But the doctor had other ideas. After cutting the cord and wrapping a length of flannel around the tiny little girl, he carried her to Loris and placed her in her mother's arms.

"I thought you were sure it was going to be a boy, Connor," his mother-in-law said, her voice teasing him.

"I did think that," he said, "but I'm just as happy with this little rosebud. Just look at her," he said proudly. "Isn't she beautiful?"

"Of course she is. She's my grandchild, isn't she?"

"Well, I'm the one that did all the work," Loris said. "And I think she's the prettiest little thing I've ever seen." She held the infant against her breasts, nuzzling the tiny head and kissing the sweet skin that smelled like the most beautiful flowers she'd ever known to exist.

"My daughter," Connor said, as if tasting the words

to see how they fit on his tongue. "I'll have to write to James and tell him."

"He'll be pleased," Loris said. "His last letter sounded like he was a little worried."

"I know," Connor said. "But I wasn't. I knew this baby was meant to be, as will the rest of them we have. Isn't that right, honey?"

Loris hesitated, then smiled. "Just don't get carried away, Connor. I won't be ready for another baby for a little while."

"You haven't even begun to recuperate from this one yet," the doctor said sternly. "You just behave yourself for a while, young lady. No more babies for at least a year and a half. Two years is even better."

"Yes, well you'd better tell Connor that," Loris said, gazing on the babe she held.

"I'll have a talk with him later on," the doctor told her. "But for now, I think we need to leave you to rest, while we wash up that baby and let your father know what's going on in here. And Cora is champing at the bit, waiting to get a peek at the both of you."

Loris's eyes were closing as the baby was taken from her arms, and the door closed quietly, leaving her alone with Connor.

"I'm sleepy," she said, stifling a yawn.

"You've done a hard day's work, delivering our daughter," he told her. "Why don't I just snuggle up here next to you and you can go to sleep in my arms?"

"That sounds about right to me," she told him. "I'm happiest right here, with you."

"I'm planning on spending every night of my life in this bed with you, sweetheart," he said quietly, planning their future aloud. "We'll live here, in this house, with our children growing up around us, sharing more happiness than you can shake a stick at."

"I didn't realize how wonderful it would be to be your wife," she said quietly. "I'm so glad you found me here that day, that you wouldn't take no for an answer, and that you married me."

"We were meant to be together, Loris. From the beginning. For all the years God gives us together, we'll love and be loved."

* * * * *